In the Mean Time

"Paul Tremblay's *In the Mean Time* is a dark, heart-twisting collection of short fiction which defies categorization and requires your complete attention. The children, parents, and teachers who inhabit these stories exist in the ways we all exist—through those old historical longings which are rarely answered. Tremblay offers no solutions, but in the end, somehow, we walk away with a greater understanding of ourselves. Or, at the very least, the kind of selves we are but rarely see."

—Jessica Anthony, author of *The Convalescent*

"Paul Tremblay creates images of terror and wonder. Lean, mean, and just a bit on the nasty side, he's a hardnosed prose stylist with a heavyweight punch. Tremblay is a bona fide contender."

—Laird Barron, author of *The Imago Sequence* and *Occultation*

"*In the Mean Time* is a formidable collection, as disquieting as it is beautiful. They shock and they gleam, these stories, and the moods they provoke linger powerfully in the imagination: the dread of those who see the trouble coming and the strange relief of those upon whom it has already fallen."

—Kevin Brockmeier, author of *The Brief History of the Dead*

"Rumor has it that the world will end in fire and ice, but then again, if Paul Tremblay is to be believed, it may conclude in preternaturally active plants, amusement parks, sudden brain aneurisms, and silence. In *Mean Time*, end of the world scenarios brush up against the traumas of more personal apocalypses. The resulting stories are as stressful and quietly traumatic as they are fluidly and lucidly written."

—Brian Evenson, author of *Last Days* and *Fugue State*

"The power of these stories is that you think you're reading them, that there's that distance, but really you're living them, experiencing them, and that's how you remember them later. Not as something you read, but an event, lived."

—Stephen Graham Jones, author of *Demon Theory* and *The Ones That Almost Got Away*

"*In the Mean Time* is a miscellany of voices—witty, wise, weird, assured. These stories push at boundaries, not just within genre; they play alongside the uneasy undercurrents of lives we'd usually call ordinary. Stories to read and read again."

—Helen Oyeyemi, author of *White is for Witching*

"Paul Tremblay's stories sneak up on you quietly and then . . . wow! You don't know what hit you, but you like it. And you want more. Powerful, emotional and unforgettable; these are stories that work their way into your brain and into your heart. Highly recommended."

—Ann Vandermeer, Hugo Award-winning editor of *Weird Tales*

"Paul Tremblay disappears into the dark places that most writers are afraid to venture, and he returns with something gleaming and beautiful, stories that are absolutely unforgettable. In Tremblay's work, once the thrilling shock of seeing a two-headed girl wears off, he reminds you of what's most important, the single beating heart inside of her. With this collection, Tremblay announces himself as a master of the fantastic, and I look forward to reading each new word he writes."

—Kevin Wilson, author of *Tunneling to the Center of the Earth*

IN THE MEAN TIME

PAUL TREMBLAY

ChiZine Publications

FIRST EDITION

In the Mean Time © 2010 by Paul Tremblay
Jacket design © 2010 by Erik Mohr
Interior design © 2010 by C. A. Lewis
Interior illustrations © 2010 by Mara Sternberg
All Rights Reserved.

Library and Archives Canada Cataloguing in Publication

Tremblay, Paul
          In the mean time / Paul Tremblay.

Short stories.
ISBN 978-1-926851-06-8

          I. Title.

PS3620.R445I68 2010   813'.6   C2010-903996-3

CHIZINE PUBLICATIONS
Toronto, Canada
www.chizinepub.com
info@chizinepub.com

Edited by Helen Marshall
Copyedited and proofread by Shirarose Wilensky
Printed in Canada

always, for Lisa, Cole, Emma,

sometimes, for me

IN THE MEAN TIME

TABLE OF CONTENTS

"Perhaps in time the so-called Dark Ages
will be thought of as including our own."
—Georg C. Licthenberg

"All good things arrive unto them
that wait—and don't die in the meantime."
—Mark Twain

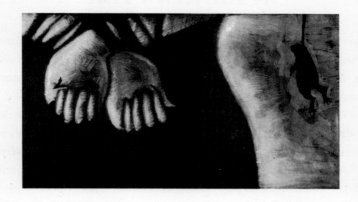

THE TEACHER

We loved him before we walked into the room. We loved him when we saw his name on our schedules. Mr. Sorent says, "All right, this is going to be a special class." We love him because of the music and movie posters on his walls, the black stud earring in his left ear, his shoulder-length hair. We love him because of those black horn-rimmed glasses; the same glasses we see people wearing on TV and in movies. We love him because he looks like us.

He stands at his podium. We love him because bumper stickers, many with political messages we want to understand, cover that podium. He says, "Because you guys are seniors and you're going to be outta here and out *there*," and he points out the window with his miniature baseball bat, and we love him for that, too. "We're going to learn more than just AP American History." We love him because he wears jeans. We love him because he makes fun of teachers we don't like. We love him because he plays guitar and he knows our songs.

There are only eight of us in his very special class. Four girls and four boys. We sit at a circular table. There are no desks. His is the only room in the school designed this way. He passes that smile around the circle. That smile we share, that smile we hoard for ourselves. He says, "We will be doing things outside of the book: special lessons. These lessons won't be every day or even every week, but they will be important. They will have weight and meaning. Certainly more meaning than the AP test you'll take next May."

We love him because he tells us the truth. Mr. Sorent leaves the podium and sits on a stool. "Just know the after school rules apply to our special lessons." We love him because he lets us talk to him after school. He lets us be confidential. He lets us talk about beer and parties and drugs and parents and abortions. "This is so exciting. I really can't wait. Maybe we'll have a lesson tomorrow." We love him because he is the promise that growing old doesn't mean becoming irrelevant.

At dinner Mom asks me about my soccer game even though she watched it. She's dressed in a sweatsuit as bright yellow as our kitchen. She leans over her plate to hear my answer. She's eager. She wants the coach to put her in the game. I tell her it was good because we won. Mom then answers her own question by announcing that those girls on the other team were playing dirty. Dad apologizes for missing the first game of the year, but it's perfunctory. He's wearing a yellow sweatsuit too. He doesn't want to be left out. I tell him it's okay and there'll be other games. My brother Lance is six years old and stirs around the unwanted green beans. I stare at his dinosaur plate and Spider-Man fork and wonder why everything has to be something. It's my turn to ask Lance how was his day. This is what we do at dinner. We ask about each other's day as if it was an actual object, something that could be held and presented. Lance giggles, covers his face, and tells us normal stuff happened. Everyone smiles even though we have no idea what normal stuff is. Dad asks me more questions and I try some humor; I say, "How could I possibly describe my day in a manner that would truly communicate my individual experience and world view concerning what had happened in that randomly delineated time period?" My parents laugh, and make we're-impressed faces. Dad says, "Did you learn that in school today, Kate?" He manages enough sarcasm for my approval. Mom shakes her head, then grabs my nose. Her fingers are cold. I look just like Mom. Right there, in the middle of my stir-fry, I make a solemn promise to never colour my brown hair auburn, or wear a yellow sweatsuit.

After dinner, I go to my room to do homework and Facebook my friends. Dialogue boxes pop up on the lower right corner of my screen. We type messages on walls. We don't capitalize. We use bad grammar and code words. We chat about who is seeing whom and how far each couple has gone. We chat about TV and we chat about Mr. Sorent. We chat about weekends past and future and we chat about nothing, and it's a comfort. I don't hear my friends' voices but I know all their secret names.

A TV on a rolling stand replaces his podium. Mr. Sorent is a live wire. His hands are pissed-off birds that keep landing on his face and then flying away. We sit and whisper jokes about Molly's short skirt and Miles's porn moustache, but we don't take our eyes off Mr. Sorent.

He says, "There will be more films and even some live demonstrations, but today's clip is the arc of the course." One of us turns out the lights without being asked, and the TV turns on.

A black-and-white security video of a classroom. There are finger paintings and posters with big happy letters on the walls. Stacks of blocks and toys and chairs that look like toys are strewn on the floor. There is no sound with the video, and we don't make any sounds. Five preschoolers run around the room, two more are standing on chairs and trying to knock each other off. The teacher is a young woman. She wears white, unflattering khakis and a collared shirt with the school's logo above the breast. Her hair is tied up tight behind her head, a fistful of piano wire. She breaks up the fight on the chairs, and then another child runs into her leg and falls to the ground. She picks up the squirming child, grabbing one arm and leg. She spins, giving a brief airplane ride, but then she lets go. Mr. Sorent pauses the video, and we know the teacher did not simply let go.

Mr. Sorent doesn't say anything until we're all looking at him. He says, "I don't want to say too much about this." He edges the video ahead by one frame. The airborne child is a boy with straight blond hair. We can't see his face, and he's horizontal, trapped in the black-and-white ether three feet above the carpeted floor. "Your individual reactions will be your guide, your teacher." The video goes ahead another frame. The boy's classmates haven't had time to react. The teacher still has her arms extended out. If someone were to walk in now and see this, I imagine they'd want to believe she was readying to catch the child. Not the opposite, not what really happened. Mr. Sorent moves the video ahead another frame and a wall comes into view, stage right. Class ends, and none of us will go see Mr. Sorent after school.

At dinner we eat spaghetti, and we're quiet. Everyone's day is a guarded secret. My parents missed my soccer game and when they ask about it, I tell them I scored a goal when I didn't. I think they know I'm making it up; my parents are smart, but they don't call me on it. They're still dressed in their work clothes, not their usual sweatsuit dining wear. Mom sits up straight and I can almost hear her spine straining into its perfect posture. Dad crouches behind a glass of water. Lance won't speak to us. He shrugs and grunts when we ask him questions. Dad sighs, which means he is pissed. Mom tells Lance it's okay to have a cranky day. I imagine Lance flying through the air, toward a wall, and I get the same stomach dropping feeling I get sometimes when I think about the future.

I don't eat much and I go up to my room early to Facebook. My friends are all here on my computer. No one talks about the video. We know the rules. But no one knows what they're supposed to write in their notebooks. Mr. Sorent handed us special-lesson composition notebooks that he wants us to decorate. We're supposed to write down diary entries or essays or stories or doodles or anything we're moved to do after reflecting upon the lesson. My notebook is open but empty, a pen lying in the spine. I've tried to write something, but there's nothing, and I get that afraid-of-the-future feeling again.

Days and weeks pass without another special lesson. We've had plenty of time to waste. Our first term grades are good and we lose ourselves in the responsibilities of senior year: college recommendations and applications and social requirements.

On the first day of winter term the TV returns. Mr. Sorent doesn't have to tell us what to do. We pull our chairs in tight and put away our books. Mr. Sorent says, "Lesson Two, gang."

There is a collage of clips and images—nothing in focus for more than a second or two—of car accidents. The kind of stuff some of us saw in driver's ed. The images of crushed and limbless and decapitated bodies are intercut with scenes from funerals, and there are red-eyed family members, the ones who never saw any of it coming, wailing and crying and breaking apart. Then the video ends with a teenage boy, alone in his room. There's no sound. His head is shaved to black stubble and he wears a sleeveless white T-shirt. The room is dark, and he scowls. There's no warning and he puts a handgun in his mouth and pulls the trigger. A dark mist forms behind his head and then he falls out of the picture. Mr. Sorent switches to the preschool video, still paused where he left it. He runs the video for a frame, then a second. The boy is still floating and horizontal, but getting closer to the wall. On the wall, bottoms of the finger paintings are curling up, heading toward the ceiling as if everything could fly. None of the boy's classmates know what is happening yet. But we know.

Mr. Sorent says, "Don't forget to do your homework."

There was this time I was waiting for Mom to come home. I had a Little League game in an hour. I wore my white uniform and black cleats, ponytail sticking through the back of my hat. I was in front of my house skipping rope, even though I didn't like skipping rope, but I liked the sounds my cleats made on the pavement. I was nine years old but if anyone asked I pretended I was ten. Three neighbourhood boys, three teammates dressed in their white baseball uniforms, came by, grabbed me, and forced me into one of their backyards. I didn't resist much as they used the jump rope to tie my arms behind my back, but I screamed a little, just enough to let them know that I didn't fully approve, especially since they never talked to me at baseball practice or games because I was a girl. They led me toward the edge of a stranger's wooded property, to a woodpile buried in dried pine needles and spiderwebs. They'd hanged a bullfrog by its neck from a piece of twine. It was as big as a puppy, kicking its legs out and covering itself in web and debris. The jump rope went slack on my arms but the boys didn't care. They told me to watch. They threw rocks. They had a BB gun and shot out one of the frog's eyes. Then they took turns pulling and pinching the frog, dancing at the base of the woodpile in their bright white baseball uniforms. Everything was white. They had a book of matches.

I left the jump rope in the grass like a dead snake and walked home and sat down in front of the TV. Nothing was on. Mom was late coming home and we missed the first inning of my game. When it was my turn to be the pitcher, I closed my eyes before releasing every pitch, afraid of what might happen.

Jake sits in a chair at the front of the room. Jake is elderly and has no hair. His face is a rotting fruit, and he moves like a marionette with tangled strings. He grins. Big yellow teeth break through his purple lips. He wears only a hospital gown, blue and white socks, and brown slippers. None of us wants to be here. Jake says, "Thanks to the loving support of family and friends, even if I don't beat this disease, I'll still have won, you know what I mean?" We don't know what he means. We couldn't possibly know. He says more heroic things, things that win us over, things that speak to the indomitable human spirit we always hear about, things that inspire us, that make us want to be better people, things that make us believe.

Then Mr. Sorent says, "Okay, Jake." Jake drops the curtain on his yellow teeth and he slouches into his chair, his marionette stings cut. He tells us everything he's just said is bullshit. He tells us to fuck off. He hates our fucking guts because of our health and youth and beauty. He hates us because we expect and demand him to be brave in facing his own withering existence, because we expect him to make our own lives seem better, or tolerable. He tells us we're selfish and that he'll die angry and bitter if he wants, that he's not here to die the right way for us, fuck you, you fucks he tells us, he doesn't give two shits about us and he tells us that we'll all die the ame way he will. Alone. He limps out of the room, limbs shaking and moving in the wrong directions.

Mr. Sorent says, "Look here," and he points with his bat. We hate that stupid bat now. We want to steal it or break it or burn it. It's meaningless to us. The bat points at the TV screen tucked away in a corner of the room, framed by all those posters that are no longer cool, but trying too hard to be cool. We want to destroy those too. We want to destroy everything. Mr. Sorent is still pointing with that ridiculous bat at the floating-boy video. It moves ahead another frame. Class dismissed.

I help Lance with his homework. Lance sighs like Dad whenever we finish a problem, as if he'd just completed the world's most demanding task. I tell him he'd better get used to it. His eyebrows are two little caterpillars fighting on his forehead. I want to tell him about the bullfrog and about pitching with your eyes closed.

My cell phone rings and Lance ducks under the couch cushions. He thinks he's funny. Caller ID says it's Tom, my boyfriend, and I crawl under the cushions next to Lance. Lance giggles and tries to push me out, kicking me in the head and chest. Tom hasn't called me all week. I hold the ringing phone against Lance's ear, and mock screams mix with his giggles. My last date with Tom was a movie. We watched the previews intently. During the movie, I wouldn't let him stick his hand into my jeans. I told him to stick his hand in his own pants. I thought I was funny. He pouted the rest of the night. I don't and won't answer Tom's phone call. I'm going to break up with him. He's starting to scare me. Lance and I emerge from the couch after the phone stops ringing, and Lance rushes through the rest of his assignment, his eights looking like crumbling buildings.

I go upstairs to the computer. I tell everyone that I'm going to break up with Tom before I tell Tom. Tom hears it from somebody else and he yells at me through cyberspace: capital letters and multiple exclamation marks and no smiley faces. I make jokes about him masturbating to porn. I make jokes about the size and smell of his dick. I don't do any homework for Mr. Sorent's class.

All eight of us in Mr. Sorent's special class, our grades aren't good anymore. We are not in good academic standing. Some of us drink. Some of us smoke. Some of us will fuck anyone and everyone, or we punch and kick and destroy, or we drive really fast and late at night, or we stay locked in our rooms. Teachers openly talk about the changes, our senior slides, our early spring fever, and they pretend to be more knowing than they are. But they don't know anything and they won't do anything.

Mr. Sorent has stopped teaching us AP American History because we don't listen. Most days he sits at his desk and reads the paper, smelling of old cigarettes and something else, something organic none of us cares to identify. His hair is greasy and formless. His jeans don't fit his waist correctly, not cut to the length and style we want. He doesn't shave and his beard grows in patchy and rough. He wears old glasses now, the lenses too big. He is an old man trying to act young. He's a fraud. He knows nothing. He can teach us nothing. We know this now, even if we didn't know it then. We've stripped his podium of the bumper stickers, stolen his CDs and his miniature bat.

We only listen to Mr. Sorent during the special lessons. One class he showed us a PowerPoint presentation of crime scene photos: there was a man beaten to death with a bat, only his sausage-sized lips were a recognizable part of his face, and there was an old man hacked to death with a samurai sword, and there was a woman who shot herself in the chest with a shotgun, she was a junky and so withered you couldn't tell she was female, even with her shirt off. Another class was war footage, soldiers and civilians in pieces and burnt and eaten away by the chemicals neither side was using. Another class was snuff and torture films and the sound was the worst part. In other classes we saw the Columbine video, terrorists beheading kidnap victims, grainy newsreel stuff from Chernobyl and Hiroshima, and from Auschwitz and Cambodia and Rwanda and Kosovo and their endless piles of bodies.

And there's still the floating-boy video. Moving only frame to frame with each new day. Some days we can believe there has been no progress, as if that boy will be trapped in the amber of TV forever, but that's not right. He has progressed. He's almost at the wall.

No one talks at dinner. Just forks on plates. Mom says she already ate and then goes out wearing heels and sunglasses and not her yellow sweatsuit. Dad takes off his tie and unbuttons his shirt and dumps Lance in front of the TV with his dinosaur plate and Spider-Man fork. Lance has dark, purple circles under his eyes, his skin carrying something heavy. In all the hours of TV Lance has already logged, I wonder if he's seen the floating boy. Dad disappears into his bedroom, and then the master bathroom. Both doors shut at the same time. I'm the only one eating at the table. Maybe this is how it always was. I go upstairs. Online I find my friends arguing without me. Tomorrow is our last class with Mr. Sorent. Its arrival will be unheralded and inevitable. I still haven't written anything in my notebook. I can't decide if I want that to mean anything. If I were to write something down, I'd tell Mr. Sorent about the bullfrog. No, maybe I'd just tell him about me pitching in the Little League game. Tell him how when I closed my eyes, I hoped the ball would stop somewhere between me and the catcher and just float. I would hope so hard I'd believe it was really happening. With my eyes closed, I'd see that ball just hovering and spinning and I'd follow the path of those angry red stitches along with everyone else; we'd all stare it for hours, even when it got dark. But then I would hear the ball hitting the catcher's mitt, or the bat, or the dull thud of the ball smacking into the batter's back, and open my eyes.

Mr. Sorent has shaved and cleaned himself up, has a new mini-bat, bumper stickers back on his podium. He's a cicada, emerging fresh from his seven-year sleep. He says, "You think you know why I'm

IN THE MEAN TIME

doing this. But you don't," which is something so teacherly to say and utterly void of credibility or relevance. "So let's begin again."

We're tired and old, and we've experienced more and know more than he does. We know we can't ever begin again. We hand in our special notebooks. They are decorated and filled with our blood, except for one notebook that is empty. One of us closes our eyes after releasing the empty notebook, refusing to watch its path to the teacher's desk.

Mr. Sorent turns on the TV and the floating-boy video. The boy's head is only inches away from the wall. Some of his classmates are watching now, but they probably don't know what is really going on, or even what is going to happen. We hope they don't know. We hope they aren't like us. The teacher has retracted her arms and is facing the boy and the wall. Her face is blurry and because we haven't seen the entire video at normal speed, we don't know if this means she's trying to look away or if it's just a quirk of the video or if there's some other meaning that we haven't unearthed, or if it's all meaningless.

Mr. Sorent rewinds the video, the boy flies backward and into the teacher's embrace. We know it won't last. He says, "I need a volunteer."

This isn't fair. He is trying to break us apart, turning we into me. Doesn't he know that we'll hate the volunteer? The volunteer won't be able to rewind back into the we. We will never be the same. Maybe we are being melodramatic but we don't care. We believe the volunteer to be irreversible; there is no begin again, Mr. Sorent, why can't you understand that? But I volunteer anyway.

I leave our circle and it becomes *their* circle. I walk to the front of the class, next to the TV, and I imagine the floating boy finally hitting his wall and then smashing through the right side of the television and into me, into my arms.

"Stand here and face that wall."

I do as he says. I feel their eyes on me. Them who used to be we.

"Please walk halfway toward the wall. Everyone else watch the video." I take four steps and stop; the TV is behind me so I can't see the screen. "Please halve the distance again, Kate." I take two steps.

When I move I hear the DVD player whir into action and then pause when I pause. "Again, Kate." I take one step. I could touch the wall now, if I wanted, and rip down the movie posters that we once tore down.

"If you keep halving the distance, Kate, will you ever get there? Is forever that far away, or that close? What do you think, class?" He says *class* like it's the dirtiest of words. I close my eyes, and take a half step, then a quarter-step, an eighth-step, and I still haven't hit the wall.

"That's good enough, Kate." I don't move, but not because of what he said.

"Go back to your seat and we'll let you decide whether or not this little boy will ever hit the wall." I don't move. My eyes are still closed and I'll stay here until I'm removed. I haven't touched it yet, but the wall is intimately close. It's impending, and it's always there. Mr. Sorent says something to me but I'm not listening and I'm not going to move. I'll stay here with my eyes closed and pretend that where I am is where I'll always be. Where am I? I'm at the dinner table discussing days with my dissatisfied parents. I'm helping Lance and his caterpillars with homework. I'm at the computer instant messaging secrets to secret friends.

"Return to your seat so we may finally watch the video, Kate."

No. I'm staying where I am. I'm the baseball pitch that stops before home. I'm an empty notebook. I'm half the distance to the wall. I'm the video with an ending that I won't ever watch.

THE TWO-HEADED GIRL

1

I have to keep swinging an extra fifteen minutes before I can go downtown and to the Little Red Bookstore, because Mom wants to run the dishwasher and the blender tonight. I wonder if my time on the swing will generate enough extra juice for those appliances, or even if she's telling me the truth. I've been having a hard time with telling-truth or truth-telling.

Anne Frank is on my left again. I only ever get to see her in profile. Whenever I'm around a mirror she is always someone else. Today, she's the early-in-her diary Anne, the same age as me. Anne spent most of my swinging afternoon pining for Peter, but now she wants to talk to Lies, her best friend before the war.

She says, "I feel so guilty, Lies. I wish I could take you into hiding with me."

I get this odd, stomach-knotty thrill and I pretend that she really knows me and she is really talking to me. But at the same time, I don't like it when she calls me Lies. I say, "I'm sorry, Anne, but I'm Veronica." The words come out louder than I intended. I'm not mad at her. I could never be mad at Anne. It's just hard to speak normally when on the downswing.

Anne moves on, talks about her parents and older sister, and then how much she dislikes that ungrateful dentist they took in.

"Nobody likes dentists," I say and I want her to laugh. She doesn't. I only hear dead leaves making their autumn sounds as they blow up against the neighbor's giant fence and our swing set and generator

Mom sticks her only head out of the kitchen window and yells, "Looks like we need another fifteen minutes, sorry, honey. I promise I'll get Mr. Bob out here tomorrow to tune everything up."

This is not good news. My back hurts and my legs are numb already. She's promised me Mr. Bob every day for a week. She's made a lot of promises.

"Hi, Veronica." It's that little blond boy from across the street. He's become part of my daily routine: when I come out, he hides in our thick bushes, then sneaks along the perimeter of my neighbor's beanstalk-tall, wood plank fence, and then sits next to the swing set and generator.

"Hi, Jeffrey," I say. Anne is quiet. Jeffrey has a withered left arm. Both of us try not to stare at it.

He says, "Where's your Dad?" His little kindergarten voice makes me smile, even though I'm sick of that particular question.

"I don't know, Jeffrey, just like I didn't know yesterday, and the day before yesterday." I try not to be mean or curt with him. He's the only kid in town who talks to me.

Anne says, "My Dad is hiding in the annex."

Jeffrey stays on my right, which is closer to my head. He only talks to me. I know it makes Anne lonely and sad, which makes me lonely and sad, just like her diary did. I don't remember what came first: me reading the diary or Anne making a regular rotation as my other head.

Jeffrey says, "You should ask your Mom or somebody where he is."

I know Jeffrey doesn't realize what he's asking of me. I know people never realize how much their words hurt, sometimes almost as much as what isn't said.

I say what I always say. "I'll think about it."

"Can I ride on the swing?"

Anne is mumbling something under her breath. My heart breaks all over again. I say, "No, sorry, Jeffrey. I can't let you. You'd have to ask my mother." I find it easier to blame everything on Mom, even if it isn't fair.

Jeffrey mashes his fully developed right fist into his cheek, an overly dramatic but effective pantomime of I-never-get-to-do-anything-fun.

I say, "Do you want to walk downtown with me when I'm done?"

He nods.

"Go ask your parents first."

Jeffrey runs off. With his little legs pumping and back turned to me, I let myself stare at the flopping and mostly empty left arm of his thin, grey sweatshirt. He scoots onto his front lawn and past a sagging scarecrow, a decoration left out too long.

My legs tingle with pins and needles, and Anne is crying. I wish I could console her, but I can't. Now I'm thinking about the question I've always wanted to ask Anne, but never have because I'm a coward. I could ask her now, but it isn't the right time, or at least, that's what I tell myself. So we just keep swinging: a pendulum of her tears and me.

2

Jeffrey and I are downtown, playing a game on the cobblestones. I have to step on stones in a diagonal pattern. Jeffrey has to step on the darkest stones. I've seen him miss a few but I won't call him on it. I'll let him win.

Anne is gone and Medusa has taken her place. She is my least favourite head but not because she is a gorgon. I wish she were more gorgon-esque. Medusa is completely un-aggressive, head and eyes always turned down and she doesn't say boo. I feel bad for her, and I hate Athena for turning Medusa into a hideous monster because she had the audacity to be raped by Poseidon in Athena's temple. Athena was the one with the big-time jealousy and beauty issues, kind of like my mother. I used to try and talk to Medusa, to make her feel better about herself. I'd tell her that her physical or social appearance doesn't measure her worth and that her name means *sovereign female wisdom*, which I think is really cool for a name, so much cooler than my name which means *true image*. But she never says anything back and when I talk her snakes tickle my neck with their forked tongues.

Jeffrey shouts, "I'm winning," even though he keeps falling off dark stones onto light stones. Balancing with only one arm must be difficult.

I say, "You're really good at this game."

It's getting dark and I know Mom will be mad at me for being so late, but I'm allowing myself to champion the petty act of defiance. We make it to the Little Red Bookstore with its clapboard walls, cathedral ceiling, and giant mahogany bookcases with the customer scaffolding planks jutting out at the higher levels. There are people everywhere. Customers occupy the plush reading chairs and couches, the planks, and the seven rolling stack-ladders. I hold Jeffrey's hand as we wade through the crowd toward the fiction section. No one notices us.

Jeffrey is as patient as he can be, but soon he's tugging at my arm and skirt, asking if we can find dinosaur books, then asking if we can go home. I need a stack-ladder to go after the books I want. They're still all taken. Even if I could get a ladder, I can't leave Jeffrey unattended and he can't climb the ladder and walk the bookcase scaffolding with me. So I grab a random book, something I've never heard of by someone I've never heard of, because I have to buy something. Then I walk Jeffrey to the kid section and to some dinosaur books. He sits on the ground with a pop-up book in his lap. He knows all the dinosaur names, even the complex ones with silent letters and ph's everywhere, and I've never understood why boys love the monsters that scare them so much. Above my heads, people climb in and out of the ladders and platforms and book stacks.

I say to Medusa, "I think they look like bees in a honeycomb." Medusa sighs and doesn't lift her head.

Jeffrey sounds out an armored dinosaur's name, an-kie-low-saur-us, ankylosaurus, then he stands and swings an imaginary tail at me.

I say to Medusa, "Come on. Tell me what you think. Something. Anything!"

Medusa's snakes stir, rubbing up against my neck. She says, "Unlike my sisters, I'm mortal."

Everyone in and above the stacks stops what they are doing and looks at us, looks at Medusa, who for once returns their stares. No one turns to stone, at least not against their will, and I know it's time for us to go. The customers are upset with us, likely because we're talking about mortality in a bookstore.

I brush a particularly frisky snake off my neck and I say, "Me, too," but enough time has passed so I'm not sure if Medusa knows I'm responding to what she said. Communication is so difficult sometimes.

We walk to the register and pay for the book I don't want.

3

It's dark when I get home. Mom is sitting at the kitchen table. She's dressed to go out, even though she won't, wearing a tight candy-red top, the same red as her lipstick, with a black poodle skirt. Her black hair bobs at her shoulders. She could be my sister back from college ready to tell me all she's learned about life and love as a woman. But she's not my sister.

There are two white Irish-knit turtleneck sweaters on her lap. On the counter, the blender is dirty with its plastic walls dripping something creamy. The dishwasher is in a loud rinse cycle. My dinner is on a plate, hidden under a crinkled, re-used piece of tinfoil.

Mom says, "You shouldn't keep Jeffrey out so late. He's only five years old. You know better than that." Her voice is naturally loud. She looks at me quick, like a jab. Then she goes up the left side of one sweater with the scissors.

She's right, but I'm not going to acknowledge her rightness. Just like Mom won't acknowledge that my other head is Jeanne D'Arc. I say, "Jeffrey had a great time at the bookstore and his parents were fine with it." Suddenly not quite ready for an argument to start, I add, "Everything okay with the blender and dishwasher?"

Jeanne whispers a prayer, coving her face with my left hand, very pious and humble.

Mom says, "So far so good, thanks for asking. You're such a sweetheart." Mom goes up the right side of the other sweater. She works so very fast. "It's going to be cold out tomorrow, so I'm making you a nice, warm, and presentable sweater." She says presentable as if anyone will see me. Mom gets up and goes to her sewing machine next to the kitchen table. I wonder if Mom planned the sewing machine into this evening's allotment of electricity and then I'm worried that I didn't spend enough time on the swing today, and then I hate myself for being so trained.

I say, "What's for dinner?"

"Mushroom chicken, corn, rice pilaf. Go wash up first. And you are going to do your math and science homework tonight, Veronica. No excuses. I can't put off your exams any longer. They're due in the post in three days."

I mix truth with a lie. "I bought a book that I really want to read first."

"Tomorrow night is your book club and the next night you have to take the exams. You are going to do your homework tonight."

Mom is always so reasonable, and I hate it. Makes me feel like I'm the bad one for wanting to fight. I say, "I don't care," but not very loud. I think Mom is going to let it slide, but then she breaks protocol by commenting on my other head.

"Why is there a boy on your shoulder?"

Jeanne crosses herself.

IN THE MEAN TIME

I don't know what to say. Other than when she's making two-headed clothing, Mom usually ignores my other head. I manage to say, "Real nice, Mom. She's Joan of Arc." I don't say her name in French because I don't want to remind Mom that she hasn't given me a French unit to work on in almost two weeks.

"I didn't say that to be mean, Veronica."

"Then why did you say it?"

She stares at me. "I won't let you start another fight with me over nothing," she says and turns on the sewing machine.

I throw myself into a chair and pick at my lukewarm dinner. I don't wait for Jeanne to say grace.

There's a spider fern hanging above Mom and the sewing machine, some of its leaves are browning. With the machine's vibrations, some leaves break off and fall onto Mom's head. She sews quickly and the result is a beautiful Irish-knit turtleneck sweater with two turtlenecks. No visible seams where two different sweaters come together. She is very talented, and I hate her. Okay, I don't hate her but she makes me very angry without me being able to rationally explain why. Yesterday, I constructed an elaborate Cinderella fantasy where my father, a man I no longer remember, was driven off by my evil and shrewish mother. I suppose it's the only desertion scenario that doesn't hurt me.

I offer Jeanne some of my food but she is fasting. Now I feel guilty. I struggle to finish what's on my plate. I think about Jeffrey insisting that I ask Mom where my father is, or better yet, how come he doesn't see me if he really lives in the same town as us, but I know tonight is not the night for that conversation.

Mom says, "Try the sweater on, sweetie. Make sure it fits."

I pull the scratchy wool over our heads. Jeanne doesn't like it.

Mom tugs at the shoulders, waist, and sleeves, inspecting her work. She says, "This fits nice. Very nice. You look great." Mom is still at least six inches taller than me. I don't know if I'll ever catch up. Mom folds her arms over her thin chest, her defense and attack posture. Big smile, quite satisfied with herself, with what she's done for her daughter. It's a very intimidating look. One I don't know how to overcome.

She says, "Homework time. I'll check your answers when you're done."

I leave the kitchen with a full belly and empty of fight. As I walk into the living room and past the snarling fireplace, Jeanne closes her eyes and says, *"Allez!"* which means *go!* I already feel bad about the food so I hurry away from the fire, but I trip and fall, my hands scraping on the brick landing in front of the fireplace. Jeanne spasms and twitches, trying to remove herself from my body and away from the fire, and I'm crying, but not because of the pain, and somehow this must be all Mom's fault too.

"Sorry!" I get up and dash up the stairs to my bedroom. My hands sting and I look at them. The palms are all scraped up and bloody.

Jeanne says, "It's only stigmata. But keep it secret. Go wash it off and don't tell your mother."

At least, that's what I think she says. My French is a little rusty.

4

Mr. Bob was my science teacher when I went to school. I don't miss school and the taunts and the stares and how incredibly lonely I could be in a lunchroom full of other people. Nor do I miss Mr. Bob, even though he's always been nice to me.

Mom and I are standing next to the swing set, watching Mr. Bob. Odd and misshapen tools that couldn't possibly fix anything fill Mr. Bob's fists and spill out of his tight, too short, and paint-stained overalls.

My mother says, "Can you fix this?"

Mr. Bob says, "No sweat."

My other head is Marie Curie, child-aged, so no one recognizes her. She's very plain and I find that beautiful. Marie says something in Russian that sounds vaguely commiserative. Mom ignores this head.

IN THE MEAN TIME

Unprompted, Mr. Bob launches into an explanation of how the swing set works. Maybe he does know that I have young Madame Curie with me and he's trying to impress her. If so, that's really creepy.

Mr. Bob says, "This swing set is one big friction machine. Mounted on the horizontal bar above is an axle with circular plates, each plate turning and rubbing against pads when you swing, making an electrical charge. The prime conductors, your long brass pipes, follow the frame of the swing set. The ends of these conductors carry metallic combs with points bent toward the faces of the glass plates. The combs collect the charge, and the pipes bring the charge to the collector/generator and then to your house. Really it's very simple, but not very efficient."

Mom says, "Nothing Veronica's father did was very efficient."

I want to tell Marie Curie the obvious, that my father made this swing set, but he isn't here anymore and I don't know where he is but supposedly he's still in town, somewhere. I don't think Marie has learned English yet. The next time I go to the bookstore, I'll get her biography, and maybe some books on electricity and friction machines so I can fix this without any help.

Mr. Bob climbs a ladder to get at the axle. Tools drip and drop like a lazy rain. As much as I'd like the swing to be tuned up so it'll be more efficient, I don't want Mr. Bob touching any of it. The swing is my only connection to my father and I'm afraid Mr. Bob will ruin everything. Wanting to be random and unpredictable, but knowing different, I blurt out, "Where's my father?"

Mom folds her arms across her chest and says, "Why don't you go inside and wash up. Don't forget you're hosting the book club tonight and you haven't prepared any of the hors d'oeuvres."

I stare at Mom and I want to cry. Marie stares at Mr. Bob and clucks her tongue at his apparent incompetence. Marie says something in Russian that I think would translate as: "I'd like to see this contraption's schematic, you talentless monkey."

Mom softens, and bends to whisper in my ear. She says, "We can talk about this later if you really want to. If you need to. But it's for the best, Veronica. Really. Go on, now. Set up for your book club."

5

My book club is here. Six women, ages ranging from Peg Dower's somehow rheumy thirty-six to Cleo Stanton-Meyer's health-club fifty-three. Our chairs and bodies make a circle, a book club Stonehenge, but with an end table loaded with coffee, tea, water, chips and spinach dip, and biscotti at the center. Everyone has their dog-eared copy of *Mrs. Dalloway* by Virginia Woolf on their slacks-clad laps.

Mom stays in the kitchen and doesn't participate in the discussions, even though she reads all the books. She insists this is my *thing*. I hear the sewing machine turn on and off sporadically.

Bev Bentley, white-blonde and DD chest (Mom is so jealous), says, "Excuse me, but is that her, Veronica? Will we be able ask her questions?" Hands cover faces all over the circle. Peg and Cleo groan much like a crowd at a sporting event when something bad happens. Bev is the something bad happening. She asks me the same question every meeting. And every meeting I answer: "Sorry, Bev, she's not the author of this book." It is rather insulting for her to continually think that my other head is that simple or predictable, but I don't tell them my other head is Sylvia Plath. They should be able to figure that out on their own. Sylvia just smirks and takes it all in, burning Bev down with a look that could shame an entire culture.

Our discussion begins with Peg trying to compare Clarissa Dalloway to Catherine from *Wuthering Heights*, but no one agrees with her. Sylvia laughs but it sounds sad. I redirect the discussion to the book's themes of insanity and suicide and reality and the critique of the social system. None of us says anything that's new or important, but it is still satisfying to discuss something that matters to us. Cleo wonders aloud how autobiographical this novel was for Woolf, and I wonder how hard Sylvia is biting her tongue or maybe she just doesn't care enough to join in. I'll need to keep me and her out of the kitchen and away from the oven.

Then book talk is over before everyone's teacups and coffee mugs are empty. And as usual, our talk deteriorates into town gossip.

"Darla has been sleeping with that new pharmacist."

"William Boyle?"

"He's the one."

"He must be ten years younger than Darla."

"Fifteen."

"And her divorce isn't even final yet."

They move on to discuss the high school gym teacher and his secret gay lover. As best as I can figure, this mysterious lover is more abstract ideal than reality. Sylvia is still disinterested. She's flipping through my copy of *Mrs. Dalloway* and doodling in the margins. And there's more of the who's-sleeping-with-who talk followed up with who's-not-sleeping-with-who talk, which includes Cleo's third husband's erectile dysfunction diagnosis and her daily countdown until he fills one of those blue pill prescriptions, likely to be handed out by the philandering pharmacist.

The sewing machine in the kitchen is quiet and has been for a while. Mom stopped sewing once the book discussion ended. I know Mom thinks this book-club-cum-gossip-session is a substitute for all the wonderful teenage conversations I don't have with other teenagers. I don't know if it is or not, since I'm not having those teenage conversations with other teenagers. I generally don't mind the town dish as I do find it entertaining, but tonight it seems wrong, especially on the heels of Woolf's book. I mean, this was what she was railing against.

So, inspired by Virginia to say something meaningful, or at the very least to yank everyone out of complacency, I say, "Does anyone know where my father lives?"

In the kitchen, the sewing machine roars to life, stitching its angry stitches. Sylvia whispers, "Atta, girl," into my ear. I look out into the newly silent Stonehenge of women. All of them here, all of them totems in my living room only because my mother asked them to be here. I love Mom and I hate her for the book club; not either/or but both at the same time.

The women, they shrug or shake their heads or say a weak *no*. Then they fill their plates with chips and biscotti. I know it's not fair to make them uncomfortable, but why should I always be the only one?

Our discussion slowly turns toward TV shows and movies, and then what book should we read next. Peg finds the book I didn't want to buy sitting unread on the mantel. She passes it around. Everyone claims to have heard about the book that no one has heard about. They mumble agreeable sentiments about it being challenging, something new, having buzz, and they decide, without asking me and before the book makes it way around the circle back to me, to make it our next book club selection. Sylvia thumbs through it and doesn't say anything.

Mom reappears from the kitchen with everyone's coats in her arms. Polite, light-pats-on-the-back hugs are passed back and forth, even when I insist upon handshakes, and then everyone leaves. I'm left with Sylvia, no answers to my father question, a mother pouting and sewing in the kitchen, loads of dishes and cups and trays to wash, and a book in my hands that I don't want to read.

6

I am up and out of the house before Mom wakes up. We haven't said anything to each other since the book club. Getting up and eating breakfast alone quickly becomes an hour on the swing set. It's cold and there's no way of knowing if Mr. Bob's tune-up did any good. The swing doesn't seem any different, or more efficient.

I really don't want to do this today. It's not helping that my other head is changing by the downswing, almost too many heads to keep up with. There's been Cleopatra, Bonnie Parker, Marsha Brady, Fay Wray, Emily Brontë, Cindy Lou Who, Janis Joplin, and even that vacuous snot, Joan Rivers.

My heads never change this fast, and I hate it. I really wanted nothing more than to sit out here and talk with one of the heads, have someone help me decide what to do, or what to think. I don't know why finding my father is all of a sudden so important to me. Last week and pretty much all the weeks before that week, he was never more than a fleeting thought, a forgotten dream.

The swing coupled with my changing heads are making me dizzy, so I put my legs down, scraping my sneakers on the sand, digging an even deeper rut, and I stop swinging. Then I go and sit up against the neighbour's wooden fence with my head in my hands, trying to regain some level of equilibrium. Joan Rivers is yammering in my ear about my terrible clothes and iffy skin. The leaves I'm sitting on are cold and wet. I get up and walk.

I walk downtown to the cobblestones and the Little Red Bookstore and Joan Rivers becomes Lauren Bacall becomes Calpurnia becomes Scout becomes Boo Radley's mother, which is confusing. I stand outside with my hands cupped on the bookstore's bay window. The place is empty and I'd have the shelves to myself but I keep walking, past the Little Red Grocery and Little Red Hardware and the Little Red Candy Shoppe and the Little Red Bank, and out of the downtown area and through the town square, and Boo Radley's mother becomes Lucille Ball becomes Karen Silkwood becomes Mary Shelley becomes Susan Faludi. I walk past the Little Red Library and the Little Red Schoolhouse, which was where I dropped out during my sixth-grade year. Tommy Gallahue showing up to school with a papier-mâché second head was my last day of sixth-grade. Susan Faludi becomes Blanche DuBois becomes Alice in Wonderland. I walk past the town high school and I walk past without any regrets. Alice becomes Rosa Parks becomes Vivien Leigh. I walk through residential neighbourhoods, peeking over fences and into yards randomly, looking for the man I don't remember, looking for the man I know I'll never find. Vivien Leigh becomes a starving Ethiopian girl that I don't know but have seen on commercials becomes Zelda becomes Flannery O'Connor. I don't have a watch but it must be noon as the sun is directly over my head and I'm very hungry, so I start walking back home, taking a different route back, staying in the small neighbourhoods, still looking through fences and even inside a few mailboxes, for what? I'm not sure. And Flannery O'Connor becomes Oprah becomes Nancy Drew becomes Maya Angelou becomes Shirley Temple becomes Eponine becomes Little Orphan Annie becomes Amelia Earhart and I'm home.

My mother is on the swing. She's actually sitting on the swing that apparently is not calibrated to precisely my weight. But she's not really swinging. She's sitting, her legs folded under, her toes tickling the rut in the sand, her face in her hands, and I can't be sure, but I think she's crying. She's wearing an Irish-knit turtleneck sweater like mine, but with only one turtleneck. Amelia Earhart becomes Shirley Jackson becomes Hester Prynne. I'm hiding where Jeffrey usually hides, in the thinning shrubbery next to our neighbour's fence. Then Jeffrey runs out of his house, across the street and to my mother. No one has seen me yet. Jeffrey is talking with her. I guess, for him, it doesn't matter who is swinging. I won't hold it against him. He's only five. I wonder if he asks her the same questions he asks me. Mom laughs then scoops up Jeffrey into her lap and they swing together. Hester Prynne becomes the witch accusing Abigail, and I'm angry-jealous, or jealous-angry, and maybe they're the same emotion, each just wearing something a little different. I walk out of the bushes and to the swing. Abigail doesn't say anything but just points with my left index finger.

Jeffrey says, "Hi, Veronica!" between giggles.

"Hi."

Mom stops the swing. She says, "Jeffrey, you can swing by yourself, as long as you promise not to go too high. Promise?" If she was crying before, there is no sign of it now.

Jeffrey puffs out his chest. "I promise."

I want to ask how Jeffrey is going to manage this with his withered arm. But he hops right on the swing, tucks the left chain of the swing under his armpit, grabs the other chain with his good arm and starts pumping. We watch him swing for a few minutes and Abigail has become someone else but I haven't bothered to look and see who it is.

IN THE MEAN TIME

Mom says, "We'll be right back, Jeffrey. I need to talk to Veronica for a bit. Keep pumping, kid." She puts a hand on my shoulder and guides me to the house. After a few paces, she says, "What?" like I've been staring at her expectantly, but I haven't. Then she says, "I need someone on that swing today. I need the juice to vacuum the floors later."

7

We're in the kitchen. I sit down. Mom stands and paces. She doesn't wait for me to say anything and starts right in with a simple declarative.

"You and I came home early one afternoon and I found more than the expected amount of heads in my bedroom."

I say, "How old was I?"

"One."

My other head is Mom. Mom when she was my age. Despite her pigtails, she manages older-Mom's fierce, intimidating look. I don't know what she's thinking, and I'm tired of trying to figure out who's thinking what.

I ask, "Who was he with?"

"Does it matter?" Mom doesn't waver, doesn't get all choked up or anything like that, not that I expected her to.

"I don't know if it matters, Mom. That's why I'm asking."

"The woman was the middle school science teacher that Mr. Bob replaced. She doesn't live in town anymore."

I imagine a woman who looks like Mr. Bob. She wears baggy clothes that have chemical stains and Bunsen burner singe marks. She has short, straight hair, mousey brown, wears thick glasses, and no makeup. Pretty in a smart way, maybe. I imagine Mom finding her in the bedroom with my father, who I can't describe in such physical detail, no matter how hard I try to conjure him.

Young-Mom doesn't say anything but just stares at her older self. Is this look of hers studied observation or soul-deep sadness?

"Did he leave after you caught him?"

"The very next morning."

"Did you tell him he had to leave?"

"No."

Young-Mom says, "Do you really need to know any more of this?" which I don't think is a very fair question. It's not fair to be double-teamed by Mom like this, even though I know that I can't always blame everything on Mom. I fight the urge to tell the Young-Mom to shut up.

I say, "That's terrible. I'm sorry that happened, Mom. I really am."

"Thank you." Mom says it like she's accepting a throwaway compliment about her shoes. Young-Mom pouts. They are both so intimidating but I stand up and stutter-walk to Mom and give her a hug. She doesn't uncross her arms off her chest so the hug isn't soft and comfortable. I make contact mostly with the angles of her bones and the points of her elbows and the sweater wool scratches my face, but Mom does kiss the top of my head, twice. That's something, maybe even enough.

"Thanks again, sweetie."

I break the one-sided hug and say, "What did he look like?"

"You."

"Can I ask where he lives?"

Young-Mom sighs and shakes her head. Her pigtails tickle my neck, feeling eerily similar to Medusa's snakes, but I don't mind them as much.

"I thought I was ready to tell you, Veronica, but I'm not."

I want to ask if she knows who my other head is. I want to ask if she knows what it means. I want to ask if she knows that most days I dream about becoming her.

She continues, "It's not you anymore. I know you can handle it now, but you'll just have to give me more time." Mom uncrosses her arms and looks around the kitchen, at the cluttered counter and the sewing machine, looking for something to do.

Young-Mom turns, whispers directly into my ear, "Are you happy, now?"

I unroll the neck of the sweater and pull it up over her mouth and nose. She doesn't stop me or say anything else.

I say, "Okay, Mom," but I don't know if it is okay and I don't know if I feel guilty or satisfied or sad or angry or scared. What I'm feeling no one has bothered to name or classify or dissect, or maybe this feeling has already been outed by somebody else and I just haven't stumbled across it, and that seems likely but at the same time it doesn't, and then I think about all the books in my bedroom and the giant stacks of books in my Little Red Bookstore and I wonder if *it* is there or here or anywhere else other than inside me.

Mom says, "All right, back to work, then." She claps her hands and I feel my other head change but I won't look to see who it is yet. "Could you go and take over for Jeffrey on the swing? He's making me nervous. I appreciate it, honey. And don't forget about your big tests later."

8

It's windy and cold, the temperature dropping by the minute. Jeffrey stops swinging but stays on the seat. "Do I have to stop now?"

"Yes, my mother wants me to take over."

He doesn't argue, but he hasn't moved off the seat either. He releases the swing chain that was tucked under his armpit. "You and your Mom had a talk?"

"Yes, Jeffrey." I notice I'm standing in my Mom's pose, but I don't change it.

"Did you ask her about your Dad?"

"I did."

"Did she tell you?"

"Tell me what?"

"Tell you where he is."

"No, not yet."

Jeffrey nods like he understands. Maybe he does. He says, "Maybe you should ask someone else."

"Like who?"

"Me?" He says it like a question, almost like he doesn't know who *me* is.

I play along. Anything to keep me off the swing for another few minutes. "Okay, Jeffrey. Do you know where my father is?"

He nearly shouts, "Yes."

My arms wrap tighter around my chest. This isn't fun anymore. "Then where is he?"

Jeffrey scoots off the swing and points behind him. He points at the neighbor's big wooden fence. "He lives there. Right next door."

That's impossible. Isn't it? Wouldn't I have seen him by now? I think about who lives there and I can't come up with anyone. Is that right? Has he been this close all along and I just haven't noticed, or haven't wanted to notice?

Jeffrey says, "I'm not lying, Veronica. I've seen him."

"I didn't say you were lying."

He says, "I think he's even out in the yard right now. Go and see."

I look at the fence, seven feet high, completely wrapping around the property. "How?"

"There's a knothole in the fence behind your bushes. You know, I usually hide in your bushes."

I snort, ready to charge. "Okay. Jeffrey, go home please."

He reacts like I hit him, and tears well up.

I soften. "You can come back over later, but I need to do this by myself."

Jeffrey nods, still fighting those tears, then sprints home, this time gripping the empty arm of his sweater. I walk to the bushes, to where Jeffrey hides, the same bushes I hid in earlier. There is a knothole in the fence, the size of a quarter, plenty big to see through. I should've seen this earlier, but I guess I wasn't looking for it.

I remember my second head. The turtleneck is still rolled over her nose and mouth. I roll it down and find Anne, again. Only this Anne is older, older than me, even older than the one in her diary. Her skin has sores and is sallow and tight on her face, deepening and widening her already big eyes. Her hair has thinned and I see white scalp in too many places. This Anne doesn't ask any questions. This

IN THE MEAN TIME

Anne isn't chatty. This is the Anne that no one dares imagine after reading her diary. I want to help her, take care of her somehow, and I think she senses this, because she points at the knothole with my left hand and nods. Before I look into the hole, I think, selfishly, that this might be the right Anne for the question I've always wanted to ask.

There's a man in the backyard. He's wearing jeans and a moth-worn, olive-green sweater, sleeves pushed up to his elbows. He's raking leaves with his back turned to me. When he stops raking, he walks over to a tire-swing tied to a thick branch of an oak tree. The branch has an axle and generator set-up similar to my swing set, but no one is riding the tire-swing. There are rocks duct-taped to the bottom of the tire. He pushes the tire-swing a few times, to get the pendulum moving, then goes back to raking leaves. This man has two heads.

I wait and watch. He rakes and pushes, but he doesn't turn around so I can see either of his faces. His hair is brown and short on each head, and now I wish I never looked through the hole.

Anne says, "Why has he never contacted you? Why does he hide so close to home? Does he do this so he can see you when he wants? Or is he just being cruel, mocking you, mocking your mother?"

I want to stay crouched in this spot and let leaves and snow gather on me and never stop watching, but I do pull my eye away from the knothole. Anne and I scan the length and height of the fence. I don't know the answer to Anne's questions and I know the likelihood is that I may never know.

I decide to ask Anne *the* question. I hope it doesn't seem callous or even cruel to her. I understand how it could be interpreted that way, but I hope she understands me and why I do what I do. I still hope.

I say, "Anne, in your last diary entry, you wrote something that . . . that I need to ask you about. This *you* in particular. Do you know what I mean by *this you*?"

"Yes."

I say it. "Do you still believe that people are really good at heart?"

Anne sighs and closes her eyes and it's terrible because it makes her look dead. She holds my left hand, the fingers suddenly and dangerously skinny, over her mouth and chin. She's thinking and I know she will give me an answer. But now that I've asked, the answer isn't as important to me as it was a few days ago, or even a few seconds ago. Because no matter what she says, I'll go back to my swing set and to feeding my house what it needs and I won't tell Mom that I know where he is and I'll take my tests tonight and try my best and help her with the dishes and then talk to her about *Mrs. Dalloway* and the women in my book club and maybe even convince Mom to become an official member. Because, maybe foolishly, I still hope.

But I'll sit in the bushes and wait as long as is necessary to hear what Anne has to say. I owe us that much.

THE STRANGE CASE OF NICHOLAS THOMAS: AN EXCERPT FROM A HISTORY OF THE LONGESIAN LIBRARY

Edited by Paul G. Tremblay

***Editor's Note:

Transcribed below are the notes left behind by our most infamous and mysterious librarian, Nicholas Thomas. Be advised the original notes were handwritten; I've made no changes to spelling or grammar; I've used ellipses where Mr. Thomas trailed off and underscores where he wrote illegibly. You will be spared further editorial commentary until after you've read the notes in their entirety. However, I can't resist beginning with a juicy quote. P.G.T.***

"The Balloons of Annotte in all their implausibility, absurdity, allure, inevitability, mystery, promise (to some), and menace serve only as symbols, and as constant reminders, of the irrational and capricious nature of our City-lives, of our very existence."

—Gwyneth Ann Thomas

FROM NOTES FOR "THE BALLOONS OF ANNOTTE: A MODERN VIEW"

AUTOBIOGRAPHICAL POINTS OF INTEREST:

——Nicholas Thomas, age thirty one, head librarian of the Longesian Library, the largest of City's three public libraries (maybe include a brief or anecdotal history of the Longesian—the only library with an academic display devoted to the Balloons—possibly as a way to introduce or preface the book?), earned a Masters of Library and Information Science from City University and lower degrees in antiquity verification/cataloguing and a degree in City-folklore literature, founder and moderator of the highly successful City Arts discussion group (meeting weekly in the Longesian's Green Room). This is to be the author's first published work of non-fiction.

OBSERVATIONS:

12/17, 12:34 PM

——During these weeks before December 19th, City newspapers devoted pages of ink and text (thirty-three articles to my count . . . I need to remember to scan them into the office computer) to the Balloons of Annotte: fourteen articles detailing what had happened during the most recent occurrence and speculation on what may happen on the 19th, ten articles declaring the Balloons a hoax and outlining how—and by whom—such a hoax might be pulled off, two articles (these appearing in the underground religious publication, *The Temple*) more than intimating the Balloons were proof of God or other supernatural entities pertaining to God, three articles satirizing the event (two with a political bent, and another hilariously imagining the Balloons landing in other parts of the City, including the Pier and in the sex-and-drug-crazed Zone), and five articles written with bureaucratically mind-numbing detail about City's planned and rather draconian response to a Balloon occurrence and the riots that have historically ensued.

——To emphasize a modern view I probably should mention there is countless more text and video devoted to the Balloons on City Television and on the Internet (though nothing from those mediums is worth documenting in the opinion of this author). One sophomoric website claims to have the only existing photograph of a Balloon; however, after a brief viewing, it screams hoax, and a poor one at that. Someone photographed a ludicrous pink balloon, its Happy Birthday message still visible, hovering over a building, a building clearly not from Annotte.

12/18, 5:59 PM

——While working to set up a mini-observatory on my beloved library's roof, someone deposited a truly strange publication into the library's return-slot. A publication that I'm convinced is not authentic, or at the very least, flawed, if not purposefully so. *An Essay on the Strange Case of the Balloons of Annotte* is thin, pamphlet-sized, nineteen-pages long, soft-bound with crude cover art depicting a Balloon hanging over the towers and spires of Annotte, and written by none other than Gwyneth Ann Thomas, my dear mother who passed away eighteen years ago this very week. I was hoping to keep any personal history from seeping into my scholarly endeavor, however, as December 19th approaches, it seems I may have little choice. There is no doubt the woman in the grainy, black-and-white photo on the back cover is my mother. There's no mistaking those owl-eyes, her sloped nose, and ghostly pallor (she was often besieged by a chorus of "You look so pale. Are you feeling all right?" at any gathering of friends or family), all of which I inherited and earned through a mostly secluded and indoor life at my library.

——The essay's publication date must be an error. According to an age-weathered copyright page the publication is only a year old, which isn't possible as both of my parents have been in their graves for almost two decades. I wonder if a former co-worker of hers, possibly someone who was her research assistant once-upon-a-time, is publishing this posthumously. I wonder if someone is trying to make me the butt of a nasty joke. Most likely the Catholic priest from next door, he tends to be surly and mischievous, more so than usual so close to his Messiah's birthday. This is an unexpected and unwelcome intrusion upon my research, and only two days before the event. I vow not to read the essay until after the 19th. I need to remain on task.

——I had planned on dedicating my book to my mother, and now there's this essay. City University Press is the publisher. Must make a note to call them tomorrow and ask about this copyright date.

12/18, 6:49 PM

——I broke down and read half of my mother's essay. I'll include some marked passages (with commentary) below. Perhaps her essay will be more help than hindrance to my academic cause. If nothing else, I will ensure I do not duplicate my mother's work and conclusions.

——From page one, second paragraph:

Only in City does the implausible become expected, miracle become the mundane. While I will not turn this essay into yet another discourse on the nature, the who, the why, or the how of the great wooden Pier beneath City (many a scholar, most more talented than I, have dedicated millions of words to the Pier question without any verifiable answer), I find it important that we so readily accept and take for granted the two-hundred-foot tall wooden posts, and the practically infinite in their number wooden struts and beams that lift City above the coastline. Such City-wide social attitudes are important because we—especially the people living in Annotte—have the same attitude toward the enigmatic Balloons, despite the consequences often attributed to their appearance.

While my mother was certainly a gifted writer, with obvious abilities to sway the reader, I'm surprised by the level (or lack) of academic rigor. I suppose I have to remind myself this is an essay, not a detailed thesis. As seen in this paragraph, she offers no documentation or research to back her claims of City's societal beliefs. After a quick flip through the publication, I found no footnotes or other sources cited. I wonder if this was published unfinished and without my mother's permission. Perhaps I should contact the family lawyer to enquire about the legality of such a publication.

——From page three, ninth paragraph:

Annotte is generally regarded as the birthplace of City. A common debate, even heard among the populace walking City's streets, is whether the Pier was built before Annotte or somehow built underneath the existing City-section. Compelling anecdotal evidence of Annotte being populated with pillars and spires and other rotund architectures— many of the buildings seemingly Pier-like—is used to argue both sides. While Annottites wear their ancient and mysterious City Pier heritage as a badge, it is the Balloons that infect their everyday lives, despite the nineteen-year period between occurrences.

Its cobblestone streets and quaint shops are so unspoiled by comparison to the rest of City. Annotte, decades ago declared the historical section of City, has been seemingly inoculated against the technological onslaught and organized crime encroachment. As a boy who grew up in Annotte (and now as an adult who longs to again make that quaint place his home), I remember the pride, the reverence with which we spoke of our Annotte, even during the anxious weeks leading up to the only Balloon occurrence I experienced.

——I can't resist adding this (though I doubt my editor will have the same problem trimming my personal background information): My father was a mason, and he owned a three-story cylindrical-shaped (as is the case with most of the older dwellings in Annotte) apartment building, and we lived on its third floor. Mother rode a fire-red bicycle to the University. She kept odd hours, which enabled her to stay home with me while father worked early morning jobs. On Mondays we had an odd little ritual. My mother would move furniture to clear a path spanning the circumference of our apartment, and she'd let me ride her bike. She didn't want me riding on the cobblestones and having to dodge the many vendors and their carts. Around and around I rode the entire morning away. Eventually, I wore out a rut in the hardwood floor that my father had to sand out. While I rode, Mother read her books, or if she had no projects due, she clapped and sang silly folksongs, even one about the Balloons. But of course, I don't remember that song, and I've yet to stumble across the ditty in my research.

——From page four, eighth paragraph:

> I wish I could speak to common folklore regarding the Balloons, because there's very little common among the many tales and legends surrounding the Balloons other than their appearing every nineteen years on the nineteenth day of December. Whether the Balloons are to be laughed at, ignored, feared, or welcomed depends upon whom you ask. While not a particularly religious community as a whole, Annottites seem to find their religion every nineteen years.

IN THE MEAN TIME

Obviously, I do not fear the Balloons. But neither am I a zealot or enthusiast. However, I do fear the mobs. One such ruinous group takes to the streets and tears apart any person who dares announce they see a Balloon, or any person claiming to be chosen as a Balloon recipient. Like the torch-and-pitchfork-wielding peasants in Shelley's *Frankenstein* this mob's goal is to keep the occurrence from happening. In addition, as has been the case historically, a second mob patrols the streets displaying any number of bizarre prayers and homegrown incantations supposedly to aid the coming of the Balloons while violently clashing with anyone who voices a dissenting view. Throughout Annotte's recorded history, mob and riot casualties have increased with each occurrence. This is why I shall be an impartial observer, overlooking Annotte from the relative safety of my library roof. The Longesian abuts Annotte, and from the roof, there's a wondrous view of the ancient City-section.

12/19 10:54 AM

———I had planned a final walk through before the evening's events and possibly to conduct some interviews, but the police have closed Annotte to all non-residents. Wooden barriers manned by small patrols block each of the nineteen streets leading into and out of Annotte. I was surprised to hear City was organizing an evacuation as well, but from what I've heard, no one was leaving. I will need to confirm or deny the rumor officially. Yet another phone call to make.

———We've been forced to close the library as the turned-away crowds were making themselves a nuisance among our stacks.

———Just off the phone with City University Press: A representative (don't know how much faith I have in the woman, as I had to spell "Longesian" for her) told me they have no such publication as my mother's essay in their catalogue, nor any record of its impending release. Surely this lends credence to my joke-theory, and a cruel joke at that.

————Rereading the copyright page, it seems I have made a mistake, although I'd swear that I read City University Press, originally. The publisher's credit reads: CUPress, which could conceivably be a publisher different than City University Press. But there's the new problem of who CUPress is.

12/19 3:16 PM

————I've read more of my mother's essay. The question of by whom and why this was published is a mystery that will have to wait until after this evening. Despite the alarming and often contradictory information contained within, I've decided that she was indeed the author. I've read enough of my mother's scholarly works to know the essay's voice and style is as unmistakable as the photo on the back cover.

————What follows are some excerpts taken from her set of interviews conducted the day after the most recent Balloon occurrence.

————From page twelve, seventh paragraph:

This from a market owner who wished to remain anonymous:

"My family was upstairs and I was standing on my shop stoop, holding my shotgun. I'll be damned if I was going to let some group of Balloon-crazies bust up my shop. Anyway, it was snowing hard. And damn my eyes they [the Balloons] were actually falling out of the sky, but slow, and with a weird kind of aim. Am I making any sense? I'm saying they were falling like they knew where they were falling. Too many to count. And one was coming toward me, no bigger than a small dog. Even in the snow, I saw this one was red, so red almost purple, like a wine, and hanging under it was a string as thin as a hair strand. It didn't really look all that different than a plain old kiddie balloon, but, at the same time, it looked different. I don't know, sounds silly, right? Me being scared of a goddamn balloon. But just seeing it and how it floated with purpose. I've never been so afraid in my life. Hands, arms, legs, everything was shaking and it felt like . . . I don't know, like I was dying. Then I heard one of those mobs yelling and coming up my road and the damned Balloon was still getting closer. And then I saw some sort of picture on the Balloon's face but I shot at it before I saw what the picture was. I didn't want to see it. You know, I used to laugh at all those stories . . . So I just fired and didn't even bother with getting the thing in my sights. I fired two wild shots. I'm sorry, and I hope I didn't end up hitting another house or store or God forbid, anyone else. I did what I had to do. Then I looked up and didn't see the Balloon anywhere. I ran inside and upstairs into my apartment. The mob came and started busting up my shop and I just sat with my wife and kid in my arms, and we were crying."

While estimates run higher, City Hospital reported two fatalities and thirty-eight injuries solely due to firearm wounds on the 19th. Both fatalities and approximately half of the injuries occurred within the safety of their own homes, with the injured individuals (along with eyewitnesses) claiming stray bullets fired from the street were the culprits.

Thinking about the stray bullets: perhaps my roof observatory won't be as safe as I imagined it to be. Regardless, I find it interesting my mother did not directly comment upon the interviewee's story, or his obvious (and frightening, if his viewpoint is to in any way represent the attitudes of some Annottites) paranoia.

———From page thirteen, sixth paragraph:

This from Aubrey Haas, self-proclaimed Balloon enthusiast:

"Yes, I've seen plenty of Balloons and I've received their messages. No,

I won't describe what I saw, because they are beyond words, and to try to describe them to a non-believer, such as you, is tantamount to blasphemy. What is also blasphemy are the lies you and people like you spread about the supposed disappearances and gory deaths associated with the Balloons. It's obvious these people are vagrants or victims of the anti-Balloon mobs. I've seen Balloons and many of my friends have seen them, even touched them. None of us have disappeared. Yet our secular press run by our secular Government continues the lies in attempt to squash any and all religious fervor. Don't you see? We've been witness to a true miracle. Proof of God's existence and His greatness. That is all I have to say to you."

As I tried to explain to Ms. Haas before she dismissed me, many estimates run higher—as these are only the cases being officially reported—but in the five days since the 19th twenty-two Annotte residents have been reported as missing to the City Police Department, along with sixteen cause-unknown fatalities.

Again, the interviewee's zealot attitude disturbs me as much as the cold statistics my mother quotes.

——While my mother was not a religious person, she celebrated spiritual diversity, as most true academes do (though she never gave credence to the cult-like worshippers of the Balloons). When I was a child, she encouraged me to find my own beliefs, my own spirituality. She used to bring home tomes of the many different religions practised in our City so we could discuss, dissect, and compare. Probably not a typical mother-son activity, but one I cherished. This essay reminds me how much I miss my parents, my mother, my kindred academic-spirit, in particular. The timing of this sentimentality couldn't be worse in terms of my planned research; however, I know the trips and turns of everyday life cannot be planned and/or catalogued.

IN THE MEAN TIME

——From page fourteen, fifth paragraph:

This brief interview was the most difficult I've ever experienced. To be honest, I'm not very proud of myself for conducting it, and less so for publishing it. Regardless, it does belong here, in this essay. While gathering data at Police Headquarters, I saw a man, an Annottite, whom I knew very well (I'm keeping his name anonymous). He left the building in tears and screaming obscenities. I followed and despite having no pen or paper, or recorder, our conversation is burned into my memory. This is an exact transcription:

Anon: She's gone.

Me: Who?

Anon: My daughter.

Me: My goodness, S____? Oh, I'm so sorry. Is there anything I can do?

Anon: No. There's nothing. Nothing.

Me: Forgive me for pressing, but what happened?

Anon: Come on, Gwyn. You know what happened.

Me: I do?

Anon: Yes, you're writing your damned book about it, aren't you?

Me: About what?

Anon: I locked her bedroom window. I know I did. I stayed up late, patting her head, watching her window, watching the snow, watching her sleep, and then thinking it'd all passed before I went to my wife and bed. And in the morning, I went into her room and it was so cold because the window was open. She was sleeping, so I didn't wake her, even though I wanted to know why the window was open. At breakfast she was so quiet, keeping her eyes on the table. I thought she was just tired, probably didn't get much sleep. And like a fool, the goddamn fool that I am, I pushed it all aside, you know? Like we all do. Like we all try to ignore the everyday evils. We'll read about City's drugs, murder, and homeless, but we don't really see it. None of us do. We close our eyes and whistle past the graveyard, hoping and praying the not-my-family prayer, wishing all the bad away to never come back. And we Annottites simply wish the evil away for another nineteen years. My wish didn't come true this time,

Gwyn. That morning, I left for work, and J____ sent S____ to school . . .
and . . . and she hasn't come home. She hasn't come home, Gwyn.

Sometimes I feel like I've been punished for my part in this interview.
An irrational feeling, but one I can't shake. It's been nineteen years and
I haven't forgotten this conversation, this interview, or the parallels to
my life. Forgive this author's melodramatic indulgence, but this essay—
started all those years ago—has become one of loss and tears.

I've stared at the ominous phrase "or the parallels to my life" for a
better part of the afternoon. I don't know what that means, or to
what she was referring. And her writing about the nineteen years
certainly gives the impression that this essay was written recently
(all dates quoted in the essay refer to the most recent Balloon
occurrence), which is an impossibility. The numbers aren't adding
up. Despite its apparent authenticity, this can't have been written by
my mother. Or at least, the dates and text were fudged and doctored.
Yet, I'm still reading it.

——December 19th, nineteen years ago: I remember locking and
barricading our doors and shutters against the mobs. We were
tightly shut in. We did our best to ignore what was happening
outside. Mother played jazz records on her antique phonograph. The
horns, bass, and piano almost drowned out the shouts and cries of
the streets. Father and I played cards in his bedroom, playing well
past midnight and playing until Mother joined us. Or did she? I
don't remember. I remember their bedroom with its yellow walls
turned amber in the lantern's glow. I remember hearing shouts and
screams and cheering and gunshots. I remember my father telling
me over and over, "It will be all right, son." I remember being afraid,
but exhilarated. I remember being bored with the hours of card
play (though I don't remember what games we played). I remember
asking to ride the bike around the apartment. I remember the bike
was stowed in my parents' room for the evening (though I don't
remember the reason). Riding was forbidden on that evening, but I

was allowed to sit on the red bike, and I remember pretending I was, of all things, a Balloon: I was a Balloon circling my home, floating like a fat snowflake in a squall, descending upon the streets and manic crowds, laughing at the juxtaposed looks of joy and fear on those City faces.

——Rereading my notes: there's still much I don't remember about that evening and the days that followed. I'll admit I started this project with more than academic ambitions. There are holes, personal holes, to be filled. But they only seem to be growing deeper.

12/19 6:49 PM

——From page nineteen (the last page), final three paragraphs:

> *Time heals all wounds*: a cliché we've all heard and very likely spoken in an effort to comfort the grief-stricken. However, denizens of Annotte know better. Here, every nineteen years, old wounds are reopened and bleed anew. My own wounds: one week after the 19th, my husband and my son— my wonderful, magical, curious son—disappeared, never returning from their Sunday trip to the Longesian Library. This is something I'm only able to write about now that nineteen years have passed, and now that the Balloons are due to make their fateful return. There isn't a day that goes by without my thoughts and broken heart going out to them, and to myself.

> Academes often write with the lofty goal of serving the populace, of performing the often thankless task of imparting information crucial to one's daily life. I have a greater hope for this, my last essay. My hope is that this modest essay will heal better than the overrated salve of time. Simply put: this is my reaching out to all Annottites who have suffered as I have. This is a commiseration from which I hope others gain strength.

> In the end, all we have are the big questions: Why Balloons? What connection do they have to Annotte? Why the violence? Why the

disappearances? What does it all mean? I don't know and I don't offer any solutions or explanations, meanings or reasons. To look for such in the Balloon occurrence is folly. Ultimately, there is no meaning to the Balloon's existence, as there's no meaning to be taken from the presumed death and disappearance of my or anyone else's family. The Balloons of Annotte in all their implausibility, absurdity, allure, inevitability, mystery, promise (to some), and menace serve only as symbols, and as constant reminders, of the irrational and capricious nature of our City-lives, of our very existence.

This essay has so turned my head around. I've been pacing my office, like that long-ago little boy who once circled his parents' home while riding his mother's red bicycle. The contradictory information, the cruel joke upon my mother's memory, the undeniable effect it is having on me while mere hours from the most important night of my academic life. I vow to strike this essay from my notes, first thing in the morning. Removing the damnable essay from my memory won't be so easy.

12/19 8:11 PM

———I've manned my mini-observatory. Oak desk and chair, telescope, all resting upon a flattened section of library roof and pushed as close to a ledge as is permitted by the Longesian. Visibility is clear, though snow squalls are in the forecast. Spread out before me, Annotte: the column-like buildings pointing to the sky, like skinny fingers. City below and all around is quiet.

12/19 9:19 PM

———They came with the snow, I don't know if that's something that has always occurred (as documented, it was snowing during the last occurrence), or just simple chance, there's a cluster of three or four, or maybe five, hanging over the northern section, they're only dark blobs at this distance, the telescope is too unwieldy and

IN THE MEAN TIME

the lens keeps gathering snow . . . there's more, two hover over
Tanner's Market . . . ___ having a hard time keeping up with my
pencil and keeping the snow off the paper . . . there's another cluster
over the Cribbage Street tenements, they're circling the buildings,
I've lost sight of some of them, can't see their color yet, a strange
scene to try to describe, they look like they belong there, floating
above Annotte, their movement is slow, almost too slow to perceive
such movement from this distance, but they are moving, they are
falling, my God, I just lost one, it just disappeared, it just ___ . . .
looking higher and there must be hundreds, hundreds of the things,
and there is yelling and screaming, breaking glass, lights blink on
and off in houses and buildings, adding a strobe effect to the snowy
night sky, I can't see the cobblestone streets, but there's a glow, they
must be lighting fires, the mobs, it's going to be real bad this year, I
just ___ it . . . snow is making the writing difficult, hope these notes
survive, just across the Longesian, I see two Balloons bouncing off
the side of the Buertin Bed and Breakfast as if they're feeling the
building for weak spots, looking for entry, ___ there's an explosion!
and a huge fire in Annotte's center, in Travis Square, maybe one of
the breweries, the Balloons are patient shadows in the fire's light,
still floating, dropping, falling . . . what's ___ ? this can't be ___,
there's a Balloon floating directly above me it's by itself twenty feet
above maybe it's an illusion like an Escher painting it really isn't
directly above me it only appears that way I'm not in Annotte it only
appears ___ no it's dropping gliding descending bathed in the fire's
back glow I feel the fire's heat I hear it's crackle I see the Balloon is
blue a sky blue no a dark blue and there's a picture on its face a little
red bicycle maddening in its detail in miniature in minutia I want to
___ I have to ___ I have to run grabbing what I ___ . . . ___ back in
the office my hands shaking more explosions rip through the night
oh this will be the worst night in City's history what I felt when it
was almost on me what I felt it's hard I can only think about the door
to the roof and did the creaky rusty old flimsy roof door ___ behind
me the lights are out I'm huddled under my desk and I hear oh God
I hear something gliding passing floating and I can hear floating

PAUL TREMBLAY

I ____ MOMMY I'M SO SORRY IT WAS ME I KNOW I WASN'T SUPPOSED TO BUT I OPENED THE WINDOW DADDY FELL ASLEEP AND INSTEAD OF COMING TO GET YOU I OPENED THE WINDOW I JUST WANTED TO SEE ONE COME IN AND IT WAS SO PRETTY MOM ALMOST AS BIG AS MY KITE AND SO RED LIKE YOUR BIKE OUR BIKE IT FLEW RIGHT INTO MY ARMS IT WAS WARM IT HAD A SOUND WHEN I CAUGHT IT IT WAS SOFT NOT LIKE A RUBBER BALLOON AT ALL FELT LIKE THE CANVAS YOU HAVE AT SCHOOL MOM IT FELT LIKE A SECRET INSIDE OF ME THEN I PRESSED MY FACE AGAINST IT LOOKING THROUGH IT INSIDE IT I SAW ALL OF US AND WE WERE IN THE LIVING ROOM PLAYING LAUGHING CLAPPING WE TOOK TURNS RIDING THE BIKE AROUND THE HOUSE AROUND AND AROUND AND AROUND AND I WATCHED ALL OF US RIDING IT MADE ME SO HAPPY SO I WOKE DADDY AND GAVE HIM THE BALLOON HE HELD IT AND LOOKED INSIDE HE HAD THE SADDEST HAPPY FACE I'D EVER SEEN LIKE THE FACE YOU HAD THAT MORNING WE LEFT FOR THE LIBRARY I DIDN'T TELL YOU THAT AND I'M SORRY MOM I DIDN'T TELL YOU WE WERE KEEPING THIS SECRET INSIDE OF US I JUST WANTED TO RIDE AROUND MOM REALLY WE LET IT FLY BACK OUT THE WINDOW I THINK I CAN'T REMEMBER MOM I CAN'T REMEMBER MOM MOMMY I'M SO SORRY IT WAS ME I KNOW I WASN'T SUPPOSED TO BUT I OPENED THE WINDOW I JUST WANTED TO SEE ONE COME IN AND IT WAS SO PRETTY MOM ALMOST AS BIG AS MY KITE AND SO RED LIKE YOUR BIKE OUR BIKE IT FLEW RIGHT INTO MY ARMS IT WAS WARM IT HAD A SOUND WHEN I CAUGHT IT IT WAS SOFT NOT LIKE A RUBBER BALLOON AT ALL FELT LIKE THE CANVAS YOU HAVE AT SCHOOL MOM. . . .

***Editor's note:

In the interest of authenticity, I did not add punctuation to the last entry. However, I decided to change fonts where the notes changed in its handwriting: the final part of the original 12/19 9:19 PM notes section

59

IN THE MEAN TIME

was in block letters, as if written by a child. This child-scribble repeats itself (starting with "Mommy I'm so sorry" and ending with "I can't remember Mom") for 361 pages.

Other points of note:

Going back almost four hundred years, the Longesian's employee-ledger has no record of a Nicholas Thomas having ever worked among the many book stacks.

Neither Gwyneth Ann Thomas nor CUPress were willing to comment upon Nicholas Thomas's notes, the pages of which were found the morning of December 20th, spread on the Longesian's foyer floor, in the shape of a Balloon and Its string. DNA and handwriting tests proved inconclusive, and no one (other than Nicholas Thomas) has claimed ownership of the notes.

The missing person file belonging to Gwyneth's son, Nicholas Thomas, is entering its third decade as unsolved but still filed as **active** with Annotte's police, presumably by request of Ms. Gwyneth Thomas (Annotte law allows for parents to petition the police to keep missing person files active indefinitely). While the police would not release the file numbers, they did confirm Nicholas and his father's files had sequential numbers.

I'm leaving this particular chapter of the Longesian's history purposefully ambiguous. As a proud employee of the Longesian, I wouldn't dream of crying hoax or debunking any of the mystery surrounding Nicholas Thomas—City's legendary librarian. I will do as any good historian should do: present the findings, with little to no pontificating from my editorial soapbox, and let the reader come to their own conclusions. P.G.T.***

FEEDING THE MACHINE

It's Friday. There are plans for this day, and after. So many things supposed to happen. But you aren't doing anything to prepare. Instead, you linger in front of the refrigerator. It's open, and you itemize: eggs, low-fat milk, her soy milk, orange juice, V8, caffeine-free Coke cans sharing space with bottled waters, assorted fruits and veggies in ragged plastic bags and containers, two-night's-ago Lo mein and Kung Pao leftovers in those white cardboard cartons emanating their funky gone-bad-already smell, and three mystery-filled Tupperware cases you don't want to open.

Lower back aches. It's been getting worse. You remember thinking morning sickness used to be bad, but now you'd trade in this back pain for a little AM vomit in a heartbeat.

You're still standing in front of the stocked fridge. You rub your back, then your pregnant belly, and you feel yourself detaching, fading out, going to that place you don't want to go. But you can't stop it. Just like you couldn't stop yourself from reading her diary.

Her diary: You didn't know she had one, but it wasn't a surprise. You made sure to put it back, exactly where you found it, which was on top of her dresser: alone, on display. You hate yourself for reading it, but a diary was a wink and a nudge. It had no lock, no key, no password; just flimsy leather and cardboard keeping the pages shut. A diary was a dare: daring you to choose between trust and the truth. And you read it. You wanted to read it again and again until you memorized it, until you chewed all her words to pulp, all those words of blame and guilt and sadness she no longer shares with you. All those words she should be saying to your face, those words she couldn't say to you last night and for the past two months of last nights are in your head now, bouncing around, and you stretch and squeeze and roll them into a ball, trying to milk out all possible interpretations and meanings, but it's getting messy. You're already forgetting and mixing up what she wrote with what you thought about it.

This was hard.

This was being us. The new us. The somebody-went-and-got-pregnant us.

The first time it had happened, my doctor said Pica is the craving or eating of items that aren't food. He said Pica (which sounds like pie-kah) means "magpie" in Latin. Magpies were nature's garbage disposals; they feed on everything they find. There was a fat joke in there somewhere.

We'd got back from the hospital ten minutes before. I'd been sitting at the kitchen table watching Cassie make some tea. She was still in her work clothes. Dark blue skirt and light blue button-down shirt. It was her nicest skirt, but it looked a little tight on her. There were slight bulges at her hips and waistline that never used to be there, not that it mattered to me in any physical-attraction sense. I was still very much in love with and attracted to Cassie. No, I was not trying to convince myself. Since my first Pica-episode two months ago, Cassie had stopped jogging and stopped going to the gym. She had gained almost as much weight as I had, not that I pointed it out. I know the weight gain was bothering her, although she hadn't said anything to me about it. She hadn't said a lot of anything to me lately. But I wasn't really being fair, laying all this (this was hard, this was being us, the new us. . . .) on her.

Standing in front of the stove, her back turned to me, Cassie said, "You feel up to some tea? I think we have some honey left."

The second time it had happened my doctor said Pica is prevalent in animals. He said for some animals eating dirt is a weapon in the battle between plants and animals. Yes, he said weapon. He said animals use Pica as a weapon against plant reproduction strategy. I was still not sure why he told me that, or even what it meant. But I did know I was getting sick of him comparing me to magpies and animals.

You shake the fading embers of her lost, never-spoken words from your head and dive back into the fridge. Food is again priority number-one. Everything else can wait. You're elbow-deep, pushing aside the standard food items, looking for that one thing your body craves and by proxy, the baby craves. Your doctor and all those baby magazines and the *What to Expect When You're Expecting* books have been less than subtle in hammering home the point that what you eat is what the baby eats. But what they didn't tell you was that you have about as much choice in choosing your fuel as a car does. You-the-machine wants what it wants. And it needs what it needs.

Jars of barbeque and spaghetti and soy sauces, salad dressing, cream cheese, ketchup, mustard, maple syrup, relish, mayo, grated parmesan cheese, butter, jam, baking soda, and an empty jar of honey. You don't think about why she left an empty jar in the refrigerator. You don't think about what it means, or if there is any meaning.

Your thoughts are becoming objective, antiseptic. You are detaching, watching two hands pick up and reject all the jars and bottles and containers. You are the machine.

I said, probably too loud, exaggerating my enthusiasm, "I'd like some tea, Cassie. Not too much though. I'm still feeling . . ." and then I paused, and even after living with Pica for two months, I wasn't sure how to describe what I was feeling. ". . . all blocked up, if that makes sense." But that wasn't exactly right, either.

IN THE MEAN TIME

Cassie said, "I bet," and disappeared into the pantry.

We had to talk, but there were so many things to say. It was overwhelming. Both of us afraid if we said the wrong thing there'd be no way to fix it. And saying the wrong thing would blow up into the wrong conversation: one wrong word leading to the next and the next and the next in some predetermined, logical chain that must be followed, like the code to a computer virus, one misstatement permanently infecting and crashing our hard drives, crashing us. We had been like this since the day we decided to keep the baby and each day that passed made everything worse. Like a pair of cowards, we ran away from each other, or worse, stood hand-in-hand with our other hands covering our mouths or our ears. We were walking hear-n'-speak-no-evil monkeys.

Jesus. Now I was comparing us to animals.

Cassie emerged from the pantry with the little, yellow jar of honey. "There's not much left."

I said, "That's okay, then. You take it. I don't need it."

Cassie loved her honey. I was stunned there wasn't another full jar or two in the pantry already. There being no honey left was disturbing. She was really losing herself.

Cassie put honey on bread, on her salads, in summer she made her own honey-bbq sauce, and she put honey in tea and an assortment of other drinks. My first time at a bar with her, she'd had a little bottle inside her jacket and she kept pouring dollops into her draft IPA. She didn't stir it in though. I watched the little blob of honey sink, keeping its droplet-shape and then resting on the bottom of the glass. When she brought the pint to her mouth the honey-blob rolled up the glass but stopped short of her lips. I asked her if she could even taste it. She said she could and then offered me a sip. I gulped, trying to suck in the honey-blob but couldn't catch it. After, I wiped my mouth on my sleeve, flashed my most petite and demure smile, and told her I couldn't taste the honey and that it looked like the bartender had hocked a loogie at the bottom of her glass. She laughed, shaking our uneven, glass-topped table for two. I loved her laugh. So loud. So out of control. I imagined when other people heard her laughing, they might think she was faking, or crying hysterically, or going nuts. Still laughing, she told me she wished all her dates would work *loogie* into conversation. She downed the rest of her beer, and insisted you could taste the honey, only you had to be paying attention to do so. She winked, ordered another round, and eventually took me home and poured what was left of the honey all over me.

Cassie scraped the jar's sides with a spoon and then dunked it into my teacup. She said, "Don't be silly. You can have the last of it."

I wished fixing us was as easy as another loogie joke. And maybe it was, and we were just too stubborn to see it.

The next time it had happened my doctor said that Pica was a misunderstood problem and there were many reasons why people ate dirt or other non-food items. He said to be diagnosed a person must have symptoms for about a month. He said there was no diagnostic or medical test for Pica and usually it was only caught when the eating complications force the person to seek medical attention. Well, at least he'd stopped comparing me to animals.

Closing the refrigerator door, you turn. There's the mica countertop with the breadbox you've already poked around in, four times to be exact but who's counting. There's a yellow beam of sunlight trapping dust like prehistoric bugs in amber. There's the dishwasher with its full load but you won't put the dishes away. Even if you wanted to, Cassie would be bullshit at your token foray into manual labour; she's so rabid with preggo-support it's depressing, depressing because you learned in those diary pages that it's all a show.

There are glossy and cheesy entertainment magazines on the kitchen table and you think about lining your stomach with all those photos of toothy and plastic and unreal women, like that would be a suitable revenge for what life has done to you, for what you've done to yourself, for what you've done to Cassie, but you're not so far gone to know you don't want to eat the magazines, at least not yet. There are the cabinets underneath the sink and all those poisons contained within, and you think about how you probably need to put some sort of safety lock on those to protect the baby. You tighten your white bathrobe and you're still hungry. There's the sunbeam again, its wattage weakening, and now the spotlighted dust is plankton floating at the ocean surface, just waiting to kick-start the food chain. You try to avoid the beam on the way to the cupboard, but it hits your leg and you feel its weak heat, and you know there's no stopping this. And there's the walk-in cupboard across from the L-shaped mica counter, and you go through the sliding doors, and your robot-hands walk over boxes of pasta, crouton bags, cans of peas and corn and soup, rice, cereal, and a canister of bread crumbs, and then onto the non-food items, and it's here that the hands hesitate and study the olive oil and flour, and you eye the tarragon and crushed oregano and the little vanilla extract bottle like a hawk eyeing a field of mice.

Sipping my tea like it was medicine I didn't want to take, the proverbial bitter pill, I said, "Thank you, Cassie." I tasted the honey this time, but it tasted old somehow. I wondered if she knew that pregnant women weren't supposed to eat honey. If I told her that, would it have sounded like some terrible joke, or a really good one? I didn't know. I noticed how everything meant something when we weren't talking.

She said, "So Phil will be here on Friday night."

Right. Her brother Phil. I'd seen pictures but I'd never met him. He was to be my new babysitter. I'd got him a fill-in job at a small and local private boys high school, teaching math for a month. The job ended when I was to go on maternity leave so he could help me take care of the house, and help me take care of me. But there was still that month we all had to get through.

"Lots of stuff happening this Friday," I said and then laughed, but Cassie didn't join in.

Friday: Valentine's Day (no matter how much we said the Hallmark-holiday meant nothing, it meant something, probably more this year than any other), the math department at UVM was throwing me a good-luck-on-preggo-leave party, even though I wasn't scheduled to leave until mid-March. And, Friday was Phil's arrival day.

I said, "You're okay with me going to my party by myself, right?" I knew what her answer would be, even if she didn't mean it. Wasn't I just a drama preggo-lesbo-queen? But did I mention that the Daddy would be at the party? It was all Cassie was thinking about.

The next time it had happened my doctor said the non-food items that are typically ingested are dirt, clay, chalk, sand, potting soil, cigarette or fireplace ashes, paint, starch, plaster, gravel, and rocks. Then he said the person suffering from Pica might eat just about anything.

The Daddy used to be my best friend. Carlos Greene. He and I had gone through college, then the UVM master's program, then had earned PhDs together. We had both been offered tenure-tracked teaching jobs. Last year we had joint-published our first research project: *Matrices, Hyperbolic Curves, and Mars' Gravitational Effects on the Human Brain*. Yeah, I was wicked smart. Except six months ago, while Cassie was away on business, I got piss-drunk at our school's beginning of the year party, blacked out, and woke up next to a naked (and appallingly hairy) Carlos. That wasn't wicked smart.

While staring at the bottom of her un-honeyed cup, Cassie said, "I'm okay with it. You don't have to keep asking me. I trust you."

I put my cup down and looked at her. I stared, waiting for her to pick up her eyes and send them down her sharp and elegant nose at me. And I wanted to scream at her, make her tell me what she really felt, to make her say I'm okay with the party because I know at least this time you're already pregnant and probably won't get sloppy-drunk and then fuck Carlos. I would've been okay if she said that.

The next time it had happened my doctor said complications of Pica can include malnutrition, intestinal obstruction or infections or soil-borne parasites, anaemia, mercury or lead poisoning, liver and kidney damage, constipation and abdominal problems. He said Pica can be harmless, but obviously, eating certain material could lead to death. Just so much to look forward to.

IN THE MEAN TIME

In this final, tenuous moment before surrendering to the machine, you want to blame Cassie and her diary for starting this. You want to blame her for your emptiness even though you know you've been complicit, a full-fledged partner in adding to the empty. Losing yourself now and forgiving yourself after would be so much easier if you could blame someone else. But you can't do that and be fair. So you'll feel guilt. Oh yeah, you'll double that order, but it won't fill you.

All of which means this will most certainly happen again. Your own rolling wheel of guilt and emptiness and the need to fill it.

I didn't press her further on the party. I was all talk and just as comfortable saying nothing, adding to our nothing. How could we both be so empty of things to say?

"What are you and your brother going to do on Friday?"

"I don't know. Depends on what time he gets here." She laughed through her nose and folded her arms across her chest. Doing that made her look younger, and small. "Not sure if I'm ready to take Phil out on the town. I'd have to work up to that."

The next time it had happened my doctor said there is no cure for Pica. Sometimes giving nutritional supplements help. He said sometimes again, and then wrote a prescription and encouraged me to eat appropriate, healthy, nutritional foods. That list didn't include my recent à-la-carte items: cardboard, newspaper, or kitty litter.

I said, "I can't wait to meet Phil. I'm going to bombard him with questions about his growing up with the one-time young . . ."

"Hey! I'm still young," she said, and gave me the first real smile of the night, maybe of the week.

". . . and uncorrupted Cassandra Evans."

"You won't get anything out of him."

The next time it had happened my doctor said typical Pica patients are people who are poor or have nutrition and vitamin deficiency or a family history of Pica, or even people with ethnic customs who live in cultures where it is practiced. Oh, and as a throwaway, he added that Pica is very common among pregnant women. I had resisted the urge to thank Doctor Obvious.

Cassie sat next to me at our little kitchen table. Another of our antiques. This one we'd stripped and lacquered ourselves on a breezy fall Sunday. The wind had kept sticking leaves on the table while we'd worked. If you were looking for it, you could see three different leaf-outlines in the table's finish. My teacup was resting on one. This table was my favourite piece of furniture in the house.

She said, "Can I ask you something?"

"Please do."

"How does it happen? I mean, what are you thinking when it happens?"

The next time it happened my doctor said that even in America the eating of clay is common and sold as edible in some states. He said some people believe that eating clay will help with morning sickness. He said pregnant Nigerian women will eat calcium-rich clay because there are no calcium-rich foods in their usual diet.

Cassie had taken out books and talked to my doctor, but this was the first time she'd asked me about it. This was a good thing. Although I had no idea what to say, because I really didn't know the answer.

The next time it had happened my doctor said Pica in pregnant women tended to go away after childbirth but sometimes it occurs post partum. Again, he said sometimes.

I decided to try this:

"I never sense when an episode is coming on. Usually, I fake myself out. I'll be reading or teaching or watching TV, and then I'll start thinking about the disease and worry about what it could do to me and the baby, almost convincing myself that an episode is going to happen. But then it doesn't.

"When it happens for real, I don't really notice there's anything wrong, but at the same time I do. I don't know if that makes any sense. But I guess there is a sense of something about to happen, I can remember that, but I'm calm and there's no worry or panic, like my body knows there won't be any thinking or worrying getting in the way of what it wants. I don't know, I guess the best way to describe it is that it takes over, without any real struggle on my part. Like being hypnotized, or anaesthetized. Any memory of the actual eating is fuzzy at best, like remembering a scene from a long-ago-watched movie or TV show."

Cassie grabbed my hand and said, "You can stop now."

It was too much for her. She got up, tried to offer me a smile, but it was broken, and she walked out of the kitchen, walking like there was a somewhere else for her to go. I heard our bedroom door close, and I closed my eyes and got this sudden vision of unused honey at the bottom of my teacup, and somehow that seemed like the saddest thing in the world.

After it had happened earlier that day, my doctor said that there is talk about Pica possibly being more psychological than physical, the ingesting of toxic or harmful non-food items as a form of self-abuse.

Self-abuse. We were good at that.

So you-the-machine walk out of the cupboard, ploughing through the sunbeam. You-the-machine doesn't notice. Then across the kitchen to the back door and out that door onto the three-season porch. You-the-machine doesn't see how clean it is, how Cassie must've dusted and washed everything: mini-blinds, walls, wicker table and chairs, everything, because today is Friday, the day of plans. You-the-machine notes the change in temperature on the porch, but only in an instinctual, gooseflesh way. You-the-machine does not notice your frosty breath, your exhaust, nor do you look out the windows to see the still-going-strong snow cover. You-the-machine walks to the porch corner that is adjacent to the garage entry. Resting on the floor and tucked into the corner like a poorly kept secret, are a bag of potting soil and a box of powder laundry detergent. You-the-machine doesn't care that the soil was a house-warming gift that has sat in the same spot for the two years you've lived at the house. You-the-machine doesn't care that the detergent has been there as long as the soil, something you bought before learning Cassie only used liquid detergent.

One robot-hand goes inside the soil bag, satisfied with the cold and crumbling clod it snatches, and the other into the detergent box and its white chemical sand.

After, there will be no going-on-leave math department party and you won't meet Cassie's brother Phil. The Friday, and all the days after, you planned, will not exist, as if it ever did.

After, and *this* after will only be if Cassie comes home and finds you in time, you'll be in an ambulance that shouts all the way to the hospital and you'll only faintly remember the rest: mouth opening, a foggy notion of taste, of enriched mineral and earth filling your mouth and mixing with the tang and burn of chemical, and before the pain is the initial opiate-like rush and relief of a full stomach, of filling the empty, of feeding the machine.

FIGURE 5

(co-written with M. Thomas)

1

Anderbine has watched her for seventy-two days. Each morning, as the sun spills around the spires of the Ministry of Bone, Midria pauses on the eighty-seventh step of the Grand Hundred stairs and throws back her tattered hood. Plague victims who pass her on the stairs never show their faces. The city sprawls below her on precarious ridges carved from bloodless limestone and greywacke cliffs. The guards on the eastern edge of the Grand Hundred stairs do not pass the plague barrier, but some throw ugly slurs her way, which she ignores.

Anderbine's Figure 1 is a triptych on wood. Only minute manifestations of the plague are visible on the first panel: cold sores and rashes around the eyes and mouth, along the cheeks, jaw, forehead, and into the hair. Such manifestations are the only evidence necessary for quarantine. In panel two, the lesions suppurate and the pus congeals into a tough, honey-coloured scab too painful to remove. It sloughs off eventually along with hair and eyelashes, as is evident in the third panel, leaving behind the nacreous sheen of the new flesh called the Caul. The Caul will be lost too, eventually. The ears draw closer to the head as the lesion seams heal tightly, leaving the cartilage of the ear flap to stick out in ridges along the jaw. In the beginning, change was the only constant, fluid in its speed, and he sketched madly for hours. Now her metamorphosis has slowed, if not stopped.

Anderbine sits in his studio, holding a pencil and sketchpad, and looking out his high window. He tries to catch sight of her hands, which will accept her daily allotment of water from the plague well: the well once reserved, in better times, for penitents and holy days. Midria has not changed since the preceding night. She keeps her hands hidden in her sleeves.

In Figure 2, a full-length portrait, Anderbine has paid special attention to the milky sheen of her Caul, the strange bulges and bumps of the new bone growth underneath or rather, the rearrangement of the chin, cheeks, eyebrow ridges, and jaw, which narrow and elongate. The Grand Hundred stairs are littered with teeth that fall out during this stage and they crack like shale underfoot of the plague victims.

Figure 3 is a simple line drawing, no shading, only lines to show the sharp new edges of her and the new eyes, three of them along her forehead. They pressed and bulged against the Caul until they burst through, doe-ish and dry.

In Figure 4, chalk on gray pulp-print, the Caul is completely worn away and hangs from her in strips. Days ago, he doesn't remember how many, she scratched at and pulled off the Caul. Its thin swaths dropped onto the stairs among the teeth. Underneath the Caul was a smooth, white carapace, which reddened, then browned in the sun, looking like a finely polished wooden mask.

Midria pauses to search the high houses on the eastern side of the stairs, and her gaze lingers on familiar places: the Salons, the rock gardens, the terrace restaurants, the libraries. Then she is gone again, her hood replaced. She rejoins the anonymous crowd of hoods and slumped shoulders climbing up from the bottom of the Grand Hundred to their water, to prolong their death sentence with the barest of comforts.

Anderbine leaves his window and considers his final canvas. It is Figure 5 he cannot complete. Midria has remained unchanged, or unfinished, locked in the Figure 4 stage for a week now. There have been no reports of plague victims surviving for long after the shedding of the Caul.

"Gravis," Anderbine calls, and his aged and stooped servant appears immediately. "A fish for dinner, I think. And some apples, if you can get them."

Gravis, the only member of his staff to stay after she left, says, "Yes, sir." They still address each other formally, though stubborn adherence to social mores is meaningless with no one present to observe it. Gravis disappears from the room, thrifty and economical in all his ways. Anderbine doesn't blame the others for leaving.

Anderbine walks the dark and cobwebbed hallways to the dining room. The house is too much for Gravis, but there are few left to hire. Those who come try to hide the rashes with makeup and scarves, increasingly bizarre wigs, strange jewellery pressed through open sores to seem like ornaments. In the dining room, candles are lit beside a single place setting at the head of the long table. Ministry portraits, arranged chronologically, hang on the walls, safe in their shadow. Anderbine sits and wipes the silverware with his napkin, then traces scratches and gouges in the wooden table with a tine of his fork, following them as if on a path, or solving a maze. But he is thinking only of his Figure 5 and whether Midria will live long enough for him to paint it.

2

Summoned by messenger that afternoon, Anderbine takes a curtained rickshaw to the locks, away from the Grand Hundred stairs. He waits patiently in his private boat until it is raised to the Ministry landing. Once inside the Ministry, he ensconces himself in a sanitized balcony encased in glass, a thin, white baton in his left hand.

Ten feet below is the operating room and its lone table. On the table is the nude body of a Figure 2 plague victim, a young male, whose Caul is misshapen and protruding concave bony plates. Three Figure 1 plague victims stand around the table, having already been trained and initiated into Anderbine's surgical strategies, trading their plague zone detention for the relative comfort of spending the rest of their lives cloistered within the walls of the Ministry. Anderbine doesn't fool himself into believing that it is a fair trade, but his work must be done. It is important work, work worth their lives. They stare up at him, their eyes and mouths rumours within the lesions that will take over their faces. They are ready to begin.

Anderbine lifts the baton and his conscripted surgical assistants take scalpels, clamps, and bone saws into their hands. Flesh and bone are rent, limbs and organs removed, everything catalogued according to the precise and fluid motion of his baton. Anderbine scribbles notes onto personal copies of his four complete Figures, replicas of which hang from the balcony and operating room walls, slide off instrument trays, lie under the feet of his surgical assistants, and are covered in old notes and fresh blood and gore.

Anderbine halts his baton, allowing the assistants a short reprieve. One of the assistants, a male with black ringlet hair that will fall out in clumps soon enough, leaves his position at the operating table and surveys the walls and its wallpaper of Figures. He gently places his hands on the replica drawings, obscuring her many faces with a bloody palm print. It's as if the young plague victim cannot bear to see his future, and the desperation of this act fills Anderbine with sadness, albeit distant. The work must go on.

He taps on the balcony glass and flicks his wand harshly, demanding the autopsy begin anew. The other two assistants scurry and fill their hands with instruments and flesh. But the first assistant chooses a Figure from the floor instead of a scalpel. He turns, holds up the Figure 4 replica toward the surgeon's balcony, and points.

IN THE MEAN TIME

Anderbine turns and jabs the baton, twisting and arcing it into a new set of directions.

The assistant wets his finger inside the cadaver's chest and writes a message on the Figure:

I know who she is.

Anderbine pauses. The young man rewrites the message.

Anderbine calls the guards and has the operating room cleared. He ties a black mask over his nose and mouth, and leaves the balcony. In the decontaminant vestibule, he covers the rest of his body in clear plastic, and then enters the operating room. The young man steps toward him, head tipped up. Anderbine is not prepared for the rich baritone that emerges from the ugly scab of a mouth.

"There was a man came out healed from the Ministry. 'Healed,' they said. She took him as her lover, but he did not give her the plague that way. He gave it to her because she asked him to. It was a gift. And she gives it to us."

No one has been released from the Ministry healed. There are Ministry agents who spread lies within the plague zone, to keep the infected from rushing the border guards and checkpoints. Anderbine knows that most of what this man says is myth, but for every myth there's a kernel of truth. Why did she seek a life so far removed from the one she had with him?

Anderbine decides the distant view from his window is no longer sufficient. He says, "Do you know where she is?"

"Yes. Everyone does."

3

The Ministry rickshaw burrows into the plague zone. Following the canal and moving past the base of the Grand Hundred stairs, Anderbine looks out the window to the east, trying to find his house, trying to find her view of what was once their home.

To justify this trip, Anderbine called on all his Ministry favours. He is dressed in layer upon layer of protective gear: gloves and hose and scarves and a ridiculous hat that covers his rapidly greying hair.

Two members of his surgical team, the extensions of his hands, draw the rickshaw along the seaside base of the city, after lowering from the locks. The rickshaw windows are poor glass. Through them the plague zone appears watery, riddled with bubbles of air, stone turned the colour of thunderheads by the smoke of endless fires. The plague zone is too small for its inhabitants, and they camp crowded against the lanes in blanket tents, fouling the roofs of houses on the ledges below with their night-pots and oyster shells. The stench comes in through the cracks around the windows and through his protective scarf, a rotting flesh and vegetable smell.

The rickshaw pulls up outside a shanty deep within the zone. It has a curious space around it; even the plagued masses give it a hole, a burrow of its own. The door is torn away, for firewood perhaps, and only a tatter of cloth covers the entrance. He draws it aside gently, and though he cannot feel the cloth through all the protective layers, he is treated to a memory of a slim dress she wore once, the way it spilled into his hands when she shrugged it from her shoulders.

There is a table in the center of the shack, and on it rotting fruit, bread, fish, an oil lamp burning. Outside the lamp's light are thick nests of debris: seaweed and deep piles of shells, the barnacled slats of wrecked ship hulls, furniture, clothes, tree branches, and, he suspects, rotting pelts of dead animals. On top of it all are blue teacups, an alarm clock with rusty bells, a dulled letter opener with etched vines, and an empty suitcase, all of which came from his house. The debris is artfully arranged, rising and falling, mimicking tsunamis and a voluptuous horizon.

Midria stirs, lounging in one of the piles, and the bare light of the lantern is not enough to discern where she begins, where the refuse ends.

"I've been looking for you," he says, his voice swallowed by the miserly acoustics of filth against the walls.

"No," she replies. "You have been brought to me."

"You are very ill now," he says.

"I am well," she says. "Changed, but not unhealthy."

IN THE MEAN TIME

It's too dark. Though he hears her shift, he can't see her. "You chose to live in the plague zone over living with me. You are alone."

"I am not the one who is alone."

He says, "I can still help you."

"You still assume I am diseased." Her sudden stillness in the pile of refuse is profound. "It was the same with us when we were together and I yearned for you, and you were at your work and your art. You swore it was vapours, humours, my uninhabitable womb, my fondness for smoke, some spirit possession. It was always something. You wanted so badly to heal me, but always from inside your Ministry vestibule. Glass between us when we were not in bed."

She sheds the detritus, stands, and moves forward, lamplight striking her brown mask, skimming across her new eyes, black along her forehead like a jewelled ornament. They blink, disregarding him as unimportant, roving up and around the room. Only her original eyes meet his, and they are gentle. Her limbs are elongated, arms and legs and neck, flesh strained across them so thinly he sees her veins and the ichor within them, which is black.

He says, "I only ever wanted to help you." How easily they fall into recriminations and regret.

She shifts her weight, and the tightening and relaxing of tendons is audible. "Do you still paint and sketch?"

"You," he says. "On the Grand Hundred stairs every morning. I watch from my window. I've almost completed a series of studies. I only need the fifth figure."

She runs her hand across the tabletop, plucks a soft apple from a pile and holds it in her palm. "The day before I left, I stood in front of that window. I asked you to do something. Do you remember?"

Anderbine remembers their last day together.

Despite the cold temperature they were on the terrace, seated at an outdoor table for two. A sore spotted the corner of her mouth. The indoor dining area was closed. The wait staff and bus boys wore gloves and masks. Their food was served but they weren't eating.

Anderbine had seen and known and, regrettably, already done too much.

She said, "We could leave and make a life in the territories, Anderbine. We could go anywhere and be away from the Ministry."

He said, "No," and he'd keep saying that word no matter how much he knew it tore them apart. She wouldn't look at him. He wished she would. He wished she'd share his eyes and listen to his stories from the Ministry, the stories of his lifetime of work. He'd tell her everything, and then maybe she'd understand how unreasonable and irrational her request was. He wouldn't leave the comfort the Ministry afforded him (them!) for a life unknown. He wanted to believe that she didn't understand because of her youth, but he knew better. He reached out and touched her elbow, but she flinched away. Below the terrace were quarantined sections of the city, the plague zone in infancy.

She said, "Are you that afraid? So afraid that you won't dare try to live on your own?"

Anderbine's hands went from the table, toward her, then into his lap and back to the table. They didn't know what to do without a pencil. He said, "My answer is no, Midria."

She said, "Then, I am sorry." She stood up and left the table, then broke into a jog. Anderbine watched her disappear, left a handful of money, and walked home. He went directly to his study and his canvases. But she was there, standing in front of his window, already a shadow, already a regret.

4

Midria says, "Do you remember what I asked you to do?"

"I was confused. I needed more time. If you would have waited a bit longer . . ." He lets the words die at the end of his tongue.

She ignores his lies. "Anderbine, *do* you remember?"

He says, "I didn't hear you that night. I swear."

She folds and opens her arms and legs as if staying in any one position were unbearable, seeking some perfect pose for the sham artist and lover before her. Her precise, stilted movements mock his powerlessness. She still chooses to move, to act. He is nothing but her archivist.

Midria says, "What did you say to me?"

"I asked you to move aside," he says. "I told you there was something on the Grand Hundred that I needed to sketch. A procession to the well. I swear I did not hear you."

She says, "You chose not to hear me."

Anderbine resumes his lies; he doesn't know what else to offer her. "There was the fading light of dusk on the backs of the penitents, and light at their feet, and they were bowed so perfectly for a sketch, a study of the play of light across their backs . . ."

"I said, *see me.*" Then, in his silence, she opens her mouth, lays her tongue flat, and a gray proboscis emerges from the back of her throat, contained in some physiological modification he has not seen in any of his cadavers. She inserts the needle-tip of the proboscis, glistening with saliva, into the mealy cheek of the apple, and then withdraws it.

"I make the plague victims as easily," she says. "The entire city sees us, Anderbine. In your Ministry, in your vestibule, in what you think are safe places. You see us. We die, and clog up the drains. We live, and clog up the Grand Hundred. Did they tell you how this came of a Ministry-released plague victim?"

He nods.

She says, "Rumours and lies, of course, although we both know the Ministry is far from blameless."

"There have been mistakes. . . ."

She interrupts, her voice bubbling into a higher register and volume. "I kept getting those sores. I thought they disgusted you. I thought they were something rotten in me. You knew what they were."

Anderbine whispers, "I'm sorry. I was going to help you if you had just let me."

She says, "I went looking for you in other men. There were many men, Anderbine. Men who had wives, men who visited whores." The lantern gutters, and a slow rill of black smoke rises from the wick before it rallies back brightly. "I think you should take a new rumour back to the Ministry. One that has more flair and romance, and one closer to the truth," she says. "We made this, Anderbine. You and I."

His face in his hands, Anderbine says, "I did not make this," although he no longer believes his lies.

"One of us could not see, and one of us could not wait. Vision and patience are the strategies of the wise. Aren't we terrible, terrible fools?" She drops the apple to the floor, adding to her sea of refuse, then folds herself in complicated, vertiginous ways, and scuttles back underneath everything, squelching through the wet and mulch of her nest, out of sight. Anderbine stays, waiting for what, he doesn't know. He follows her movement around the room by the rise and fall of garbage until it lies still for a long time, then returns to the rickshaw.

5

Midria rises with the sun: both are seemingly eternal. She stands on the eighty-seventh step of the Grand Hundred and throws back her hood. Anderbine has set up a canvas next to his window, ready with his charcoal. She has split open along the seam on her new, exterior skull. A clear mucus spills down her face, her proboscis flickers in and out. She sheds her cloak and is nude. Anderbine sketches. She sheds her skin as easily as the cloak. Anderbine works in a frenzy, capturing her emergence in expert lines: the red mandibles and serrated palps, the female form re-imagined in lengths and proportions dizzying, artful, delicate and savage, membrane falling away in gristly lumps, calcareous plates emerging along her legs. She flexes, and they bend backward at the knee.

The sun climbs higher, creeping up the heights of the Ministry spires. Other plague victims on the Grand Hundred remove their cloaks. They climb out of their skins and emerge as gargoyles of flesh and boney plates, their appendages as mottled clubs or scythes or greedy talons, their backs and chests covered in armour plating. There are some who sprout misshapen wings of stretched skin and tendon, wired with a network of bones reassigned and thinned. The transformed tear apart the guards and clamber over the plague barriers. Sirens and bells sound throughout the city. Ministry soldiers answer the cries quickly, but the transformed rout them, rending and shedding them as they did their old skin. Other transformed take to the sky clumsily but undeterred, their wings uneven but able to carry their weight, and they descend upon the Ministry, tearing stone, shingle, and glass from the spires.

Midria climbs past the plague barrier with the others, but does not follow their flood of violence to the Ministry. Anderbine has finished the sketch of her face, and his Figure 5 is complete for when she arrives, though he knows the sketch is frivolous, as they all were. He moves away from the window, holding his sketch as if it is a mirror. He will not impede her ingress into the room. She will stand in front of the window again. She will say, "See me now." This time, he will see her.

GROWING THINGS

1

Their father stayed in his bedroom, door locked, for almost two full days. Now he paces in the mud room, and he pauses only to pick at the splintering door jamb with a black fingernail. Muttering to himself, he shares his secrets with the weather-beaten door.

Their father has always been distant and serious to the point of being sullen, but they do love him for reasons more than his being their sole lifeline. Recently, he stopped eating and gave his share of the rations to his daughters Angie and Florida. However, the lack of food has made him squirrelly, a word their mother—who ran away more than four years ago—used liberally when describing their father. Spooked by his current erratic behaviour, and feeling guilty, as if they were the cause of his suffering, the daughters agreed to stay quiet and keep away, huddled in a living room corner, sitting in a nest of blankets and pillows, playing cards between the couch and the silent TV with its dust-covered screen. Yesterday, Florida drew a happy face in the dust, but Angie quickly erased it, turning her palm black. There is no running water with which to wash her hands.

Angie is twelve years old but only a shade taller than her seven-year-old sister. She says, "Story time." Angie has repeatedly told Florida that their mother used to tell stories, and that some of her stories were funny while others were sad or scary. Those stories, the ones Florida doesn't remember hearing, were about everyone and everything.

Florida says, "I don't want to listen to a story right now." She wants to watch her father. Florida imagines him with a bushy tail and a twitchy face full of acorns. Seeing him act squirrelly reinforces one of the few memories she has of her mother.

"It's a short one, I promise." Angie is dressed in the same cut off shorts and football shirt she's been wearing for a week. Her brown hair is black with grease, and her fair skin is a map of freckles and acne. Angie has the book in her lap. *Oh, the Places You'll Go.*

"All right," Florida says but she won't really listen. She'll continue to watch her father, who digs through the winter closet, throwing out jackets and itchy sweaters, snow pants. As far as she knows, it is still July.

The gregarious colours of Angie's book cover are muted in the darkened living room. Candles on the fireplace mantle flicker and dutifully melt away. Still, it is enough light for the sisters. They are used to it. Angie closes her eyes and opens the book randomly. She flips to a page with a cartoon New York City. The buildings are brick red and sea blue, and they crowd the page, elbowing and wrestling each other for the precious space. Florida has coloured the streets green with a crayon.

They are so used to trying not to disturb their father, Angie whispers her story. "New York City is the biggest city in the world, right? When it started growing there, it meant it could grow anywhere. It took over Central Park. The stuff just came shooting up, crowding out the grass and trees, the flowerbeds. The stuff grew a foot an hour, just like everywhere else."

Yesterday's story was about all the farms in the Midwest, and how the corn, wheat, soy, and every other crop were overrun. They couldn't stop the growing things and that was why there wasn't any more food. Florida had heard her tell that one before. Upset by both the story and that they'd been alone in the house long enough for Angie to have repeated herself, Florida cried so long and loud that their father pounded on his locked bedroom door until she stopped. Angie scolded her, saying she had to toughen up. Florida folded her thin arms and legs and crawled under her own private nook of their blanket nest, mad at her sister for making her listen again, and then, when Angie wasn't looking, Florida grabbed the storybook and drew the growing things on the New York City page with her green crayon. She coloured in the streets until the crayon was a nub smaller than the tip of her thumb.

Angie says, "The stuff poked through the cement paths, soaked up Central Park's ponds and fountains, and started filling the streets next." Angie talks like the preacher used to, back when they went, back when Mom would force them all to make the trip down the mountain, into town and to the church. Florida is a confusing combination of sad and mad that she remembers details of that old, wrinkly preacher, particularly his odd smell of baby powder mixed with something earthy, yet she has almost no memory of her mother.

Angie says, "They couldn't stop it in the city. When they cut it down, it grew back faster. People didn't know how or why it grew. There's no soil under the streets, you know, in the sewers, but it still grew. The shoots and tubers broke through windows and buildings, and some people climbed the growing things to steal food, money, and televisions, but it quickly got too crowded for people, for everything, and the giant buildings crumbled and fell. It grew fast there, faster than anywhere else, and there was nothing anyone could do."

Florida, half-listening, takes the green crayon nub out of her pyjama pocket. She changes her pyjamas every morning, unlike her sister, who doesn't change her clothes at all. She draws green lines on the hardwood floor, wanting their father to come over and catch her, and yell at her. Maybe it'll stop him from putting on all the winter clothes, stop him from being squirrelly.

Their father waddles into the living room, breathing heavy, used air falling out of his mouth, his face suddenly hard, old, and grey, and covered in sweat. He says, "We're running low. I have to go out to look for food and water." He doesn't hug or kiss his daughters, but pats their heads. Florida drops the crayon nub at his feet, and it rolls away. He turns and they know he means to leave without any promise of returning. He stops at the door, cups his mittened and gloved hands around his mouth, and shouts toward his direct left, into the kitchen, as if he hadn't left his two daughters on their pile of blankets in the living room.

"Don't answer the door for anyone! Don't answer it! Knocking means the world is over!" He opens the door, but only enough for his body to squeeze out. The daughters see nothing of the world outside but a flash of bright sunlight. A breeze bullies into their home, along with a buzz saw sound of wavering leaves.

2

Florida sits, legs crossed, a foot away from the front door. Angie is back in the nest, sleeping. Florida draws green lines on the front door. The lines are long and thick, and she draws small leaves on the ends. She's never seen the growing things, but it's what she imagines.

The shades are pulled low, drooping over the sills like limp sails, and the curtains are drawn tight. They stopped looking outside after their father begged them not to, and they won't look out the windows now that he's not here; it seems a fitting way to honour him. When it first started happening, when their father came home with the pickup truck full of food and other supplies, he stammered through complex and contradictory answers to his daughters' many questions. His knotty hands moved more than his lips, removing and replacing his soot-stained baseball cap. Florida mainly remembers that he said something about the growing things being like a combination of bamboo and kudzu. Florida tugged on his flannel shirtsleeve and asked what bamboo and kudzu were. Their father smiled but also looked away quickly, like he'd said something he shouldn't have. He didn't answer her as they had run out of words to share, and the daughters helped their father carry the big water jugs into their basement.

Outside the wind gusts and whistles around the creaky old cabin. The mud room and living room windows are dark rectangles outlined in a yellow light, and their glass rattles in the frames. Florida stares at the wooden door listening for a sound she's never heard before: a knock on her front door. She sits and listens until she can't stand it any longer. She runs upstairs to her bedroom, picks out a pair of new pyjamas, changes again in the dark, and carefully folds the dirty set and places it back in her bureau. Florida then returns to the nest and wakes her older sister.

"Is he coming back? Is he running away too?"

Angie comes to and rises slowly. She lifts the book from her lap and hugs it to her chest. Her fingers crinkle edges of the pages and worry the cardboard corners of the cover. Despite the acne, she looks younger than her twelve.

Angie shakes her head, answering a different question, one that wasn't spoken, and says, "Story time."

Florida used to enjoy the stories before they were always about the growing things. Now she wishes that Angie would stop with the stories, wishes that Angie could just be her big sister and quit trying to be like their mother.

"No more stories. Please. Just answer my questions."

Angie says, "Story first."

Florida balls her hands into fists and fights back tears. She's as angry now as she was when Angie told all the kids at the playground in town that Florida liked to catch spiders and rip off each leg with tweezers, and that she kept a jar of the their fat legless bodies in her bureau.

"I don't want to hear a story!"

"I don't care. Story first."

Angie always gets her way, even now, even as she continues to withdraw and fade, which started before their father walked out the door. She only leaves the nest to go to the bathroom and she walks like an old woman, the joints and muscles in her legs already stiff with disuse.

Florida says, "You promise to answer my questions if I listen to a story?"

All Angie says is, "Story first. Story first."

Florida isn't sure if this is a yes or not. Maybe.

Angie tells of the areas around the big cities, places called the suburbs. How the stuff ruined everyone's pretty lawns and amateur gardens, and then started taking root in the cracks of sidewalks and driveways. People poured and sprayed millions of gallons of weed killer, liquid plumber, lye, and bleach. None of it worked on the stuff, and all the chemicals leeched into the ground water. Water supplies were quickly poisoned.

Like most of Angie's stories, Florida doesn't understand everything, like what ground water is. But she still understands the story. It makes a screaming noise inside her head, and it is all that she can do to keep it from coming out.

She says, "I listened to your story, now you have to answer my question, okay?" Florida takes the book away from Angie, who surprisingly does not resist.

"I'm tired." Angie licks her dry and cracked lips.

"You promised. When is he coming back?"

"I don't know, Florida. I really don't." Angie looks smaller somehow, with the blankets curled and twisted round her legs and arms. It's as if she's been pulled apart and her pieces sprinkled about their nest.

Florida wants to shrink and crawl inside one of her sister's pockets. She asks in her smallest voice, "Was this how it happened last time?"

"What last time? What are you talking about?"

"When Mommy ran away? Was this how it happened when she ran away?"

"No. She wasn't happy so she left. He's going to get food and water."

"Is he happy? He didn't look happy when he left."

"He's happy. He's fine. He isn't leaving us."

"He's coming back though, right?"

"Yes. He'll come back."

"Do you promise?"

"I promise."

"Good."

Florida believes in her big sister, the one who, on that very same spider-story day in the playground, punched a third grader named Elizabeth in the nose for putting a Daddy Long Legs down the back of Florida's shirt.

Florida leaves the nest and resumes her post, sitting cross-legged in the mud room, in the shadow of the front door. The wind continues to increase in velocity. The house stretches, settles, and groans, the sounds eager for their chance to fill the void. Then on the other side of the front door, brushing against the wood, there's a light rapping, a knocking, but if it is a knocking, it's being done by doll-sized hands with doll-sized fingertips small enough to find the cracks in the door that nobody can see, small enough to get inside the door and come through on the other side. The inside.

Florida stays seated, but twists and yells, "Angie! I think someone is knocking on the door!" Florida covers her mouth, horrified that whoever is knocking must've heard her. Even in her terror, she realizes that the gentle sounds are so slight, small, quiet, that maybe she's making up the knocking, making up her very own story.

Angie says, "I don't hear anything."

"Someone is knocking lightly. I can hear them." Florida presses her ear against the wood, closes her eyes, and tries to finish this knocking story. Single knocks become a flurry issued by thousands of miniature doll hands, those faceless toys, maybe they crawled all the way here from New York City, and they scramble and climb over each other for a chance to knock the door down. Florida wraps her arms around her chest, terrified that the door will collapse on top of her. The knocking builds to crescendo, and then ebbs along with the dying wind.

IN THE MEAN TIME

Florida rests her forehead on the door and says, "It stopped."
Angie says, "No one's there. Don't open the door."

3

Angie hasn't eaten anything in days. They are down to a handful of beef jerky and half a box of Cheerios. In the basement, there are only two one-gallon bottles of water left, and they rest in a corner next to the staircase landing. Flashlight in hand, Florida sits on the damp wood of the landing, plastic water jugs pressing against her thigh. It's cooler down here, but her feet sweat inside her rubber rain boots. The boots are protection in case she decides to walk toward the far wall and hunt for jars of pickles or preserves her father may have stashed.

Florida has been sitting with her flashlight pointed at the earthen floor for more than two hours. When she first came down here, the tips of the growing things were subtle protrusions; hints of green and brown peeking through the sun-starved dirt. Now, the tallest spear-like stalks stretch for more than a foot above the ground. The leafy ends of the plants would tickle her knees were she to take the trip across the basement. She wonders if the leaves would feel rough against her skin. She wonders if the leaves are somehow poisonous, despite never having heard her sister describe them that way.

Earlier that morning, Florida decided she had to do something other than stare at the front door and listen for the knocking. She put herself to work and rearranged the candles around the fireplace mantle, and she lit new ones even though, according to her father, she wasn't old enough to use matches. She singed the tips of her thumb and pointing finger watching that first blue flame curl up the matchstick. After the candles, she prepared a change of clothes for Angie and left the small bundle, folded tightly, on the couch. She picked out a green dress that Angie never wore, but Florida not-so-secretly coveted. Then she swept the living room and kitchen floors. The scratch of the broom's straws on the hardwood made her uneasy.

Angie slept most of the day, waking only to tell a quick story of the growing things cracking mountains open like eggs, drowning the canyons and valleys in green and brown and drinking up all the ponds, lakes, and rivers.

Florida runs the beam of her flashlight over the stone and mortar foundation walls, but sees no cracks, and scoffs at the most recent tale of the growing things. Angie's stories had always mixed truth with exaggeration. For example, it was true that Florida used to hunt and kill spiders, and it was true that all those twitchy legs were why she killed them. Simply watching a spider crawling impossibly on the walls or ceiling and seeing all that choreographed movement set off earthquake-sized tremors somewhere deep in her brain. But she was never so cruel as to pull off their legs with tweezers, and she certainly never collected their button-sized bodies. Florida never understood why Angie would say those horrible, made-up things about her.

Still, Florida initially believed Angie's growing things stories, believed the growing things were even worse than what Angie portrayed, which is what frightened Florida the most. Now, however, seeing the sprouts and stalks living in the basement makes it all seem so much less scary. Yes, they are real, but they are not city-dissolving, mountain-destroying monsters.

Florida thinks of an experiment, a test, and shuts off the flashlight. She only hears her own breathing, a pounding base drum, so big and loud it fills her head, and in the absolute dark, her head is everything. Recognizing her body as the source of all that terrible noise is too much and she starts to panic, but she calms herself down by imagining the sounds of the tubular wooden stalks growing, stretching, reaching out and upward. She turns the flashlight on again, surveys the earthen basement floor, and she's certain there has been more growth and new sprouts emerging from the soil. The sharp and elongated tips of the tallest stalks sport clusters of shockingly green leaves the size of playing cards, the ends of which are also tapered and pointed. The stalks grow in tidy, orderly rows, although the rows grow more crowded and the formations more complex as the minutes pass. Florida repeats turning off the flashlight, sitting alone in the dark, breathing, listening, and then with the light back on, she laughs and quietly claps a free hand against her leg in recognition of the growing things' progress.

Florida indulges in a fantasy where her father returns home unharmed, arms loaded with supplies, a large happily-ever-after smile on his sallow face. He's not squirrelly anymore, and he's so pleased with how she's managed the candles, taken care of the house and Angie. They throw open the shades and curtains. He lifts her and puts her on his back. She turns her head to the side and places one cheek on the back of his neck, the lump of his vertebra familiar and comfortable. Then they're at the top of the basement stairs, and before they descend into the dark, Florida asks to keep the growing things alive in the basement. She asks if she can keep her secret garden.

What would he say to that request? She doesn't know.

The daydream ends abruptly. In a matter of days her father has become unknowable, unreachable: a single tree in a vast forest, or a story she once heard but has long forgotten. Was this how it happened with Angie and her mother? Her sister was around the same age as Florida is now when their mother ran away. To Florida, their mother is a concept, not a person. Will the same dissociation happen with their father if he doesn't come back? Florida fears that memories of him, even the small ones, will recede too far to ever be reached again. Already, she greedily clutches stored scenes of the weekly errands she ran with her father this past spring and summer while Angie was at a friend's house, how at each stop he walked his hand across the truck's bench seat and gave her knee a monkey bite, that is unless she slapped his dry, gruff hand away first, and then the rides home, how he let both daughters unbuckle their belts for the windy drive home up the mountain, Florida sandwiched in the middle, so they could see-saw slide on the bench seat along with the turns. Did he only tolerate their wild laughter and mock screams as they slid into each other and him, hiding a simmering disapproval, or did he join the game, leaning left and right along with the truck, adding to the chorus of his daughter's screams? She already doesn't remember. Florida cannot verbalize this, but the idea of a world where people disappear like days on a calendar is what truly terrifies her, and she wants nothing more than herself and her loved ones to remain rooted to a particular spot and to never move again.

Florida considers asking Angie all these questions about her parents and more, but she's worried about her sister. Angie is getting squirrelly. Angie didn't even open the book for this morning's story. And, when Florida left the living room to go to the basement, Angie was sleeping again, her eyelids as purple as plumbs. What if Angie runs away too, and leaves her all alone?

Florida puts the flashlight down on the landing, leaving it on and centering its yellow beam in an attempt to illuminate as much of the basement floor as possible. She lifts a one-gallon water bottle and peels away the plastic ring around the cap, and then steps off the landing and walks toward the middle of the floor, unable to see anything below her ankles, which is as low as the focused beam of light hits. Under her feet, the disturbed and clotted earth feels lumpy and even hard in places, a message in Braille she cannot decipher. She hopes she is not stepping on any of the new shoots.

She pries off the cap, jarring the balance of the bottle in her arms, spilling water onto her hand and her pyjama shorts. Her forearms tremble with the bulky jug set in the crooks of her pointy elbows. Water continues to spill out spastically and gathers on the leaves. She knows they can't spare much, so she only pours out a little, then a little more, hoping the water reaches the roots.

Florida puts the cap on the bottle and walks back to the landing. She'll bring the water upstairs, pour two cups, and give one to her sister, force her to drink. Then she'll curl up in the nest with Angie and sleep, thinking about her plants in the basement. She will do all that and more, but only after she sits on the landing, shuts off the flashlight, listens in the dark to the song of the growing things, and listens some more, and then, eventually, turns the flashlight back on.

IN THE MEAN TIME

4

She did not blow out the candles before collapsing and falling asleep on their nest of blankets. All but three candles have burnt out, or melted away. Wax stalagmites hang from the fireplace mantle. Florida wakes on her left side, and is nose to nose with her sister. Having gone many days without being able to bathe or wash, Angie's acne has intensified, ravaging her face. Whiteheads and hard, painful looking red bumps mottle her skin, creating the appearance of fissures, as if her grease slicked face is a mask on the verge of breaking up and falling away. Florida wonders if the same will happen to her.

Angie opens her eyes; her pupils and deep brown irises are almost indistinguishable from each other. She says, "The growing things will continue to grow until there aren't any more stories." Her voice is scratchy, obsolete, packed away somewhere inside her chest like a holiday sweater that was a gift from some forgotten relative.

Florida says, "Please don't say that. There will be more stories and you have to tell them." She reaches out to hug her sister but Angie buries her face in a blanket, and tightens into a ball. Florida sits up, and the urge to be the next one who runs away from this house is a compulsion. Maybe the people who run away are the ones who are not alone. Maybe there's a place where they gather and say things like *what is to be done with all the foolish people left behind*?

Florida asks, "How are you feeling today, Angie? Did you drink your water?" On the end table between them and couch is the answer to her question: the glass of water that she poured last night is full. "What are you doing, Angie? You have to drink something!" An all-consuming anger co-opts her manic urge for flight, and Florida alternates hitting her sister and tearing the layers of blankets and sheets away from the nest. It comes apart easy. She throws *Oh, the Places You'll Go* over her head. It thuds somewhere behind her. Angie doesn't move and remains curled in her ball, even after Florida dumps the water on her head.

Florida kneels beside her prone sister and covers her face in her hands, hiding what she's done from herself. Eventually she musters the courage to look again, and she says, "Tell me a story about our father, Angie. About him coming back. Please?"

"There are no more stories."

Florida pats Angie's damp shoulder and says, "No. It's okay. I'm sorry. I'll clean this up, Angie. I can fix this." She'll gather their nest blankets and sheets, and she'll dry her sister and the rest of the water spill, force her to change out of the wet clothes and into the green dress, then they'll really talk about what to do, where they should go if their father isn't coming back.

Florida stands and turns around. The nest blankets Florida threw into the middle of the living room have become three knee-high tents, each sporting sharp, abrupt poles raising their cloth above the floor. The poles don't waver and appear to be supremely sturdy, as if they would stand and continue standing regardless if the world fell apart around them.

Florida puts her fingers in her mouth. Everything in the living room is quiet. She whispers Angie's name at the tents, as if that is their name. She bends down slowly, grabs the plush corners of the blankets, and pulls them away quickly, the flourish to a magician's act. Three stalks and their tubular wooden trunks have penetrated the living room floor, along with smaller tips of other stalks just beginning to poke through. The hardwood floor is the melted wax of the candles. The hardwood floor is the poor blighted skin of Angie's face. Warped and cracked, curling and bubbling up, the floor is a landscape Florida no longer recognizes.

She believes with a child's unwavering certainty that this is all her fault because she watered the growing things in the basement. Florida tries to pull Angie up off the floor, but can't. She says, "We can't stay down here. You have to go upstairs. To our room. Go upstairs, Angie! I'll get the rest of the water." She wants to confess to having poured almost half the one-gallon jug on the growing things, but instead she says, "We'll need the water upstairs, Angie. We'll be very, very thirsty."

Florida maps out a set of precise steps. The newly malformed floorboards squawk and complain under her careful feet. Green leaves and shoots on the tips of the exposed stalks whisper against her skin as she makes her too slow progress across the living room. She imagines going so slow that the stalks continue to grow beneath her, pick her up like an unwanted hitchhiker and carry her through the ceiling, the second floor bedrooms, and then the roof of the house, and into the clouds, then farther, past the moon and the sun, to wherever it is they're going.

Florida pauses at the edge of the living room and kitchen, near the mud room, and there is someone rapping on the front door again. The knocking is light, breezy, but insistent, frantic. She's not supposed to open the door, and despite her absolute terror, she wants to, almost needs to open the door, to see who or what is on the other side. Instead, Florida turns and yells back to Angie, who hasn't moved from her spot. Florida urges her to wake, to go upstairs where they'll be safe. There are shoots and stalk tips breaking through the floor in the area of the nest now.

Florida runs into the kitchen, and while there are the beginnings of stalk tips in the linoleum, the damage doesn't appear as severe as it is in the living room. She takes the flashlight off the counter and opens the door to the basement stairwell. She expects a lush, impenetrable forest in the doorway, but the stairs are still there, and very much passable; her own path into the basement, to her garden, it's preserved. She ducks under one thick, wooden stalk that acts as a beam, outlining the length of ceiling, and she descends to the landing, where the bottles of water remain intact.

Once on the landing, which is pushed up like a tongue trying to catch a raindrop or a snowflake, Florida adjusts for balance and gropes for the water bottles. She tries picking up both, but she's only strong enough to take the one full bottle and hold the flashlight at the same time. She contemplates making a second trip, but doesn't want to come back down here. The half-full second bottle will have to be a sacrifice.

Before going up the stairs, she points her flashlight into the heart of the basement, starting at the floor, which is green with countless new shoots. She aims the flashlight up next and counts twelve stalks making contact with the ceiling, then traces their lengths downward. The tallest stalks have large clumps of dirt randomly stuck and impaled upon their wooden shafts. There are six clumps; she counts them three times. One clump is as big as a soccer ball but is more oval shaped. Four of the other dirt clods are elongated, skinny, curled, and hang from the stalks like odd, over-ripened and blackened vegetables. Three stalks in the middle of the basement share and hold up the largest of the dirt formations; rectangular and almost the size of Florida herself, it's pressed against the ceiling.

Florida rests the flashlight beam on this last and largest dirt clod. Something else is hanging from it, almost dripping or leaking out of the packed dirt. After staring for as long as she can stare, and as her house breaks into pieces above her, Florida realizes what she is looking at is a swatch of cloth, perhaps the hem of dress. She can almost make out its colour. Green maybe. Or blue.

Although the previous night was more about the rush of her discovery, of the growing things, and of her flashlight game, looking at the basement now and seeing what she sees, specifically the cloth, Florida remembers walking the basement floor in her rubber boots, walking on what she couldn't see. She remembers what it felt like: the unexpectedly hard and lumpy soil, and she now knows she was walking upon the bones of the one who disappeared, of the runaway.

Florida shuts off the flashlight and throws it into the basement. Leaves rustle and there's a soft thud. She climbs the stairs in the dark, thinking of all of the bones beneath her feet, thinking of stories about spiders getting their arms and legs torn off by tweezers. Florida is furious with herself for not recognizing those bones last night, but how could she be blamed? She never really knew her mother.

Florida runs up the basement steps into the kitchen and stumbles over and past the continued growth. The knocking on the front door is no longer subtle, no more a mysterious collection of doll's hands. The sound of the knocking is itself a force. It's a pounding by a singular and determined fist, as big as her shrinking old world, maybe as big as the growing new one. The door rattles in the frame, and Florida screams out with each pounding.

She shuffles away from the mud room, and into the living room. Angie is still there, but is up and out of the nest. She's kneeled between the stalks that have erupted through the floor. She pinches the shoots and leaves between her fingers, plucks them away, and puts them in her mouth.

The pounding on the front door intensifies. Her father said if there was a knocking on the door, then the world was over. A voice now accompanies the unrelenting hammering on the door. "Let me in!" The voice is as ragged and splintered as the living room floor.

Florida shouts, "We need to go upstairs, Angie! Now now now!"

More pounding. More screaming. "Let me in!"

Florida imagines the growing things gathered outside her door, woven into a fist as big as their house. The leaves shake in unison and in rhythm, their collected rustling forming their one true voice.

Florida imagines her father outside the door. The one she never knew, eyes wide, white froth and foam around his mouth, spitting his demand to be allowed entry into his home, the place he built, the place he forged out of rock, wood, and dirt—all dead things. His three-word command is what heralds the end of everything. She imagines her father breaking the door down, seeing his oldest daughter eating the leaves that won't stop growing, and seeing what his youngest daughter knows is written on her face as plain as any storybook.

Angie doesn't look at her sister as she gorges on the leaves and shoots. Then Angie stops eating abruptly, her head tilts back, her eyelids flutter, and she falls to the floor.

Florida drops the water jug, covers her ears, and goes to Angie, even if Angie was wrong about there being no more stories.

Florida tells Angie another story. Florida will get her up and bring her upstairs to their bedroom. She'll let Angie choose what she wants to wear instead of trying to force the green dress on her. They'll always ignore the pounding on the door, and when they're safe and when everything is okay, Florida will ask Angie two questions: What if it isn't him outside the door? What if it is?

HAROLD THE SPIDER MAN

Most people don't like spiders: all those twitchy, crawly legs, the white thread that spills out of their abdomens and how it feels when you walk into their webs, like something trying to get inside your skin and poke around, maybe snack on your blood and innards, and maybe it's one of those horribly special spiders from Japan, the kind that eats your secrets.

If there's a spider in a house, most people squish or squash or vacuum it up, or they run away while flailing their own twitchy appendages and then beg for someone else to do their squish-squashing for them. No one really seems to be deterred by the threat of bringing rain with the death of a spider anymore. Even if the house is a hovel or unkempt or as messy as the messiest mess you can imagine, the owners of the messiest-mess house would likely kill the spider and wrap it up neatly in a wad of toilet paper, then flush it down the toilet.

Harold wasn't afraid of spiders though. Harold does seem like a silly name for The Spider Man (no, not the superhero or even a regular run-of-the-mill hero), but it was his name and we can't fix that. He never killed spiders in his house. And after his brittle bride Alicia died, Harold shared his home with countless spiders.

Alicia was sickly and thin and was always melodramatically suffering from various flavour-of-the-week ailments. Most thought she was a hypochondriac, but as if to prove the naysayers wrong, she went to bed early one night and never woke up.

After the brief and ill-attended funeral, Harold let the everyday house spider go wherever it wanted, which was usually inside his bathtub or sink, or in the corners of his ceilings. Daddy Long Legs liked his finished basement, hanging out by the air hockey table that no one used anymore. Harold went out to his yard and the wooded area across from his house and relocated scores of local arachnids. He transferred white egg sacks and hung them off light fixtures and doorknobs. Spiders that he found under heavy rocks he placed gently under his end tables. Garden spiders set up shop in his kitchen, spinning webs between his box of Frosted Flakes and a bag of pretzel rods. He went to his computer and he made phone calls, purchasing carton-loads of spiders, spiders, spiders. After those packages arrived, there were tarantulas tickling the keys of his great-great-great grandfather's piano, their songs always tense and high-pitched. Brown Recluse spiders hid and kept to themselves. Jumping spiders jumped on the guest bed that no one guested on. Hunting spiders wandered the house in packs and attacked the phone whenever it rang, which wasn't all that often. Harold had to keep his living room desert warm so the trap-door spiders living inside his couch and using the cushions as trap-doors would be comfortable. He had fisher spiders hanging out above bowls of water, bird-catching spiders in the upstairs guest room, and funnel-web spiders in the doorways. He even had some of those crazy secret-eating spiders from Japan that just had to be seen to be believed.

Harold briefly emerged from his home to accept condolences and well-wishes from his neighbours. He told some of them that Alicia fell victim to a nasty case of Lyme disease, while he told others she died from an esoteric flu, and yet to others he blamed her death on a mosquito bite and eastern equine encephalitis. Regardless, Harold explained that while he wasn't afraid of spiders, he was deathly afraid of ticks, and that he was also afraid of the fleas that lived on mice and rats, and he was afraid of the rats themselves, and birds, and mosquitoes, and flies. He was afraid of all these creatures because they carried the diseases that felled his Alicia. They carried diseases with horrible nicknames like Black Death, or viruses named only by capital letters and numbers, or diseases named after someone who likely isn't too happy with having a disease with their name on it, or diseases that sounded vaguely exotic but were extremely painful and deadly. Harold reasoned that spiders ate mosquitoes and fleas and ticks and flies, and there were larger species of spiders that even ate mice and birds, and if he surrounded himself with spiders he'd never catch Alicia's diseases. He'd be safe.

Suffice to say, no one wanted to visit Harold's house anymore. No matter how much you say you're not afraid of spiders, try confronting a houseful of them. And all those webs everywhere you went! For the few brave souls who insisted upon visiting The Spider Man, Harold took to greeting them in this way: "So, Miss Muffet, where will you be sitting? Ha ha!" Not a very funny or pleasant way to enter The Spider Man's house: in fact most agreed it was rather creepy, even sinister, especially after he tried to force curds and whey upon them (curds and whey, of course, being slightly more frightening than the spiders from Japan). So they stopped going to Harold's house. Even his parents discontinued their visits and only called.

Harold became infamous, with legends of his deeds and misdeeds springing up instantly among the children in his neighbourhood. The younger kids believed he could talk to spiders, and some believed his late wife had transformed into a spider that he kept and fed, and she would use a giant web to catch and devour any child foolish enough to walk near their house. The older brothers and sisters of the neighbourhood insisted that they, in fact, once knew a boy (whose name no one could remember) who had disappeared after last being seen near Harold's house, and that all that was left of the boy was a sneaker they found in the woods, hanging in a large web.

The adults in the neighbourhood gossiped about Harold too, and they guessed at the secrets his house of spiders might hold. Their tales generally concerned his relationship with Alicia and the nature of her demise. Their stories were cruel, salacious, and hardly worth mentioning.

Everyone left Harold alone. He almost never left the house, and on the few occasions that he did, he took a pocketful of spiders with him.

Harold's spiders weren't all that appreciative of his efforts. Because of the sheer number of spiders in the house, there wasn't enough food to go around. Initially, Harold would open windows and use lamps to attract moths, or bring in boxes full of mealworms but it still wasn't enough, would never be enough. The funnel-web spiders didn't like mealworms and bird-catching spiders didn't like moths and the secret-eating spiders from Japan didn't—well, you get the idea. So the spiders were forced to eat each other.

The tarantulas didn't have their hearts in it when they attacked the raft spider, and the trap-door spiders didn't move so fast when dragging nursery-web spiders underneath the couch cushions. The secret-eating spiders from Japan didn't do or eat much of anything. They were too depressed as Harold refused to feed them what they needed.

It was obvious, even to Harold, that he hadn't thought things through. He did miss having visitors and playing air hockey in his basement, and he felt terrible that his spiders were eating each other, but he did not have a solution. He wasn't about to bring in the food his spiders really wanted.

Harold didn't know what to do, so he continued mindlessly catching and ordering more spiders to replace the eaten ones. He couldn't keep pace with their appetites. The more spiders he brought home, the faster they disappeared, even the spiders in his pocket turned on each other. Eventually, the only spiders left in his house were two of the secret-eating spiders from Japan.

Harold still lives alone with the two secret-eating spiders. Some days they clean his house, tearing down the other spiders' webs and traps and food stores before they dutifully deposit these remnants of their old comrades into the trash. Most days the two secret-eating spiders follow Harold around the house. They glide on his carpets and tickle the linoleum in the kitchen, each with one of their arms wrapped around one of the other's arms as if holding hands. When Harold The Spider Man rests, they sit at his feet like trained dogs.

Harold stares at the secret-eating spiders. He thinks of Alicia and is resolute and tight-lipped. And the secret-eating spiders stare at him. They stare and they are patient, waiting to finally be fed.

RHYMES WITH JEW

Diane rhymed words with "Jew." They were silly, nonsensical rhymes. She was in love with the simple rhythm, the hard monosyllables ending with lips pursing into the *ooo* sound repeatedly. As a child, she drove her mother crazy with it. Mom, in her English sprinkled with Yiddish, said her daughter was a *schlemiel*, said her daughter was a giant pain in the *tuchis*, said she wasn't respecting their heritage, said people would think she was a *shikseh*.

It's approaching sundown on the Sabbath. Diane was too weak to go to Temple today. But she said a *Kaddish* for her mother. Now in the middle of her tea, there's a knock on her door. This older-than-Abraham woman who now forgets more than she remembers finds two Jews (she notices the delicious rhyme) on her doorstep. Two young men she has seen at Temple, two young men said to be attending a secret *yeshiva*, two young men wearing tattered and worn suits (she knows the suits likely comprise their entire wardrobe), two young men wearing *yarmulkes*. She marvels at their *chutzpah* for being so public with their faith. Yes, she supposes there are still a few of them left. A few Jews. Mm, that rhyme. . . .

The young men don't have to tell Diane why they are here. No need to talk about the new Homeland Faith taxes placed upon synagogues, and the purchase of kosher foods and all things Jewish are so burdensome, so aggressive, so clear in their message. Like so many young people, they are poor in pocket and in spirit. She knows they want to leave the Red States and go to the Blue, but they don't know how to leave and they don't know where the Blue States are. They haven't found the Blue in their libraries or on televisions and computers. Even their rabbi only has rumours, and of course, Diane's name and address.

Diane invites the young men into her home and offers them *bailies* despite the late hour.

She tells them, "Sit."

She tells them, "I'm not what I used to be, but I can still talk, and drink. We'll drink, fill our lungs with cigarette smoke and die sooner rather than later, if we're lucky."

Two weeks before the government grants and subsidies expired, Gail Goodwin (who had earned millions with home alarms and other personal security products) privatized and financed a social work department loosely affiliated with Charlotte State Hospital. One year after her start, Gail hired Diane, despite her apparent status as grossly under-qualified. Gail wore turtleneck sweaters even in summer, jeans, thick glasses, and chewed gum to keep from smoking. Gail was always as serious as her sweaters.

This is how Diane remembers their first conversation:

Gail said, "I hate gum."

Diane said, "So do I. Makes me feel like a cow working a cud."

Gail said, "We live in the eighth poorest county in the country."

Diane said, "When I left the house to come to this interview, my mother said what I had on was a *shmatteh*, a rag. But I think I look appropriate, if not nice."

Gail said, "Racial, religious, and ethnic discrimination coupled with the price structure of consumer fashion makes it easy for poor people to appear to be middle class."

Diane said, "Am I allowed to smoke anywhere in the hospital?"

Gail said, "Many of our clients believe they are a part of the disappearing middle class. They have no job security. Everything they own is on credit. They are living one pay check away from homelessness, but believe they are middle class and they believe that what is good for government and corporations is good for them."

Diane said, "Could I have a piece of gum?"

Gail said, "While it's not difficult to appear economically stable, it is difficult for the poor to get enough to eat and to keep warm."

Diane said, "I have no prior professional experience in this area, only amateur experience. I've spent my lifetime in a family desperately trying to appear economically stable."

Gail said, "Obesity is the new disease of poverty because the poor can only afford to eat the wrong things."

Diane said, "My mother wants me to work here. She says I'd be mixed up, lost, *farblonjet* without this good work."

Gail said, "Recently, one client of ours ran naked through a local swamp, then emptied his shotgun into a small herd of cows that belonged to a neighbouring farm, still pumping and shooting even after being out of ammo. We have too many clients who periodically exhibit the kind of violent behaviour that warrants a stay in our hospital. But you know what? They recover after about two weeks of food. These people's nutritional needs are so far from being met that two weeks of hospital food changes them. Nine months out of the year they eat rice, cornmeal, sawmill gravy, maybe a vegetable if it's summer, maybe fast food if they have a little money, maybe meat from a stolen hog off one of the farms."

Diane said, "Pigs aren't kosher."

Gail said, "You start tomorrow."

This conversation may or may not have happened as described. It is more likely an amalgam of twenty-five-plus years of her relationship with and memories of Gail. Regardless, the reciting of this conversation confuses the young men. They tell Diane they don't understand what any of this has to do with getting them to the Blue States.

Diane tells them, "Stop *nuhdzing* and hush up." She appreciates, even envies their impatience. Impatience means they hope.

She tells them, "In due time, you will hear what you need to know."

She tells them, "You will hear everything. You will hear about Sandra first." Diane pulls yellowed newspaper clippings from the top of her refrigerator: an obituary paper-clipped to a short two-piece article. They shake in her hand but only because her hand is always shaking.

Unlike the greying memories of Gail, Mom, and just about everyone else who was important to her, Diane remembers Sandra.

On the morning of Diane's first day as a caseworker the President announced his budget, which included 20 billion dollars cut from domestic programs. Millions of dollars of funding cut from the three largest federal food programs: food stamps, school lunches, and the Special Supplemental Nutrition Program for Women, Infants and Children (WIC). One-hundred-and-fifty social programs shrunk or eliminated outright. According to The Department of Agriculture, 36.3 million people lived in homes without enough food. The National Low Income Housing Coalition found there was no place in the Red States where a person earning as much as $9.17 an hour could afford a modest two-bedroom apartment. A quarter of the national workforce earned $9.17 an hour or less—about $19,000 annually, only fifty dollars more than the official federal poverty level for a family of four.

Sandra's case report made mention of her $12,000 income working second-shift janitorial at a William Morris office building. Her one-bedroom apartment rent was $1000 per month. Both income and rent numbers were the average for an adult citizen of the one-time textile city of Lawrence, North Carolina.

Winter, and the temperature had dropped below forty degrees.

Drug paraphernalia littered the front-stoop and hallways of Sandra's apartment building. The case report made mention of Sandra having passed her last three random drug tests. Sandra was trying. Inside the building wasn't warmer than outside. Diane's breath was white exhaust while walking the hallways and staircases.

Diane knocked on door # 213. A young woman, a teenager, a girl (Mom would've called her a *pisher*) opened the door, and held her baby, a moth-worn sweater concealing her cigarette-thin arms. This was Sandra. Diane mentally went through her checklist for signs of malnutrition: dry hair, red and cracked lips, glassy eyes, yellowing and dry skin. Diane reminded herself to watch for irritability, poor memory, strange or obsessive behaviour.

Her baby's name was Drew. He was six months old and wrapped in a blanket. His file was included with Sandra's case report folder.

Diane entered and saw the electric stove on and open. The only heat in the apartment. She said, "The heat seems to be out in the whole building."

Sandra said, "You're the woman I talked to on the phone? From the hospital?"

"Yes." Diane extended a hand. Sandra's hand was limp and cold. "I was happy to read that you agreed to continue the center's counselling."

"I'll take all the help I can get. Does it say in that folder of yours that my landlord is missing along with the building's heating oil?" Sandra put the baby in a bassinette near the oven. Her lips moved but she wasn't talking. With the baby down, she rubbed her eyes, once, then twice, then a third time. Her lips formed silent words again.

Diane made her mental notes.

Sandra said, "You're new to the center?"

"Yes and no."

"I hate that. Pick one."

"Yes. You are my first case. Congratulations."

"Then why did you say no? I get confused easy as it is without you handing me bullshit head-shrinking kind of answers." Sandra rubbed her eyes again in her three-cycle method. The skin around her eyes was now an angry, crayon-red.

Diane said, "I said *no* because I've been with the center for four months."

"What did you do before getting assigned to me?" Sandra pulled a chair up next to the oven and bassinette, then took off her sweater. A potbelly one might describe as a distended abdomen (another sign of malnutrition) pushed against a tight, green T-shirt.

Diane said, "When was the last time you ate?" Diane didn't sit, but opened the file and uncapped her pen.

"Yesterday morning."

"Can you give me a time, roughly?"

"Eight . . . maybe nine or ten."

"What did you eat?"

"Um . . . Ramen noodles, or maybe just some bullion broth. You didn't answer my question."

"What question was that?"

"What did you do before getting my case?"

Gail had instructed Diane that as a caseworker, blunt honesty would be her only chance at succeeding in gaining the people's trust in Lawrence, as the residents had been abandoned by their government and had heard every manner of bureaucratic lie imaginable. So Diane said, "My first three months I cold-called and knocked on the doors of nice white, Christian people and asked them to donate interview-worthy clothes so the lazy, fat, poor people could look for jobs, even though there were no jobs to be had within fifty miles, even though there were no more government-sponsored community action agencies or jobs training programs. Why? The young poor people that the Red States doesn't need for shit work can go into the military, avoiding the need to draft from the middle and upper classes."

Sandra's mouth had moved while Diane talked. Diane imagined this malnourished child-cum-single-mother trying to get sustenance from her words.

Sandra said, "I think you can help me and Drew."

Diane said, "That's why I'm here. When and what did Drew last eat?"

"I breastfeed Drew. He ate an hour ago. Just started him on cereal too." Sandra pointed at the all-but-barren kitchen counter. On it was a box of rice cereal for babies.

Diane wondered how much of it Sandra had eaten. She said, "Have you kept all his paediatric appointments? Has he been getting his shots?"

"Yes."

"Can you prove it?"

"Call his doctor." Sandra fished around inside her jeans pocket and pulled out a wrinkled appointment card. She gave it to Diane and she paper clipped it to the initial hospital diagnosis of postpartum depression. The diagnosis detailed episodes of Sandra wandering the halls of the hospital and, upon release, her apartment building while crying uncontrollably. The diagnosis also detailed a history of drug use, physical and mental abuse at the hands of Drew's father, and possible sexual abuse from unnamed members of her family or neighbours.

Diane said, "Have you had any uncontrollable crying fits in the last two weeks?"

"No." Sandra said it fast. A dart.

Then they talked more about Drew. Diane stayed to watch Sandra breastfeed him and wasn't convinced that Sandra was capable of producing or expressing milk. She watched Sandra mix cereal with tap water. Drew cried and shivered while eating. After Drew's lunch they discussed the day care situation (the mother of the deserting dead-beat Dad lived on the floor below and watched Drew while Sandra was at work). They talked about bills, a schedule of payment, of creating a resume and practicing job interviews.

Diane made it a point to leave multiple copies of her contact information throughout the apartment.

Diane packed up the file and readied to leave when Sandra said, "This is all well and good, but all that liberal-type stuff you were saying before, you know the government keeping people poor on purpose, and all that stuff? Well, I thought it meant you could help me."

Diane said, "It does, Sandra. And we talked about how I was going to help you."

"I want you to help me and my baby to get out. To get to the Blue States."

Diane only knew what her mother had told her when she was a child: only the rich and connected and *gentile* could leave the Red States for the fabled Blue. Diane had greeted this matronly proclamation with a *Blue-Jew* and *Jew-Blue* singsong rhyme.

Diane went against her truth-and-trust social worker paradigm and didn't tell Sandra this. She said, "I really don't know much about the Blue States."

Sandra rubbed her eyes three times, then stared hard at Drew, a look that could bore through skin. She said. "My parents escaped to the Blue States. Somewhere up north, I think. They can't contact me now because the Red States won't let 'em. But they can get me in. Didn't you know if you knew someone who lived there that you could get in? They have computerized lists at the borders. They can check that kind of stuff. I just need to get to the borders."

"I really don't know anything . . ."

Sandra said, "They help people like me in the Blue States. They'll help Drew, keep him fed, clothed, and educated. They'll know it isn't his fault that his Mom is a screw up. They won't blame him for being poor. You know, I even hear they have free hospitals, socialized medicine they call it . . ." Sandra ran out of breath and words. She rubbed her eyes.

Diane said, "I'll see what I can find out. I promise."

● ● ●

Diane shows them the obituary; a small rectangle cut from a newspaper that is decades older than the young men are:

> **Tuckett, Drew**—Of Lawrence, April 31st 20__. Beloved son of Sandra Gomes, grandson of Robert and Julia Earls, and Brenda Thatch. Funeral Service will be held at Old South United Methodist Church, 12 Conant Street, Lawrence, at 10:30 AM on May 3rd. Relatives and well-wishers are invited to attend. Internment will be at a later date and will be private. Expressions of sympathy may be made in his memory to Social Care: Charlotte State Hospital, 478 Admiral Avenue, Charlotte, NC.

Ten days after Diane had met Sandra, Diane's mother had a massive heart attack and died. Mom was sixty-four years old.

Despite the loss and while sitting *shivah* Diane met with Sandra twice that week, and every week after. She fulfilled her official caseworker responsibilities to the best of her abilities (and she picked up a new client with each passing week). But in the process, Diane broke a few of Gail's policies. She let Sandra call on her private line and initially they had chatted like old friends. When Sandra's phone was shut off, Diane gave her the cell phone that her mother had owned. They talked about Diane's mother. They talked about male-companion prospects, of which there seemed to be very few. They talked about Drew, but not in a social-service way. Though, eventually, Sandra forced the conversations to be about the Blue States. Always the Blue States, and Diane always had the same *still investigating* response.

Sandra became increasingly impatient and desperate.

After two months, Sandra was no longer eligible for food stamps or help from WIC. Diane took to treating Sandra and Drew to a lunch at a local diner once a week, money coming from her own pocket.

This is how Diane remembers her last meeting, her last lunch with Sandra:

Sandra ordered her usual, the Big Country breakfast with pancakes, grits, two eggs (always scrambled and mixed in with the grits), sausage, and a large OJ. Drew nibbled on dry toast. Diane had ordered a turkey-club, but hadn't eaten a bite.

Sandra said, "What's the matter? Not hungry?"

Diane was not hungry. She said, "Just because you get a good meal once a week doesn't mean that you can skip out on eating the rest of the week."

Despite these weekly feasts, Sandra still looked as gaunt and washed out as she had when they had met. Diane noticed Drew's new clothes. A football shirt, number twenty-seven, a logo-less blue baseball hat, and mini-work boots. Diane assumed Sandra used the once earmarked food-money (what little of it there was) to buy new clothes for Drew.

"You gonna get all professional on me now?" Sandra smiled. She meant it as a joke, but it sounded hard. Despite their apparent closeness this was a reminder that Diane did not really know Sandra. But she knew enough to know Sandra was far from well. Sandra's behaviour was still erratic; swinging from giddiness to despair like a pendulum.

"You need to eat on a consistent basis. That is priority one. You are not helping Drew by starving yourself."

Sandra aimed her eyes at her plate and filled her cheeks with food. She touched Drew lightly on his arm twice. He smiled and shoved his fist into his mouth. She said, "I bet you sound like your mother right now."

That hurt Diane. But she didn't want to show it. She went from saying nothing to saying, "My mother was *meshiginah*, crazy as a bedbug. She didn't throw anything away. Newspapers, brown paper bags, tin cans; she saved, flattened, and reused tinfoil. She took baths and pestered my father into reusing her dirty water. Last week I helped Dad empty out the house of all the stuff. I threw it all away or donated it to the center. She invited homeless people over for dinner once a week, even when we couldn't afford it. Someone new each time. We had things stolen of course, and most of those dinners were so very uncomfortable, but it never stopped her."

Sandra had an empty-screen stare, focusing somewhere beyond

Diane, and she said, "Am I you're mother's homeless person then? Your weekly charity case that makes you feel better about yourself?" Sandra jiggled her legs and banged the table with her fork like a drummer in a heavy metal band. She was a one-woman ruckus.

Drew's saucer eyes became teapots. He didn't like the sudden movement and noise. He cried and threw his toast on the floor.

Diane said, "She told me she loved everyone, even the *schmucks*. I knew who the *schmucks* were. And she told me she loved God, even when I didn't. I envied her faith. I think she saved it, but I threw it away."

Sandra's Tasmanian devil stopped spinning. She said, "I'm sorry. I don't know . . . I woke up on the wrong side of the couch this morning," then stopped, a balloon out of air.

Diane kept talking. "My mother also said God didn't make or design poverty. People did. But I think I blame both."

Sandra said, "Did you talk to your boss about the Blue States yet? You said she knew something. Can she get me in? She's rich enough. She must know how." Sandra pleaded, begged, and reached her matchstick arm across the table trying to touch Diane.

Diane thought about the case file and the details of Sandra's drug and prostitution arrests. Diane tried not to cry and she tried not to flinch away from Sandra's touch. She went one for two.

Sandra retracted her arm and wrapped it around herself. "You didn't answer my question, girlie. You not hungry?"

Diane was not hungry. She wanted to lie to Sandra.

Diane shows the young men an article. Two rectangles cut from the same newspaper in which the obituary had appeared:

MOTHER CUTS OFF INFANT'S
ARMS, CALLS 911

By *Charlotte Observer*
Staff: April 29th, 20__

Lawrence, North Carolina:
  Brian Talbot, landlord of
Conant Street Tenement said,
"It was just her and that

kid. She was quiet. Paid her rent on time."

A woman suffering from postpartum depression cut off her baby son's arms, then called 911 and her social service case manager and stayed in her apartment until the police arrived.

Her son died in the hospital, three hours after police response. Sandra Gomes, 20, was charged with first-degree murder.

Police found Gomes sitting in the common room, covered in blood. The baby was cradled in her lap. She was calm and told police she was responsible for the baby's injuries.—**continued A23**

Mother Cuts Off Infant's Arms

—continued from A2 Investigators are quiet on whether they've recovered a weapon.

"Both arms were completely severed," Chief Ryan Stanley said. "The mother was unresponsive when we left."

According to audiotapes of the 911 call obtained by the *Charlotte Observer* the operator asked if there was an emergency. Gomes calmly answered, "Yes." The operator asked, "What happened?" Gomes said, "I cut off his arms," and there is audio of the child's song, "Baby Beluga" playing in the background.

Charlotte State Hospital and Social Service representatives reported Gomes was battling chronic malnutrition along with postpartum depression, but there had been no history or signs of violence. Further, a caseworker reportedly knew Gomes had recently become despondent and had tried to visit her apartment the night before, but Gomes refused to let the caseworker in. Gomes lived at the apartment with only her infant son.

Gomes had two prior arrests for drug possession and misdemeanor solicitation. After giving birth to her son, Gomes stayed an extra two weeks at the State Hosptial due to postpartum depression symptoms. Once she was released, Gomes agreed to seek counselling. Caseworkers visited her apartment throughout the winter and early spring.

Neighbors said Gomes seemed to be a loving, attentive mother. Landlord Talbot said he saw Gomes walking with the stroller on Monday.

"She didn't give off like she was in her own world or didn't care about the baby," Mr. Talbot said.

She places the clippings back on the refrigerator, taking care to smooth out any wrinkles in the paper.

Diane says, "I'm just an old maid, and I want to lie to you. Really, I do. After Sandra, I lied. I lied for all these years and I told people what they wanted to hear. I've sent hundreds of Don Quixotes on their merry way, and I felt good with hiding truth behind hope. But I look at you fine *mensch* and know I was wrong. So I'll tell you what my beloved mentor and friend Gail told me, and what I told Sandra. I'll tell you what you already know. There are no Blue States, no *goldeneh medinah*. A myth, perpetuated by the government as much as common folklore, to have people believe change and being good to each other is as easy as going somewhere else. I am sorry, but the Blue is as much a fable as Paradise."

The young men exchange a long look and say nothing.

Diane tells them, "My mother used to say: *A mentsh on glik is a toyter mensh*. An unlucky person is a dead person." She grabs each of the young man by the wrist and says, "Come. Follow me."

She shuffles into her living room. "I was unable to do this properly because I just didn't feel like going out today. But you fine *yeshiva* students can help me. Before you leave, on this, the anniversary of my mother's death, her *yorzeit*, would you join me in lighting candles and saying a prayer? It would mean so much to me. You know, I became a good Jew in her honour." She edges deeper into her living room and the young men dutifully follow.

Diane tells them, "You are fine young men. *A leben ahf dir!* Do you know what that means? You should live! And be well and have more! You make me proud to be a Jew." Diane pauses, then adds, "It's true," and smiles.

They light candles. They pray. She tells them many more things about her mother and her childhood, all that she can remember. But Diane does not tell the young men the obvious. That Blue and Drew and true rhyme with Jew.

Dedication and special thanks to dgk "kelly" goldberg; her life, beliefs, and experiences with social service served as a model and inspiration to this story.

THE MARLBOROUGH MAN MEETS THE END

One of them yells, "I know, but the Marlborough Man is gonna go down first." Then Stephen Lee's brothers make it. They actually make it. Somehow. They shimmy up the gutters, three stories, to the roof of Eza's Brazilian Market. They still have their gasoline containers with them, and matches, though the city is already burning, the sky already ash and dead.

Eza's Market is across the street from his three-family brownstone, just one of a row of decaying three-family brownstones. Stephen Lee used to knock on Eza's plate-glass window at three o'clock and exactly at three o'clock on school days to earn a free piece of Dubble Bubble from Eza, the Brazilian widower with a smile as big as the hump on his back. Stephen Lee had to run home from school ahead of his brothers to make that free-gum deadline.

Before their climb atop the market, his brothers ripped and smashed and burned every advertisement inside Eza's, even that little cardboard Dubble Bubble display on the dusty counter.

Stephen Lee is the youngest. Too young to go on the roof with them, and now too weak; his lungs are pinched balloons. He sits in the middle of Dorchester Ave., stalled and abandoned cars around

PAUL TREMBLAY

him like a playpen. The car's drivers hidden behind ash-stained glass.

He thinks about Momma, unconscious inside their house. The smoke and chemical fumes were too much for her, too much for just about everyone. He thinks about their house, the only house on Dorchester Ave. not on fire, not dead. Thinking, focusing on any one thing is getting as difficult as breathing.

His brothers splash gasoline on the Marlborough Man billboard above the market. The thing is bigger than a school bus. Last month it was a Crown Royal ad. Before that KFC and before that Chevrolet and before that Joe Camel and before that Coca-Cola was it, and on and on. They never took down the old ads. They just pasted a new one over the old. When Stephen Lee was really young, the old and disappearing ads made him feel sad. There was the night Monday Night Football rolled over McDonald's. His friend Ronald was trapped and smothered. Gone, without ceremony or goodbyes.

Above the market now, one brother walks to the roof's edge and gives Stephen Lee a thumbs-up. His other brother chucks the gasoline canisters off the roof and they land somewhere. The smoke and ash haze is thicker now, like viewing the world through a black L'eggs stocking, but he sees each brother light a match and throw it at the billboard, at that rugged and white and smirking cowboy holding a rope in one hand and a cigarette in the other.

Stephen Lee had marked the passage of time by the billboard across from his house: he started school with Tom Cruise; some leggy perfume blonde witnessed the corner shooting last year; Taco Bell and the Chihuahua was the summer when his cousin Cayla stayed at the house.

For his last day it's the Marlborough Man, who is now burning. The Marlborough Man peels and blisters in the giant blaze aided by the surrounding fires and oxygen-feeding winds.

Stephen Lee still feels bad for all the others; Cruise, Ronald, the Colonel, and the blonde lady. He'll miss them. Beneath the fire, he sees glimpses of all his old friends, the commercial for his life.

IN THE MEAN TIME

Behind him, their house is still untouched by fire.

He cheers the death of the Marlborough Man and he cheers his brothers, who he can no longer see. Stephen Lee is proud of his brothers. They've done it. He imagines that his cheering and watching helped them take down the Marlborough Man before their house went down. He knows it did. This little victory belongs to Stephen Lee and his brothers until the very end.

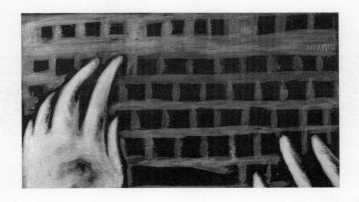

THE BLOG AT THE END OF THE WORLD

About Becca Gilman

I am twenty-something, living somewhere in Brooklyn, and am angry and scared like everyone else I know. Sometimes this B<small>LOG</small> helps me, sometimes it doesn't. I have degrees in bio and chem, but don't use them. That's all you really need to know. All right?

still here
Becca Gilman • June 17th, 2009

Barely. I thought I was ready for one more real/detailed post to the B<small>LOG</small> with a Link Roundup, but I'm not. I tried calling Mom two days ago but there was no answer and she hasn't called me back. I'm still not over G<small>RANT</small>'s passing; my personal tipping point and I hate myself for referring to Grant that way, but it's true. I haven't left my apartment in over a week. The local market I use for grocery delivery stopped answering their phone yesterday. I've only seen three cabs today. They're old and dinged up, from some independent cab company I don't recognize, and they just drive around City Line, circling, like they're stuck in some loop. They're only there because they're supposed to be. The drivers don't know what else to do. At night I count how many windows I can see with the lights on. The city was darker last night than it was last week, or the week before. I don't know if I'm doing a good job explaining all this. I'm watching the city fall apart. It's slow and subtle, but you can see it if you look hard enough. Watch. Everything is slowing down. A windup toy running down and with no one to wind it up. Everything is dying but not quite dead yet, so people just go about their days as if nothing is wrong and nothing bad can happen tomorrow.

I've had a headache for a week now, my neck hurts, and I've been really sensitive to light, to the computer screen especially. I'm scared, but not terrified anymore. There is a difference. Mostly, I'm just incredibly sad.

6 Responses to "still here"

squirrelmonkey says:

June 15, 2009 at 9:32 am

I just tried calling and left a message. I am going to stop by your place today. Please answer your buzzer.

Jenn Parker says:

June 15, 2009 at 1:12 pm

While I still offer condolences for the loss of your friend, I'm not surprised that you're experiencing headaches and the like. You're so obsessed with the textbook symptoms, you're now psychosomatically experiencing them. I am surprised it has taken this long. I had February 2009 in the pool. Get help. Psychiatric help.

beast says:

June 28, 2009 at 4:33 am

i live in new york city to last weak i saw this guy drop dead in the street he pressed a button at the traffic light on the corner and then died there was no one else around just me he wasnt old probably younger than me he died and then i saw whats really happning to everyone cause two demons fell out of the sky and landed next to him maybe they were the gargoiles from the buildings i dont know but they were big strong gray with muscles and wings and large teeth the sidewalk broke under their heavyness they growled like tigers and licked up the blood that came out of the guys ears and mouth but that wasn't good enough they broke his chest open and there was red everywere on the sidewalk and street corner i didnt know there was so much blood in us but they know they took off his arms and legs then gather him up in their big strong arms and flew away he was gone i went back and checked the next day he was gone after i walked around the city i saw the demons every were but noone saw them but me they fly and climb the buildings waiting for us to die and take us just like you i am afraid and stay in my apartment but don't look out my window any more

revelations says:

July 5, 2009 at 12:12 am

I've noticed that you haven't posted in a while. Maybe you're "fuck heaven" comments from you're earlier post caught up to you, or maybe you're fear mongering and lies have finally caught up with you. GOD punishes the wicked. He is truly just.

Jenn Parker says:

July 5, 2009 at 2:45 pm

I like beast. I want to party with you, dude!

Hey, revelations, stick to book burning and refuting evolution.

revelations says:

July 12, 2009 at 10:09 am

I can sum it all up in three words: Evolution is a lie.

Link Roundup

Becca Gilman • May 19th, 2009

I don't feel up to it, but here's a link roundup, in honor of GRANT.

—SAN JOSE MERCURY NEWS: The Silicon Valley's home sales continue to tank with the number of deals at a 40-year low. The mayor of San Jose attributes the market crisis to the glut of homes belonging to the recently deceased.

—THE BURLINGTON FREE PRESS reports that a May 3rd session of Congress ended with the sudden death of a Missouri Representative William Hightower and senator Jim Billingsly from Vermont. While neither Hightower nor Billingsly has been seen publicly since the 3rd, the offices of both congressmen have yet to make any such announcement and their only official comment is to claim the story is patently false.

—THE MIAMI HERALD reports that according to UNICEF, the populations of children in Kenya and Ethiopia have declined by a stunning 24 percent within the past year. The UN and United States government dispute the findings, claiming widespread inaccuracies in the "hurried and irresponsible" census.

8 Responses to "Link Roundup"

Jenn Parker says:

May 24th, 2009 at 7:48 pm

Another link-roundup. Reputable sources at a quick glance, but let's address each link:

The San Jose Mercury News has already issued a partial retraction HERE. The mayor of San Jose never attributed the market crisis to the supposed glut of homes belonging to the deceased. Honestly, other than within the backdrop of our collective state of paranoia/ hysteria, such a claim/statement doesn't make any economic sense. People aren't buying homes for a myriad of economic reasons, but too many deaths due to an imaginary epidemic isn't one of them.

The links to your BURLINGTON and MIAMI papers are dead. I suppose you could spin the dead links to bolster the conspiracy theory, but here in reality, the dead links serve only as a representation of your desperation to perpetuate conspiracy.

squirrelmonkey says:

May 25th, 2009 at 7:03 am

Ever heard of Google, Jenn? Those articles can still be found in the cache. It's not a hard to find. Do you want me to show you how?

Jenn Parker says:

May 25th, 2009 at 1:23 pm

Answer me this: Why were the articles almost instantaneously removed? You'll tell me it's due to some all-encompassing conspiracy, when the real answer is those papers got their stories wrong. They got their stories wrong so they had to pull the articles. That's it. Happens all the time. I guarantee retractions will be published within days. Oh-master-of-Google, prove me wrong by finding another news-outlet corroboration (and not a blog like this one) to either story. Read carefully, please. I want a news-outlet that does not site the Burlington Free Press or Miami Herald as their primary sources. If you try such a search, you'll be at it for a long time, because I can't find any other independent reports.

slugwentbad says:

May 25th, 2009 at 10:13 pm

I've called Billingsly's office on three occasions, and I've been told he's unavailable every time.

Jenn Parker says:

May 25th, 2009 at 10:23 pm

Oh, that proves everything, then.

discostewie says:

May 26th, 2009 at 8:27 am

BEES and BATS and AMPHIBIANS are disappearing, mysteriously dying off (are you going to refute that too, Jenn?). Is it so hard to believe that the same isn't happening to us?

batfan says:

June 25th, 2009 at 3:37 am

Hi, remember me? Come check out my new gambling site for the all the best poker and sports action. It's awesome. http://www.gamblor234.net

IN THE MEAN TIME

More Grant Lee
Becca Gilman • May 12th, 2009

I went to Grant's wake today. The visiting hours were only one hour. 2pm-3pm. I got there at 2. There was a line. We had some common friends but I didn't see anyone that I knew there. I didn't see his sister or recognize any family members there either. I waited in a line that started on the street. No one talked or shared eye contact. This is so hard to write. I'm trying to be clinical. The mourners were herded inside the funeral parlor, but it split into three different rooms. Grant's room was small with mahogany molding on the walls and a thick, soft tan carpet on the floor. There were flowers everywhere. The smell was overpowering and made the air thick. It was too much. The family had asked for a donation to a charity in lieu of flowers. I don't remember the charity. There was no casket. Grant wasn't there; he wasn't in the room. There wasn't a greeting line and I don't know where his family was. There was only a big flat-screen TV on the wall. The TV scrolled with images of Grant and his friends and family. I was in one of those pictures. We were at the Pizza Joint, standing next to each other, bent over, our faces perched in our hands, elbows on the counter. I had flour on the tip of my nose and he had his PJ baseball hat on backwards, his long black hair tucked behind his ears. Our smiles matched. It was one of those rare posed-pictures that still managed to capture the spirit of a candid. That picture didn't stay on the screen long enough. Other people's memories of Grant crowded it out. Also, the pictures of Grant mixed with stock photos and video clips of blue sky and rolling clouds like some ridiculous subliminal commercial for heaven. There was a soundtrack to the loop; nothing Grant liked or listened to (certainly no Slayer). The music was formless and light, with no edges or minor chords. Aural Valium. It was awful. All of it. The mourners walked around the room's perimeter in an orderly fashion. I got the sense they'd all done this before. Point A to B to C to D and out the door. I didn't follow them. I held my ground and stayed rooted to a spot as people brushed past me. No one asked if I was okay, not that I wanted them to. I watched the TV long enough to see the images loop back to its beginning, or at least the beginning that I had seen. I don't know if there was a true beginning and a true end to the loop. After seeing the loop once, I stared at the other mourner's faces. Their eyes turned red and watered when the obviously poignant images meshed with a hopeful crescendo of Muzak. The picture of a toddler-aged Grant holding hands with his parents seemed to be the cue. Then the manufactured moment passed, and everyone's faces turned blue when the TV filled with blue sky, that slickly produced loop of heaven. I wanted to shout **fuck heaven, I want Grant back and I don't want to die**. But I didn't. After an hour had passed, I was asked to leave as someone else's visiting hour was starting. They had a full schedule: every room booked throughout the afternoon and evening. I peeked in the other rooms before I left. No caskets anywhere, just TVs on the walls. Pictures. Clouds. Blue Sky. More pictures. When I went outside, there was another long line waiting for their turn to mourn properly.

I didn't cry until after I left Grant's wake. Now I'm sitting in my apartment, still crying, and thinking about my father. He died when I was four. I remember his wake. I remember crossing my arms over my chest and not letting anyone hug me. Everyone tried. I remember being bored and mad. And I remember trying to hide under the casket presentation. An Uncle that I'd never met before pulled me out of the mini-curtains below the casket. He pulled too hard on my arm and I cried. I think my tears were the equivalent of the four-year-old me saying **fuck heaven, I want my daddy back, and I don't want to die.**

I'm just rambling now. I apologize. I've turned off comments for this post. I've posted, and deleted, and then re-posted this a few times. I'm going to leave it up and as is. But no one else gets to say anything about Grant or me or anything today.

IN THE MEAN TIME

Grant Lee, RIP

Becca Gilman • May 10th, 2009

It finally happened. A very close friend of mine, Grant Lee, died two days ago. He was twenty-four. I have been unable to get much information from his family. I talked to his older sister, Claire. Grant died at work, at the Pizza Joint, two blocks from my apartment. She said his death was sudden and "catastrophic." I asked if he died from an aneurysm. Claire said the doctors told the family it was likely heart failure, but they wouldn't tell them anything specific. I then asked for information about the hospital he went to, but she rushed me off the phone, saying she had too many calls to make. I called the Pizza Joint, wanting to talk to the co-worker that had found Grant dead, but no one answered the phone. I'm going to take a walk down there after I post this. It's awful and terrifying enough that Grant died, but it looks like his cause of death will be covered up as well.

Grant. I met Grant in a video store a week after I'd moved to Brooklyn. We rented Nintendo Wii games and black and white noir flicks together. Grant ate ice cream with a fork. He always wore a white tee shirt under another shirt, even if the other shirt was another white tee shirt. Grant was tall, and slight of build, but very fast, and elegant when he moved. I'd never seen him stumble or fall down. He worked long hours at the Pizza Joint, trying to pay off the final four-grand of tuition he owed NYU so he could get his diploma. That debt wasn't Grant's fault. His father was a gambler and couldn't pay that final tab. Grant had a crooked smile and he only trusted a few of his friends. I think he trusted me. Grant liked to swear a lot. He liked fucking with the Pizza Joint customers whenever he could. Sometimes he'd greet an obnoxious-looking customer with silence and head nods only. Invariably, the obnoxious-looking customer would talk slow and loud because they assumed Grant (who was Korean) didn't speak English. They'd mumble exasperated stuff under their breath when Grant didn't respond. Finally, he'd give the customer their pizza and make some comment like, "You gonna eat all that? You leavin' town or somethin'?" and his voice was loud and had that thick Long Island accent of his. Grant drank orange soda all day long. Grant would be too quick to tease sometimes, but he always gave me an unqualified apology if I needed one. Grant was more than a collection of eccentricities or character traits, but that is what he's been reduced to. I love you and miss you, GRANT.

4 Responses to "Grant Lee, RIP"

Jenn Parker says:

May 10th, 2009 at 4:47 pm

If you are telling the truth (sorry to sound so callous, but I don't know you, and given your blogging history, your agenda, it's entirely plausible you are making this up to bolster your position, as it were), I'm very sorry for your loss.

I don't know what to believe though. Look at your first sentence: **It finally happened.** Maybe this is just a throw away phrase written while in the throes of grief, however it seems like an odd line to lead your post. **It finally happened.** It sounds like not only were you anticipating such an event, but are welcoming it so your version of reality could somehow be verified.

I find it impossible to believe that doctors would give the family of the deceased no cause of death, or a fraudulent cause of death as you are implying. To what benefit or end would such a practice serve?

And please see and respond to the links and aneurysm statistics I quoted in your earlier POST.

squirrelmonkey says:

May 10th, 2009 at 7:13 pm

I'm so, so sorry to hear this, Becca. Poor Grant.

Take care of yourself and ignore that Jenn Parker troll. Call me if you feel up to it, okay?

beast says:

May 11th, 2009 at 3:36 am

sorry about your friend its so scarey that were all gonna die

IN THE MEAN TIME

anonymous says:

May 12th, 2009 at 10:56 am

I've spent the past week doing nothing but reading obituaries from every newspaper I can find online. I read Grant Lee's obit and followed links to his MySpace and then here to your blog.

My son died last week. I was with him in the backyard when he just folded in on himself, falling to the grass. His eyes were closed and blood trickled out of his ears. He was only six. I suppose that his young age is supposed to make it worse, but it can't be any worse for me.

I'm afraid to write his name, as if writing it here makes what happened to him more final than it already is.

Someone else, not me, wrote my son's OBITUARY. I don't remember who. They did a terrible job.

When we first came home, after leaving his body at the hospital, I went into his room and found some crumpled up drawings under his bed. There were two figures in black on the paper, monstrously sized, but human, small heads, no mouths, just two circles for eyes, but all black. They had black guns and they sprayed black bullets all over the page. The bullets were hard slashes, big as knives, black too, and they curved. I have no idea what it means or where it came from.

Was it a sketch of a nightmare, did he see something on TV he shouldn't have, was he drawing these scenes with friends at school? Why did he crumple the drawings up and stuff them under his bed? Did he think that they were 'bad' that he couldn't show them to me, talk about it with me, that I'd be so upset with him that I'd feel differently about him if I were to see the pictures?

It's this last scenario that sends me to the computer and reading other people's obituaries.

PAUL TREMBLAY

A Grim Anniversary

Becca Gilman • April 12ᵗʰ, 2009

The Blog at the End of the World has been live for a year now. I thought it worth revisiting my FIRST POST. On March 20ᵗʰ, 2008, in Mansfield, MA; a fourteen-year-old boy died suddenly during his school's junior varsity's baseball practice (BOSTON GLOBE), and two days later, a fifteen-year-old-girl from the same town died at her tennis practice (BOSTON GLOBE). The two Mansfield residents both had sudden, catastrophic brain aneurysms.

So why am I bringing up those two kids again? Why am I dragging out the old news when you could open up any newspaper in the country, click on any blog or news gathering site, and read the same kind of stories only with different names and faces and places?

Despite the aid of hindsight and my general, everyday paranoia, I'm not prepared to unequivocally state that the teens mentioned ABOVE are our patient zeroes. However, I do think it worth noting those reported stories were mainstream media's **story zero** concerning the **cerebral aneurysm pandemic** and the first of their type to go national, and shortly thereafter, global.

And, finally, a one-link **Link roundup:**

—NEW YORK TIMES reports widespread shortages on a host of anti-clotting and anti-seizure drugs used to treat aneurysms. Included in the shortage, are medications that increase blood pressure, with the idea that increased blood flow through potentially narrowed vessels would prevent clots and aneurysms. Newer, more exotic drugs are also now being reported as in shortage: nimodipine (a calcium channel blocker that prevents blood vessel spasms) and glucocorticioids (anti-inflammatory steroids, not FDA approved, controversial treatment that supposedly controls swelling in the brain). The gist of the story is about the misuse of the medications (many of which are only meant for survivors of aneurysm and aren't preventative), of course, leads to a whole slew of other medical problems, including heart attack and stroke.

6 Responses to "A Grim Anniversary"

revelations says:

April 24, 2009 at 10:23 am

Your a fear monger. You spread fear and the lies of the Godless, liberal media. GOD will punish you!!!!

Jenn Parker says:

April 24, 2009 at 1:29 pm

I have no doubt the Times story is true, but only because of the panic. This story does not prove there really is a pandemic of aneurysms. Only that the general public believes there is one.

Please follow my links here, and it really is as simple as it sounds: The reality is that on average, SINCE 2000, 50,000 Americans die from brain aneurysms (spontaneous cerebral hemorrhaging) per year, with 3-6% OF ALL ADULTS having aneurysms inside their brains (fortunately, most are so small they're never noticed). There is no recorded evidence of that 50,000 number swelling to unprecedented levels. Please show me my error!

There is no conspiracy. It's the 21st Century Red Scare. Our zeitgeist is so pre-occupied with apocalypse we're making one up because the real one isn't getting here soon enough. Yes, 50K is a SMALL PERCENTAGE of the population, but it's a large enough number that if a preponderance of aneurysm cases were to get PRESS COVERAGE, as they clearly are, it gives a multi-media appearance of a pandemic and a conspiracy to cover it up. Unless you can provide some hard data/evidence—like our GOVERNMENT and the W.H.O can provide—please stop. Just stop. There're plenty more real threats (economic, environmental, geopolitical) that sorely need to be addressed.

grant says:

April 24, 2009 at 10:10 am

Has it been only a year? Fuck a flyin' fuckin' duck.

I was at the CVS pharmacy on Central Park Ave. today—just picking up "supplies" ;) —and there was a huge fucking line in the pharmacy section with two armed policeman wandering around the store. Muscles and guns and sunglasses. Some good, hot, homoeroticism there, Becks.

My fuck-headed fellow shoppers were walking all around the CVS, wearing hospital masks and emptying the already empty shelves of vitamins and who the fuck knows what else. Most of them were buying shit they'd never need, just buying stuff because it was there. It was surreal, and I gotta tell ya, they got to me! I ended up buying some leftover Easter candy. Fucking Peeps. Don't even like them, but you know, when society collapses, I just might need me some yellow fucking Peeps!

Stop by the PJ tonight, Becks. I'm working a double-shift. I'll bring the Peeps.

tiredflower says:

April 24th, 2009 at 11:36 am

I'm one of those fuckheads who wears a hospital mask when I go out now. I know it doesn't protect or save me from anything, but it makes me feel better. I know it scares other people when they see me in it, so I tried to cover it up by drawing a smile on the mask with a pink sharpie. I'd hoped it would make people smile back. I'm not a good drawer, though, and it doesn't look like a smile. It's a snarl, bared teeth, the nanosecond before a scream. It's my only mask. I should throw it away and get a new mask, but I can't. It's my good luck charm.

grant says:

April 24, 2009 at 2:15 pm

Drawing mouths on the hospital masks is fuckin' brilliant!

Becks, bring some masks (I know you have some!) to the PJ tonight. I'll help you decorate them. I've got some killer ideas. I'm serious, now, bring some masks. I want to wear one when I go out tomorrow.

bnl44 says:

September 23, 2009 at 2:34 am

I saw someone die today. We were part of a small crowd waiting for our subway train. She

IN THE MEAN TIME

was standing next to me, listening to an iPod. It was loud enough to hear the drums and baseline. Didn't recognize the song, but I tried. When our train arrived she collapsed. I felt her body part the air and despite all the noise in the station, I heard her head hit the concrete. It was a hard and soft sound. Then, her iPod tune got louder, probably because the earphones weren't in her ears anymore.

I don't know if anyone helped her or not. I'm ashamed to admit that I didn't help her. I was so scared. She fell and I raced onto the train, and waited to hear the doors shut behind me before I turned around to look. The windows in the doors were dirty, black with grime, and I didn't see anything.

THE PEOPLE WHO LIVE NEAR ME

George has been there all morning, just standing in the middle of the street. I can't quite tell what he's up to because I'm in my second-floor bedroom and he's three houses away, but something is going on with that poor guy, and I'm going to find out what it is.

Nick-Nick is downstairs pawing through my groceries. I didn't hear him come in, but there's the rustle of paper and plastic bags and the moving and stacking of my canned goods. He tries not to be loud but he's an alarm, just like every morning. He looks for the bag of peanut M&Ms. He won't find it this time because I didn't buy any. Sure, he'll pout and probably even leave a little early today, all to make me feel guilty. It takes more than that to make me feel guilty.

"It's hotter than an ass after a chilli eatin' contest," Nick-Nick says. He's trying to hide his M&M disappointment. Trying to be an adult about it. I appreciate the effort.

But he's right. It's damn hot. I say, "Don't matter. I still need my walk." I'm not going to tell him about George. I want to find out what's really going on before I get Nick-Nick's two cents. "The web MD recommends brisk exercise for men in my size and age group."

"Sure he does."

IN THE MEAN TIME

"Who says the web MD is a he?"

Nick-Nick dances two steps away from me. Afraid I'm going to whack that pointy, bald head of his, even though I've never hit him before. He says, "No one, I didn't mean anything by it."

I turn on my lawn sprinklers. Little green frogs with big sad eyes and big sad mouths surround each spigot, rigged so the water shoots out of those big sad mouths. One frog spits all over Nick-Nick's jean cut off shorts. Then we watch the frogs spit on my grass. We could watch that all day, and we have.

I say, "Whenever someone says they didn't mean anything by it, it means they meant everything by it."

Nick-Nick's mouth goes all sprinkler-frog on me. I'm not saying that he spits on me, but his mouth hangs open, big and sad. First the M&Ms and now me giving him a hard time over the web MD; he wonders why I'm pissed at him. But I'm not pissed. I'm just concerned about George, and it's making me irritable.

We walk. First, we pass the Booths' house. The empty-nesters of the neighbourhood. Biggest house in the development. Well, it isn't a development, really. More like a cul-de-sac. Their four-bedroom colonial is well kept, but their dryer is broken. Has been for two months.

Nick-Nick says, "The Booths are cheaper than a penny whore."

"Might be they're just too lazy to buy a new dryer."

Mrs. Booth doesn't want a clothesline on her land. It'd look too trashy. The Booths fly to Vegas every two months. I trust them to know what is trashy. So no clothesline, but their wet clothes are on hangers and they dangle off the gutters, windowsills on all three floors, deck, branches on their crab apple tree out back, and even on the handle of the lawnmower. When the wind kicks up, I get parachute-sized undergarments sprinkling my lawn, covering my frogs. I keep a big cardboard box on my stoop for their linen collection.

Nick-Nick pulls a can of beer out of his pocket. Up next: the Flynns' split-level ranch. Chocolate-coloured. Or mud.

I say, "Would you look at that?"

Nick-Nick says, "Flynnie has officially gone 'round the bend."

Flynnie is the Yard Guy of our neighbourhood. His lawn is immaculate, golf-course clean. He's building his third storage shed next to the other two (one red like a hydrant and the other blue like toilet bowl cleaner) and the two swing sets. Sheds and swing sets take up half of his land. He didn't get the town's permission for any of them. Proof to Nick-Nick that Flynnie is crazy.

Then there is the orthodox Jews' house. Goddamn me, I don't remember their last name. Husband's name is Howie, Israeli wife, and two kids. Nice family. Little Cape house, kind of a white-grey. Knee-high crabgrass and weeds overgrow their yard. No real lawn anywhere to be seen.

Nick-Nick says, "I wonder if mowing is against their religion."

Howie doesn't have a mower. He has a weed whacker, and he whacks those weeds maybe twice a summer. That's if his Irish-Catholic neighbour, Flynnie, doesn't mow the weeds for him. Flynnie does mow Howie's land often, but not for the right reasons.

I say, "I don't think that's funny at all."

"You know I didn't mean anything by it."

Nick-Nick falls in behind me right after he says it. We are at the end of the cul-de-sac, and George's house.

There isn't a cul-de-sac at the end of my street. Don't know why I said that. But I'll add this: the road just ends at George's house. Well, the paved road ends. There's a dirt road that continues for fifty feet, but dies out in overgrowth. Before the Booths, Flynns, Jews, and George, that dirt road spilled out onto Central Street, but with the new development (Did I say my neighbourhood wasn't a development? Well, it really is a development, all except my house, my house was here first, then everything else developed around me), they decided to close off one end of the road so us developmentees wouldn't have to deal with thru-traffic. That was nice of them, keeping our best interests in mind like that.

• • •

IN THE MEAN TIME

George is still standing in the middle of street, where the blacktop and dirt road meet, the poor bugger.

I wave and say, "How's it hanging?"

Nick-Nick burps.

George has on exactly half of his work clothes. Suit pants, tan, but he's wearing a different colour tan button-up short sleeve shirt that doesn't really go with anything. But he obviously isn't going to work.

I say, "Beautiful day, eh?"

I've always liked George. He's friendly, smiling, never yelling or building sheds or neglecting his lawn or letting underwear fly onto my yard. Quiet guy, in his late fifties. George and his father moved here about four years ago. George and his dad did everything together. They used to read the paper or play cards on their porch, take weekend trips to Canada, or to somewhere they'd never been before. George's father was a good guy too, much friendlier and outgoing, even loud, but in a good way, a way that included you in his loudness. Heck, I even played cribbage with the old fella a few times. That old Canuck used to swear at me in French, whoop my ass all over the cribbage board and laugh like crazy. George's father died a couple of years ago, and it's been just George ever since. He has a younger brother and sister who are still local, and they used to come around all the time. But since the father died, I don't remember seeing them or anyone else come to the house.

So we'll call George our Lonely Guy of the neighbourhood. The one everyone pities.

Nick-Nick answers even though I was asking George about the beautiful day. "It's prettier than that Madonna lady." Nick-Nick wanders off to the side of the road, pretending to be interested in gravel.

I say, "Playing hooky? Or is it one of those personal days that if you don't use it by the end of the quarter you lose it?"

George nods. He always sounds nervous when he's speaking. Or nodding.

Okay, so why has George spent his morning in the middle of the street? The mail hasn't come yet. He isn't gathering garbage cans. He stands at the line where the cracking pavement gives way to dirt road. He stands with his arms folded behind his back. He's hiding something.

It's tough to keep a conversation going with him, so I ask him a random question. "You ever do any acting, George?"

He shakes his head and keeps his arms folded behind his back.

"Well, I used to do some in college, and then a couple community plays after. Nothing big."

Nick-Nick walks across the street to the other side of the road, like he's that chicken in everyone's joke. He's so rude. I don't know what his problem is. He finishes his beer and says, "I bet you did some *acting* in college," but he says it with his back to us.

I ignore Nick-Nick and say, "I'm not sure why this is occurring to me, why I'm bringing it up now, but it's kind of a funny story, I think. And I like to tell funny stories. My first director was the stereotypical failed actor with the goatee, pasty skin, bald, overweight . . ." and I stumble a bit, because I just described what George looks like. To the T. Nick-Nick, of course, laughs like a clown. Big-shoed and annoying as hell. I'm going to withhold his M&Ms for a week. "I wasn't a very good actor but he gave me the only good acting advice I ever got." I stop again, making sure to draw George in.

Nick-Nick says, "Never let them see you sweat." He pulls a second beer out of his pants.

I say, "He told me when you need to act surprised, imagine someone has just snuck up behind you and stuck a broom handle in your ass." I laugh, offer my hand, and say, "All right, see you later."

George accepts my hand. He doesn't want to. Lonely Guy George isn't comfortable with contact. I see his stained-black fingernails and I feel the grit and oil on his fingers. I feel the road in his hand.

Nick-Nick raises his can. Blessedly silent because he's chewing on a mouthful of beer.

We walk back toward my house. Neither of us is sure what we'll do with the rest of the day. There's the Yard Guy, Flynnie. He's mowing Howie's weeds. He swears under his breath, cursing the

IN THE MEAN TIME

day he was burdened by the bad-lawn neighbour who goes to church (well, I know they call it Temple, but I'm sure Flynnie doesn't call it that) on Saturday.

I rub my hands together and feel the oil and grit transferred from George. I think I know what he was doing, but it makes no sense.

"Tell me what you think."

Nick-Nick says, "Would it kill you to get some M&Ms?"

I'm in my bedroom upstairs, alone. Nick-Nick went home because I wouldn't promise him his goddamn M&Ms.

Look, this isn't about me. And I won't pretend it is. So all you really need to know about me is that I've never been to Nick-Nick's house. I don't even know where he lives. I have a vague notion of the vicinity of the area in which he lives. A yellow or maybe white house, a Cape with dormers, or no dormers, or maybe a ranch, front lawn strewn with metal innards of things that he'll never finish fixing. His one-car garage has no door and is filled with things that are nothing but metal outards that won't ever be matched to those broken innards from the front lawn. Wherever Nick-Nick lives, it can't be too far away because he doesn't drive to my house.

This is about the people who live near me. And I'm predicting this just might be all about George.

From up here in my bedroom, I can see George is back out in the street. He's sitting at the road's end, right on that line between pavement and dirt. But like this morning, I'm still too far away to see exactly what he's doing. That hasn't changed.

There's a phone call. But I know it's not Nick-Nick so I let it ring.

I order Nick-Nick's M&Ms and some other groceries online. I pick up underwear off my lawn and return it to the Booths' front porch. Then I sneak past Flynnie's screaming kids. They're in Howie's yard picking dandelions and blowing the fuzz in Howie's three-year-old son Jacob's (pronounced Yakov) face. Those dandelion seeds stick in Jacob's long ringlet hair, but he's giggling. Flynnie yells at his kids, telling them to stay in their yard.

And there's George. Sitting, with his fingers digging and prying at the pavement. I walk up, as quiet as I can. His back is to me. I say, "Why are you picking apart the road?"

He doesn't look up. He doesn't act surprised. I guess I should be flattered he can't picture me coming at him with that broom handle. He says, "Oh, you know. I noticed that the pavement right at the dirt road was cracked and broken in spots." The way he says it, it almost makes sense. Like I'm silly for even asking him.

George gets a finger underneath a slab of blacktop, and picks it away.

"Doesn't that hurt?"

"No."

"Are you going to stop anytime soon?"

"I don't want the road to end at my house. I think I'd prefer it ended sooner."

I imagine what smart-ass comment Nick-Nick might have. George's fingers disappear under a piece of tar, a crack appears, and then a piece crumbles away from the road. It looks too easy. I think about asking him what he's going to do about the pre-road, grooved pavement type stuff they put down under the layer of blacktop. He couldn't possibly pick that up with his fingers. I should say something to the man. There's something obviously wrong here. Something wrong with our Lonely Guy. I've known since before the road picking. I wonder if his siblings know the kind of shape he's in. I should try and help him. It'd be the neighbourly thing to do. I mean, he's forcing me to confront some pretty strange behaviour, behaviour that I'm well within my right to comment upon as an upstanding member of the development.

Did I say that this was a development? Well, it's not. It's just a bunch of houses and people forced together by the quirks of fate and location. Like those house-sellers always say: location, location, location.

I say, "Come on, George. Talk to me. Tell me why."

"When I was seven years old, I misjudged a curb and fell off my bike, splitting my head open on some fresh blacktop. I was knocked cold for a good minute or two. When I woke, Dad scooped me up in his arms and ran with me to the hospital, which was only two blocks away. He tried to stop my crying by making ambulance noises and tickling me. But I couldn't stop crying because my head was cracking open. I still remember the pain. Between the tears I screamed, 'Why?' Dad stopped making the siren noises and he stopped tickling my legs, but he didn't answer me. He never answered me."

Well, to be honest, George didn't really say that to me. I was that kid who fell off the bike. Like I said, I like to tell good stories. And it is a good story. I thought about it right then because it might bring some sense to what George was doing if in fact that (*that* being the falling off the bike and bouncing his head off the road) had happened to him. Might explain why he wants to get rid of the road. Maybe, in his addled head, if he thinks he can tear away the road then no one would fall, no one would get hurt anymore. If there wasn't any road then loved ones would never drive away. No more ambulances or hearses to take people like his father away. Or maybe his "Why?" would finally have an answer.

But George didn't say anything to me. So I don't say anything to George, I don't tell him about falling off the bike and the little-kid me asking, "Why?" I leave our Lonely Guy to his work.

On the way back to my house:

Jacob and Flynnie's kids play on one of their swing sets. Flynnie explodes out the front door and tells his kids to come in for lunch and he tells Jacob to go home. He says it like Jacob has a long way to go before he gets home. Then Flynnie looks at me and whispers, "I just don't want to be responsible for someone else's kid, you know what I mean?" The Booths are rotating wet clothes for dry on their hangers. A Vegas-fat Elvis T-shirt hangs from the handle of the screen door.

Nick-Nick sits on my front stoop, reading the newspaper. He says, "I got my own bag."

"Swell." I put out a hand, wordless in my command for an M&M. Nick-Nick obliges, but not without a sigh, the goddamn ingrate.

• • •

Okay, okay. There's this:

George hasn't left his home in three months. Wait, that's not right. Let me fix that: he hasn't left the neighbourhood in three months. He can afford this, and a few more months if necessary. Actually, I'm just guessing at that. I haven't seen him leave in three months. I suppose it's possible he has left at one time or another. Anyway, that's not what I mean about *there's this*:

This is a funny story about me as a kid. I tell this story a lot. When I was really little, I couldn't do anything for myself. And as the youngest child, my folks indulged and cultivated my helplessness. So much so that I didn't know how to walk up stairs until I was six. It wasn't that I was physically incapable of walking up stairs. I simply didn't want to walk up stairs and my parents would carry me wherever I wanted to go. I didn't learn stairs until I held up my entire first grade class in the stairwell. I was lifting my feet up and down but not going anywhere and everyone behind me laughed and yelled at me to get moving.

At least, that's the story I was told. I really don't remember any of it. Hell, how much of first grade do you remember?

I've been thinking on this for a couple of days now. Trying to get it all sorted out. I can live with the Empty Nesters, my dryerless neighbours and their lawn invading unmentionables. I can certainly live with keep-to-themselves neighbours who don't take care of their lawn. I can even tolerate the shed-building anti-semite Yard Guy, because Flynnie is so blatantly and obviously ridiculous.

But it's official. I'm obsessed with why George is picking apart the road. I'm obsessed with the Lonely Guy. It's the third day in a row that he's out there. At first glance, he hasn't made much progress, but if you look close enough, you can tell he's made a good three feet of the road and even the pre-road disappear.

IN THE MEAN TIME

I'm tired of waiting for Nick-Nick to return with some reconnaissance-type info on George. I need to know his real story.

I wait until everyone is in their home. A quick walk. I find that he's managed to pick away another three feet of road. The road ends before his driveway now. I walk home before anyone sees me, though I'm not sure why I care if I'm seen.

Nick-Nick hasn't been by the house for days now. Maybe I should call him. But I don't think I have his number.

It's Saturday. And these are the people who live near me. Empty Nesters: washing machine is broken now, so are the dishwasher and their two toilets and showers. Mr. Booth relieves himself along their bushes in their backyard. Mrs. Booth washes herself and their dishes and clothes with the garden hose. None of their towels are dry so she lays naked on the front lawn, sunning herself like a lizard. Howie and family: wearing suits, dresses, and *yarmulkes*, walking down our little development road and then another two miles to the Temple. Everything looks normal there, except for the road they're walking on, or what's left of it. Yard Guy: Flynnie has started building his fourth shed while his kids make fun of Jacob's hair and *yarmulke* from the crow's nest perch in one of their three (yes, three now, even though I never saw him put up the third one) swing sets. Lonely Guy: still picking and plucking the road. And he's working his way past Flynnie's house now (and I'm waiting for Flynnie to call the town on George, but maybe he won't because of his illegal, permitless sheds. Flynnie is gutless like that).

What a mess. I'm staying in my house today. It seems my little quiet but quirky development has suddenly gone off the rails. I guess it isn't so sudden. It's been building for a while now.

In my own way, I love these people who share this little chunk of terra firma with me. Of course, I'm afraid of them too. And I can't help but feel a little responsible.

Where is Nick-Nick?

It's dark. I'm standing on George's back porch, peering into a black window. But I can see. His kitchen-sink overflows with dirty dishes. Bills and newspapers drip off the table and chairs, and on the floor are piles of clothes and grocery bags and boxes and trash. The hallway leading out of the kitchen looks to be in the same condition.

I wonder if all this would be as easy as knocking on the door and asking if he needs help. I'm not sure how he'd react to that. I'm not sure how I'd react to that. I'm not saying that I'm in trouble like George and that I need help. Not at all. I'm just saying that I'm trying to understand my neighbour, a fellow human being who lives in the same cul-de-sac or the same development, by understanding how I'd react if I were in his situation, his proverbial shoes. Isn't that how we all try to relate to each other? Through the filter of ourselves? The hard part is that George is probably nothing like me, but I'm trying to shoehorn him into my world so I can understand, and maybe help him.

A few minutes pass. I don't knock on his door or on his window and I don't leave a note or a six-pack of beer.

"I'm actually glad to see you today."

Nick-Nick is here. He walked right in the front door without knocking, like normal. Given all the crazy stuff happening in my neighbourhood, my home, I'll admit his arrival is a comfort, hopefully signifying a return to the routine. But there's a car in my driveway and it's not a ratty pick-up truck that I imagined he'd drive. There's a woman bent over and rummaging through the back seat. I can't really see her face from here, but she has long brown hair. Nick-Nick has three boxes of garbage bags in his arms.

I say, "About time you showed up. So what do you have on George?"

Nick-Nick says, "What do you think, is it too early for a beer?" and laughs that wild laugh of his. Today it makes me nervous. Then he says, "Look, we've been in the house and we know."

I say, "Good, lay it on me."

Nick-Nick talks and talks and tells me everything. Poor, poor

IN THE MEAN TIME

George. And now it's easy to imagine his life, how he lived, how he lives. So he lost his job, but he didn't really lose it. It's still there, he just stopped going. He saw little point to it. He has a hard enough time getting up in the morning as it is without the added stress of co-workers and supervisors and project deadlines. Besides there was no answer forthcoming to his *why* there. It's easy to imagine him after his father died. He spent his life taking care of his father, becoming his own old man in the process, hoping against hope that he was the only person who could answer the *why*. Taking care of Dad was easy. There were rules to follow, routines to maintain, orders to be taken. And then Dad was gone, making a new *why*, and there was no one there (certainly not his no good, abandoning siblings) to talk to him or to take drives or play cards or to tell him to get out of bed and go to work or buy food or put out the garbage or wash his clothes or do the dishes or change light bulbs or to go up the stairs. So now he doesn't do any of that. He doesn't wash dishes. He throws them away and buys new ones. He doesn't take out the garbage and his house is full of trash, old food and grocery bags and empty cartons and bottles and cans everywhere. He doesn't do laundry. When his clothes are dirty he buys new ones. He doesn't leave the house. He shops online, buying groceries yes, but also buying appliances that he doesn't need or already has. When something breaks he doesn't fix it, he buys a new one. It might sound crazy, but it's easy for me to imagine our neighbourhood Lonely Guy making it to advanced adulthood without being capable of forming any kind of relationship with other people. He was never taught how, or never allowed to, or it's just how he is. He's never been independent and never been able to adjust or adapt. He always lived with and for his parents, and when Mom died ten years ago he lived with and only for Dad. He let them do everything for him and they let him do nothing for himself and they let him go to school without knowing how to walk up stairs and they told him what to do his entire adult life. And now they're gone. But what I can't imagine or explain is why he's picking the road away. I feel like I'm missing something. I'm missing something and it's making me nervous again.

I look at Nick-Nick, his hands empty without a beer or a bag of M&Ms, and I don't want to talk about Lonely Guy anymore. I say, "I think Flynnie has started working on a fourth shed. Maybe we should help him."

Nick-Nick opens a garbage bag and says, "Maybe later. First you have to help us start the major cleaning in here. Then we're going to my house."

I look out the window and see the brunette woman walking up my stairs. She looks familiar. In a weird way, she looks like Nick-Nick. And she's carrying more garbage bags, too. It strikes me as funny that even though they haven't been here in ages, and even though there's no more road in front of my house, they still found a way to get here.

I say, "Why?"

Nick-Nick says nothing and opens the door for the brunette woman.

I say, "What about my M&Ms?"

THERE'S NO LIGHT BETWEEN FLOORS

My head is a box full of wet cotton and it won't hold anything else. Her voice is dust falling into my ear. She says, "There's no light between floors."

I blink. Minutes or hours pass. There is nothing to see. We're blind, but our bodies are close and we form a Ying and Yang, although I don't know who is which. She says the between floors stuff again. She speaks to my feet. They don't listen. Her feet are next to my head. I touch the bare skin of her ankle, of what I imagine to be her ankle, and it is warm and I want to leave my hand there.

She's telling me that we're trapped between floors. I add, "I think we're in the rubble of a giant building. It was thousands of miles tall. The building was big enough to go to the moon where it had a second foundation, but most people agreed the top was the moon and the bottom was us." Her feet don't move and don't listen. I don't blame them. Her toes might be under sheetrock or a steel girder. There's only enough room in here for us. Everything presses down from above, or up from below. I keep talking and my voice fills our precious space. "Wait, it can't be the moon our building was built to. Maybe another planet with revolutions and rotations and orbital paths in sync with ours so the giant building doesn't get twisted and

148

torn apart. Or maybe that's what happened; it did get twisted apart and that's why we're here." I stop talking because, like the giant building, my words fall apart and trap me.

She flexes her calf muscle. Is she shaking me away? I move my hand off her leg and I immediately regret it. I feel nothing now. Maybe her movement was just a muscle spasm. I could ask her, but that would be an awkward question depending on her answer.

She says, "There are gods moving above us. I can hear them."

I listen and I don't hear any gods. It horrifies me that I can't hear them. Makes me think I am terribly broken. There's only the sound of my breathing, and it's so loud and close, like I'm inside my own lungs.

She says, "They're the old gods, and they've been forgotten. They've returned, but they're suffering. And despite everything, they'll be forgotten again."

Maybe I'm not supposed to hear the old gods. Or maybe I do hear them and I've always heard them and their sound is nothingness, and that means we're forgotten too.

I put my hand back on her ankle. Her skin is cool now. Maybe it's my fault. My chest expands and gets tight, lungs too greedy. My head and back press against the weight around me. I'm taking up too much space. I let air and words out into the crowded void, trying to make myself small again. I say, "Did the old gods make the building? Did they tear it down? Did they do this to us? Are they angry? Why are they always so angry?"

She says, "I have a story. It's only one sentence long. There's a small child wandering a city and can't find her mother. That's it. It's sentimental and melodramatic but that doesn't mean it doesn't happen every day."

She is starting to break under the stress of our conditions. I admire that she has lasted this long, but we can't stay in this no-room-womb-tomb forever. I should keep her talking so she doesn't lose consciousness. I say, "Who are you? I'm sorry I don't remember."

She whispers. I don't hear every word so I have to fill in the gaps. "Dad died when I was four years old. He was short, bent, had those glasses that darkened automatically, and he loved flannel. At least, that's what he looked like in pictures. We had pictures all over the house, but not pictures of him, actually. My only real memory of Dad is him picking up dog shit in the backyard. It's what he did every weekend. We lived on a hill and the yard had a noticeable slant, so he stood lopsided to keep from falling. He used a gardener's trowel as a scoop and made the deposits into a plastic grocery bag. He let me hold the bag. His joke was that he was transporting not cleaning as he dumped the poop out in the woods across the street, same spot every time. It was the only time he spent out in the yard with me, cleaning our dog's shit. I don't remember our dog's name. My father and the dog are just like the old gods."

The old gods again. They make me nervous. Everything seems closer and tighter after she speaks. My eyes strain against their lids and pray for light. They want to jump out and roll away. I say, "What about the old gods?"

She says, "I still hear them. They have their own language."

I wait for another story that doesn't come. Her head is next to my feet but so far away. Her ankle feels different but that's not enough to go on. Finally, I say, "Maybe I should go find the old gods and tell them you're here, since you seem to know them. Maybe I'll apologize for not hearing them."

My elbows are pinned against my chest and I can't extend my arms. I do what I can to feel around me and around her legs. I find some space behind her left hip. I shift my weight and focus on my limited movement. Minutes and hours pass. My body turns slowly, like the hands of a clock. If the old gods are watching, even they won't be able to see the movement. Maybe that's blasphemous. I'll worry about it later. In order to turn my shoulders I have to push my chest into her legs and hips. I apologize but she doesn't say anything. I make sure I don't hit her head with my feet. I pull myself over her legs, scraping my back against the rubble above me, pressing harder against her, and I'm trying the best I can to make myself flat. It's hard to breathe, and small white stars spot the blackness. I climb over her and reach into a tunnel where I'll have to crawl like a worm or a snake, but I have arms and I wish I could leave them behind with her. I can't turn around so I roll her back with my feet into the spot I occupied. Maybe it'll be more comfortable, and after I'm through she can follow. I say, "Don't worry, I'll find your Dad," but then I remember that she told me he died. What a horrible thing for me to say.

In the tunnel opening I find a flat, square object. It's the size of my hand. The outer perimeter is metal with raised bumps that I try to read with my fingers, but they can't read. It's not their fault. I never trained them to do so. The center of the square is smooth and cool. Glass, I think. I know what it is. It's a picture frame. Hers or mine. I don't know. I slide it into my back pocket and I shimmy, still blind, always blind, into the tunnel. Everything gets tighter.

My arms are pinned to my side. My untrained hands under my pelvis. My legs and feet do the all the work. Those silly hands and useless digits fret and worry. The tunnel thins. I push with my feet and roll my stomach muscles.

The tunnel thins more. My shoulders are stuck. I can't move. Should I wait for her? She could push me through. Do I yell? Would the old gods help me then? But I'm afraid. If I yell I might start an avalanche and close the tunnel. I'm afraid they won't help me. My heart pumps and swells. There isn't any room in here for it. The white stars return. Everything is tight and hard in my chest. I feel a breeze on my face. There must be more open space ahead. One more push.

My feet are loud behind me. They're frantic rescue workers. I hope they don't panic. I need them to get through this. My shoulders ache and throb. Under the pressure. Legs muscles on fire. But I squeeze. Through. And into a chamber big enough to crawl in.

I feel around looking for openings, looking for up. I still can't see. I'll use sinus pressure and spit to determine up and down. My legs shake and I need to rest. I take out the picture frame. My hands dance all over it. Maybe it's a picture of her father in the yard. He's wearing the flannel even in summer. I remember how determined he was to keep the yard clean. He didn't care if the grass grew or if my dog dug holes, he just wanted all the shit gone.

I need to keep moving. I pocket the picture frame and listen again for the old gods. I still don't hear them. There's a wider path in the rubble, it expands and it goes up and I follow it. Dad had all kinds of picture frames that held black-and-white photos of obscure relatives or relatives who became obscure on the windowsills and hutches and almost anything with a flat, stable surface. He told me all their stories once, and I tried to listen and remember, but they're gone. After Dad died, Mom didn't take down or hide any of the pictures. She took to adding to the collection with random black-and-white photos she'd find at yard sales and antique shops. She filled the walls with them. Every couple of months, she moved and switched all the pictures around too, so we didn't know who our obscure relatives were and who were strangers. Nothing was labelled. Everyone had similar moustaches or wore the same hats and jackets and dresses and everyone was forgotten even though they were all still there. I can't help but think hidden in the stash of pictures were the old gods, and they've always been watching me.

The path in the rubble continues to expand. My crawl has become a walking crouch. There are hard lefts and rights, and I can't go too fast as I almost fall into a deep drop. Maybe it's the drop I shouldn't be concerned about. What if I should be going down instead of up? The piled rubble implies a bottom. There's no guarantee there's a top. What if she did hear the old gods but her sense of direction was all messed up? What if they're below us? Maybe that's fine too.

I continue to climb and I try to concentrate. Thinking of the picture frame helps. In our house there was a picture of a young man in an army uniform standing by himself on a beach, shirt sleeves rolled over his biceps. Probably circa-WWII but we didn't know for sure. He had an odd smirk, and like the Mona Lisa's it always followed me. I also thought his face looked painted on, and at the same time not all there, like it would float away if you stopped looking, so I stared at it, a lot. If I had to guess, I'd say that's the picture in my back pocket.

My crouch isn't necessary anymore and now I'm standing and level and the darkness isn't so dark. There are outlines and shapes, and weak light. My feet shuffle on a thin carpet. I avoid the teeth of a ruined escalator. I'm dizzy and my mouth tastes like tinfoil. There's a distant rumble and the bones of everything rattle and shake loose dust. She was right. The old gods are here. I imagine they are beautiful and horrible, and immense, and alien because they are all eyes or mouths or arms and they move the planets and stars around. I take the picture frame out of my pocket and clutch it to my chest. It's a shield. It's a teddy bear. I found it between floors. There's a jagged opening in the ruined building around me and I walk through it.

I emerge into an alien world. I'm not where I used to be. This is the top of the ruined building, or its other bottom. The air here is thick and not well. Behind me there is a section of the building's second or other foundation that is still intact. My eyes sting and my vision is blurry, but the sky is red and there are mountains of glass and mountains of brick and mountains of metal and I stand in the valley. Nothing grows here. There are eternal fires burning without smoke. Everything is so large and I am so small. There are pools of fire and a layer of grey ash on the ground and mountains. I'm alone and there's just so much space and it's beautiful, but horrible too because I can't make any sense of it and there's too much space, too much room for possibility, anything can happen here. I shouldn't be here. She was right not to follow me because I climbed through the rubble in the wrong direction and I think about going back, but then I see the old gods.

I don't know how she heard them. They're as alien or other as I imagined but not grand or powerful. They're small and fragile, like me. There is one old god between the mountains and it walks slowly toward me. The old god is naked and sloughs its dead skin, strips hanging off its fingers and elbows. Its head is all red holes and scaly, patchy skin. The old god must be at the end, or maybe the beginning, of a metamorphosis. There is another kneeling at the base of the mountain of glass. The old god's back is all oozing boils and blisters. Its hands leave skin and bloody prints on the mountain. It speaks in a language of gurgles and hard consonants that I do not understand. The old god is blessing or damning everything it touches. I don't know if there is a difference. I find more old gods lying about, some are covered in ash, and they look like the others but they are asleep and dreaming their terrible dreams. And she was right again; they are all suffering. I didn't think they were supposed to suffer like this.

I walk and it's so hard to breathe but I shouldn't be surprised given where I am. There's too much space, everything is stretched out, and I'm afraid of the red sky. Then I hear her voice. Her falling dust in my ears. She's behind me somewhere, maybe standing at the edge of our felled building and this other world. She asks me to tell the old gods that I'm sorry I forgot them. My voice isn't very loud and my throat hurts, but I tell them I am sorry. I ask her if I'm the small child in the city looking for my mother in her one-line story. She tells me the old gods have names: Dresden and Hiroshima and Nagasaki. She knows the language of the old gods and I know the words mean something but it's beyond my grasp, like the seconds previously passed, and they all will be forgotten like those pictures, and their stories, in my mother's house.

I'm still clutching the found picture frame to my chest. There's a ringing in my ears and my stomach burns. The old god walking toward me spews a gout of blood, then tremors wrack its body. Flaps of skin peel off and fall like autumn leaves. Change is always painful. I take the frame off my chest and look at it. Focusing is difficult. There's no picture. It's empty. There's only a white sticker on the glass that reads **$9.99**. I feel dizzy and I can't stay out here much longer. It's too much and minutes and hours pass with me staring at the empty picture frame, and how wrong I was, how wrong I am.

There's a great, all-encompassing, white light that momentarily bleaches the red sky and I shield my eyes with the empty frame.

Then there's a rumble that shakes the planet, and well beyond the mountains that surround me a great grey building reaches into the red sky. They're building it so fast, too fast, and that's why it'll eventually fall down because they aren't taking their time, they're not showing care. It's still an awesome sight despite what I know will happen to it. The top of the building billows out, like the cap of a mushroom, and I try to yell, "Stop!" because they are constructing the building's second foundation in the sky. The building won't be anchored to anything; the sky certainly won't hold it. It'll fall. I don't want to watch it fall. I can't. So I turn away.

She speaks to me again. She tells me to leave this place and come back. I do and I walk, trying to avoid the gaze of the old gods. They make me feel guilty. But they aren't looking at me. They cover their faces. They're afraid of the great light. Or maybe they're just tired because they've seen it all before. I walk back to our ruined building, but she's not at the opening. She's already climbing back down. I'll follow. I'll climb back down to our space between floors and bring her the picture frame. I'll tell her it's a picture of my Dad in the yard with flannel and his poop-scoop.

I ease back into the rubble, dowsing paths and gaps, climbing down, knowing eventually down will become up again. Or maybe I'll tell her it's a picture of that army guy I didn't know, him and his inscrutable Mona Lisa smirk. Did he have the confidence and bravado of immortality or was he afraid of everything? She won't be able to see the picture so I won't really be lying to her. The picture will be whatever I tell her it'll be. I won't tell her about the new giant building, the one that was grey and has a foundation in the sky.

The gaps in the rubble narrow quickly and everything is dark again. I once asked Mom why we kept all those old, black-and-white pictures and why she still bought more, and why all the walls and shelves of our house were covered with old photos and old faces, everyone anonymous, everyone dead, and she told me that they were keepsakes, little bits of history, she liked having history around, then she changed her mind and said, no, they were simply reminders. And

IN THE MEAN TIME

I asked reminders of what? And she didn't say anything but gave me that same Mona Lisa smile from the photograph, but I know hers was afraid of everything.

The picture is in my back pocket again. I am going to tell her that everyone who was ever forgotten is in the picture. We'll be in the picture too, so we won't forget again.

I'm crawling and the tunnel ahead will narrow. I can feel the difference in the air. There is another rumble above me and the bones of everything shake again, but I won't see that horrible light down here. I'll be safe. I wonder if I should've tried to help them. But what could I have done? I suppose, at the very least, I could've told the old gods that there is no light between floors.

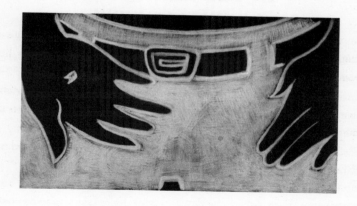

HEADSTONES IN YOUR POCKET

The sun is high but it feels low, its heat close and heavy enough to push heads down and slump shoulders. Border Patrol Agent Joe Marquez runs his hand along the tractor-trailer and chips of white paint break off and crumble to dust under his fingertips like dried leaves from a dead houseplant. There are rustling noises inside the truck, trapped spirits, humanity in a tin can. He wonders if they'll emerge in any better shape than the trailer's paint job.

Two agents pin the driver against the truck's chrome grille. He yells, claiming the hot chrome burns his skin. The agents don't care, don't say anything while they handcuff him. The smuggler is priority one. The cargo can wait.

Joe jogs the length of the trailer and yells ahead, "Let's go, get those doors open, now!"

Local commuters and smugglers and immigrants know the Tubac checkpoint's schedule. The checkpoint is thirty miles south of Tucson and thirty miles north of Nogales and the Mexico-US border. It was supposed to be closed at this mid-afternoon hour, but the Border Patrol office in Tucson, which prominently features a photo of John Wayne (circa *The Alamo*) on its wall, received an anonymous tip, a tip that turned out to be true.

IN THE MEAN TIME

One agent turns the rusted handle and throws open the trailer's doors while another agent aims his automatic rifle. Heat, sweat, and a low, desperate collected conversation rush out of the trailer and into the surrounding desert. There is no air conditioning and the temperature inside is more than 110 degrees. Flashlights penetrate the darkness and reveal a mass of bodies, scores of men picking up their heads but closing and hiding their eyes, holding out empty hands.

They'll be unarmed, they will not hurt anyone, and they'll have nothing on them. All will be processed for deportation. Joe has been a Border Patrol Agent for two years and has witnessed the same sorry scene at least twice a month.

The Tubac checkpoint is a temporary one, with its portable lights and generators resting on the shoulder of I-19, alongside its incendiary local politics. The suburbanites don't want a fixed checkpoint because checkpoint towns become a de-facto second border. The fear is that smugglers and immigrants and other dangerous (non-white) criminals would use their sleepy little towns as waystations, drug factories, and shoot 'em ups. The Border Patrol's Tucson sector comprises almost the entire Arizona-Mexico border and is the only sector without at least one fixed checkpoint.

Agents separate the fifty men into groups of ten. The men have been reduced to a task to be divvied up. They are sweaty, exhausted, and frightened, but everyone makes it out of the trailer alive and conscious. Joe's group of ten stands in a line and with their hands held out and open although he did not tell them to do so.

Joe pats down his men. The third man in line has something in the front left pocket of his jeans. Joe says, *"¿Cuál es su nombre?"* being rigidly formal in the request, Joe's intent is to give a measure of respect and dignity, but he knows it could very well be interpreted as one of *la migra* flaunting his position.

The man says, "Guillermo." He's tall, and skinny, a piece of string hanging from the leg of his cut off jeans. Guillermo has thick stubble overwriting a map of acne scars and he is likely a full decade older than Joe is, but there's no way to tell. He won't have a passport.

Joe says, "*Guillermo, dame lo que tienes un tu bolsillo. Por favor.*"

"*No es nada. No son drogas.*" It is nothing. It is not drugs. His speech pattern is as formal as Joe's. The two men are actors afraid of forgetting their lines. He reaches into his pocket and gives Joe what he wants. It is a folded rectangle of tinfoil.

"*Entonces, ¿qué es?*"

"*Es de m'hijo.*"

Joe unwraps the tinfoil slowly; the tinfoil spread open on his palm and it dances in the warm breeze. In the middle, there's a small, clear plastic baggie, and inside the baggie is a white rock. Joe takes it out and realizes it is a tooth, a baby tooth, and it's as small as a pebble and looks so inconsequential and fragile that it might blow away in the scalding desert winds, or simply disintegrate.

The lights are dim. Local country songs alternate with Johnny Cash standards on the jukebox, one that still plays scratchy 45 records instead of CDs or MP3s. Joe is purposefully early, sitting at their usual booth for two at Zula's, a restaurant in the small and impoverished border town of Nogales, their hometown. He stirs his second screwdriver with a red swizzle stick, counter clockwise, as if he can turn back the clock. The tinfoil, folded up with its secret tooth inside, is on the chipped, wooden tabletop. *Es de m'hijo. It's from my son.* Joe kept it by mistake. Before he could give the tooth back to Guillermo, he was called away to help with the smuggler's arrest and processing, and then Joe forgot he'd pocketed the tooth. The other agents deported Guillermo and the rest of the immigrants before Joe could return the harmless keepsake. There's no way he can get the tooth back to Guillermo. He can't even create a fantasy scenario where he meets the ragged man unexpectedly to return the memento, the little white tooth. The scenario that's easy to conjure is Guillermo's return home as a failure being unbearably brief and then him attempting an even more dangerous and desperate root to the US, hiking through the desert around Nogales, where the past two years has seen a more than twenty percent increase in immigrant fatalities. Post-9/11 security improvements are forcing more immigrants to attempt border crossings in further remote areas, forcing them to take their chances in the desert. Joe imagines Guillermo struggling through the barren, unforgiving landscape, then falling, twisting an ankle, getting lost, dying of heat exposure, or as has been increasingly the case, he sees Guillermo falling prey to bandits, armed Mexican nationals, or a double-crossing smuggler he paid as a guide, his body never to be found. Last winter, bandits shot a group of immigrants in an area just west of Nogales, inside the expansive and desolate Tohono O'odham Reservation. Joe helped carry one of the rescued survivors to an ambulance, an older Nicaraguan woman who had her left ear blown off. After receiving baseline medical care she was sent back to Nicaragua.

Joe checks his watch. She's late. He turns the swizzle stick again. Today was another worst day in a litany of worst days while on the job, a job that has an inexplicable hold on him, a job that says more about him than he cares to hear. He orders a third screwdriver, which means he likely won't be driving back to his Tucson apartment tonight.

Jody Fernandez finally arrives, forty minutes late, limping to their booth. "Sorry, Joe. I had a hard time escaping from my parents' house." Her voice is rough but dampened, a crinkling paper bag as it's shaped into a ball. She wears a black long-sleeved T-shirt to cover her skinny arms and jeans that are supposed to be tight, but hang off her gaunt frame like elephant skin. Her black hair is tied up in a ponytail and her skin is pale. She's in her late twenties like Joe but looks like she could be his older sister, or an aunt. Still, she's in better shape than she was a few short months ago, before the rehab stint. Jody is a meth addict.

Joe gets the sense that she's not telling him the truth, but he's okay with it. Despite everything and the relapse warning signs he's supposed to watch for, they're close enough that the little lies don't equate to betrayal. Not yet, anyway. He says, "*De nada.* I've had a long day and I'm just sitting here, unwinding."

Jody smiles, but won't show her teeth, which were ravaged by the year-plus of meth addiction. Meth is acidic, dries up the protective saliva, and while in the throes of the drug, the heavy users grind and clench their teeth to dust. She explained it to him once, saying meth mouth was like a neglected and abused engine being empty of oil but still redlining and chewing up its own gears. She says, "I see that. I guess you'll be sleeping on the couch tonight, then?"

As children, they were neighbours and best friends. Their mothers taught biology and chemistry at the regional high school and their fathers commuted to Tucson together. Joe and Jody, their names and lives almost the same until college, where both went to the University of Arizona. Jody married a physics PhD student and upon graduation got a job teaching special ed for elementary-aged children. Two years ago, after visiting her mother in Nogales, she and her husband were hit by a compact pick-up truck. The driver was a pest exterminator who fell asleep at the wheel and drifted over the center lines. Her husband died. Jody's right leg shattered in three places and her skull fractured, requiring a plate. She suffered from debilitating headaches for months and wasn't able to work, living but not living on disability insurance, so, like many of the hopeless locals of Nogales, she turned to meth.

Joe says, "Yeah, I think I might need to crash on your couch. Will that be okay?"

"Of course, but no puking allowed. I just cleaned the goddamn bathroom."

"How are you feeling?"

A waiter appears with a beer that she must've ordered before she sat down. She takes a sip big enough for the both of them, and then says, "Shitty, like I was last week. But I can deal with it."

Joe fights a growing impatience. Her lateness, her short answers that aren't really answers; he knows he can't rush her back. He wants the Jody he knew before the addiction, before the accident. He might never get her back, and that's something he needs to deal with, not her.

They both order light meals, garden salads and appetizer quesadillas. Joe orders another screwdriver. He says, "How's your mother?"

"Fine. Same old stuff. Bugging me to move back home until I *get back on my feet*. God, I hate that fucking phrase. Like me being able to simply walk around on my broken leg has anything to do with improving my shitty days."

Joe says, "I hate it when people say *cut a check*." As soon as he says it, he thinks the quip ill-timed and a terrible, miserable mistake. But she laughs, and he's flooded with relief, then shame because he shouldn't be so nervous around her.

Jody stops laughing, then leans forward, her head in the spotlight of the black pewter pot light fixture that hangs above their table like a bat. Her deep, brown eyes grow too big for her face. "All right, Joe, I wasn't at my Mom's house. I'm late because I found an old note from Steve, today." She smirks, a child caught doing something wrong, but not caring at all. But that's not right. She's no child and hasn't been one for a lifetime.

Joe says, "I'm sorry."

"Don't be. I'm not sure if I am. It was folded inside an old textbook, *Educational Philosophy*. My therapist keeps saying work is still a year or two away, but I've been looking through my old notes and textbooks, reading until the headaches take over."

Joe nods. He knows that's enough.

"I opened up to the chapter on cognitive disorders, and there it was, one of his wiseass notes, too. De-motivational aphorisms, he called them." She smiles but covers her mouth with a hand. The hand tremors and it's not enough to cover everything. "He slipped them into my notebooks and textbooks, that gloomy physics geek that he was, thinking his clever was so cute."

"What'd the note say?"

"I'll tell you if you show me what you're hiding?"

"What? I'm not hiding anything?"

"You had something out on the table and you stuffed it into your pocket when I walked over. I want to see it."

He says, "Okay. Deal. But you tell me first." Joe doesn't look forward to explaining why he has the tinfoil and what it means, but he'll play along. It's good to see her willing to play games with him, even if the game pieces aren't exactly silly.

"It said, 'Evil is a consequence of good. Cheers! Steve.'"

"That's nice. Should be a Hallmark card."

"I know. This was the only note I confronted him about. Was he implying that a gig serving special needs students was somehow a bad thing in his warped little world? He could be snotty about his field of study putting him in the supreme strata of society." Jody is talking fast, manic with her words. "If he was honest with me, if he didn't back down, he would've said something like my helping the helpless only delayed and prolonged their suffering and the suffering of their loved ones, making it all worse in the long run. He used to say shit like that at parties just to get a rise out of people. But he didn't say any of that, didn't let me put those words in his mouth. I played at being super pissed and he backed off real quick, apologizing up and down. It was the last of those notes he left in my books. Him backing down, that was my small victory, our relationship was always a competition, but now I wish he'd given me more of his pithy love notes of doom. Isn't that sad? I spent the afternoon and early evening staring it and thinking it was all quite sad."

"It is sad. But I'm glad you can talk about it."

"Stop it. You sound like my freaking therapist when you say shit like that."

"Does she say 'cut a check' too?"

"No, but I'll insist she do so from now on. Now pay up, Marquez. What are you hiding from me?"

"Uh-oh. Using the last name, she means business."

"All business, all the time."

"Okay, let's take a look." Joe takes out the tinfoil and lays it on the table. Jody furrows her brow and cocks her head to the side. Joe quickly panics, almost spilling his drink as he rushes to cover the tinfoil with his hands, a bumbling magician with nothing up his sleeves. He says, "Now, hold on a second. It's not what you think it is." He won't say *drugs*. He quickly launches into the story of Guillermo, fumbles through their roadside conversation, how this belonged to his son, and then how everything got so crazy that he forgot to give it back. The story already sounds rehearsed. Joe talks while slowly unwrapping the package, careful not to make any new folds or marks in the tinfoil, preservation somehow being of the utmost importance.

Jody leans over the table. "Well, what is it?"

He lifts the plastic bag, dangles it from his finger, and holds it across the table. "It's a tooth. His son's baby tooth. See? I feel bad, it's probably the first tooth he . . ."

Jody stands up, jumps out of her seat, and her head crashes into the pewter pot light fixture, sending its weak light arcing elsewhere into the restaurant.

"Whoa. You okay?"

She turns away from the flickering light and from him, and says, "I need to go to the bathroom." She might've only said *I need to go*, as he didn't hear her say *bathroom*. The light shines directly in his eyes, then away, then back, and Joe is unable to watch her progress through the restaurant and bar.

The waiter appears with their food, and steadies the swaying light fixture. The quesadillas are smoking and hissing on the pan. Joe wraps the little tooth back into the foil. Jody didn't just go to the bathroom; she fled from the table. He's not sure what he did, but clearly it was wrong, and he's not sure if Jody is coming back. He waits, elbows on the table, hands making a steeple, and now she has been gone long enough that he considers going to the bathroom or the parking lot to find her. But she comes back, walking as fast as her limp allows, and sits down abruptly, the final word to some inner conversation. She stabs her fork around the salad, into the cherry tomatoes, and doesn't place her napkin on her lap.

Joe says, "Hey, everything okay? I'm sorry if . . ."

"Jim Dandy," she says, but doesn't look at him.

Everything has become so difficult between them. He knows he's not being fair, but these bi-weekly dinners are becoming as tedious and futile as his job. He isn't helping anyone, isn't improving lives; if anything he's making everything worse, like that note from Steve. He orders another screwdriver.

For now, Joe won't ask Jody what's wrong because he's afraid of making it worse, and he's also being selfish. He drank too much to drive home and he needs her couch tonight, not further complications.

They walk the two blocks to Jody's one-bedroom apartment. It's late, a weeknight, and no one else is out, the streets as desolate and windswept as the desert. They don't talk. She doesn't ask Joe why he still has that tooth, why hasn't he just pitched it and moved on. Joe assumes she's just accepted it, like he has.

Her apartment is maniacally clean, antiseptic, and it smells of cleanser and air-freshener. The hardwood floor in the living room gives way to yellowed and curling linoleum tile in the kitchen. Joe falls onto the couch in front of the TV and turns it on. Jody says that she has a headache, and disappears into her bedroom, closing and locking the door.

Joe kills the lights and tries watching a baseball game between two teams he doesn't like, then shuts off the TV and reclines, sinking into the couch, and stares at the stucco ceiling. The buzz of alcohol fills the sensory void, droning in his ears and jostling his equilibrium. He closes his eyes, the room spins, he sinks deeper into the couch, and he can't sleep. He's always had trouble sleeping. As a kid, he'd lie awake for hours and obsess over his nightmares. Then he learned to trick himself to sleep. He created and choreographed his own waking-dream, some simple innocuous scene on which to focus and loop in his head until it relaxed him enough and he fell asleep.

Tonight, in Joe's crafted dream, he gets off the couch and walks into the kitchen, first pausing above the room's borderline, where the hardwood meets the cracked linoleum. He fills a glass with tap water and drinks half, dumps the rest in the sink, then walks back to the couch, lies down, and then starts it all up again, past the borderline and back to the kitchen again for his same glass of water. On one of his return trips to the sink, Joe stops filling his glass. To his right and next to Jody's bedroom is the study, and its door is open. There's no light, everything is dark, but inside the study is somehow darker than the rest of the apartment. A child, a little boy, stands in the doorway, his hands in the pockets of his jeans, hangdog in his posture. It's too dark to see any facial features, but he knows this boy. Then Joe is standing in the doorway although he doesn't want to be there, just wants to be back at the sink, filling his glass of water and making it half-empty. The boy is still in the doorway too, and he wraps his arms around Joe's legs. The embrace is brief and weak, a butterfly-wing hug, and then the boy puts his hand inside Joe's, a small, cool stone. The boy leads Joe back to the couch. There's more light here; stray neon and streetlight amber filter through the windows. The boy has thick, black hair and eyes like Jody's but not Jody's. Joe lies on the couch. He doesn't want to lie on the couch. He's tired of doing so many things that he doesn't want to do, that he can't do, not anymore. The boy smiles like Jody too, hiding his mouth behind quivering lips. It's not a smile, it's something else, recognition maybe, or acceptance. Whatever it is, it's filled with more despair than the tears to come. Then the boy does part his lips, those rusted hinges, and opens his mouth, and the teeth, an angler fish at the bottom of the deep, black ocean, his *teeth*, the stalactites and stalagmites of nightmare, angry shards of glass with thick tips curved in awkward and dangerous directions, teeth just spilling out of the boy's mouth. He climbs on top of Joe, sits on his lap, and tears the size of gumdrops roll down the boy's eyes because he doesn't know he's a monster, and it's not fair because he's not supposed to be the monster, does not deserve to be the monster. But the teeth, the *teeth*.

After he left, he realized he shouldn't have driven home. It was too late and he was too drunk. He should've stayed and slept it off, but he got into his car instead. He drove, taking the I-19, and was stopped at the Tubac checkpoint, his non-permanent checkpoint. The agents shined flashlights in his face. He knew they initially only saw a Mexican behind the wheel, and Joe knew he looked just like the men in that decaying trailer, dark skin, squinting and hands held empty and up. The agents were going to pat him down and take the tinfoil away. But the flashlights turned off as they did recognize their co-worker. Yeah, they knew him, and they knew he was drunk. They didn't arrest him, but they didn't allow him to drive home and there was an incident report filed with the Tucson office. His immediate two-week suspension was the result. Two weeks. He only left his apartment to go the liquor store. He ate meals only when he wasn't drinking, and the meals consisted of slices of American cheese, cold hot dogs, dry cereal, pretzel sticks. He removed all of the curtains and shades from his windows, and at night, turned on all the lights. He only slept when he drank himself into unconsciousness, but then didn't wake until late afternoon. He lay on the couch or on the floor and wouldn't sleep in his bedroom, convinced he'd find the little boy sitting at the foot of his bed, and the boy wouldn't say anything and wouldn't look at Joe, but he also wouldn't leave, not this time. He kept the tinfoil. He called Jody when he was awake past midnight. She didn't answer and didn't return his calls. The two weeks passed like most time does, without any acknowledgement. The two weeks were something he simply survived.

Now it's the night before Joe is to return to active duty. He is again at their booth at Zula's. He sits, a tumbleweed without a breeze, and he stares at his empty screwdriver and empty cup of coffee.

Jody isn't coming so he leaves the restaurant and walks to her apartment. This night is hotter than all the previous nights, and Joe sweats through his white T-shirt. Her door isn't locked and he lets himself in without knocking. Inside, the apartment is dark and a disaster of clothes and food and trash. It's as though the spotless apartment he saw two weeks ago never existed, or maybe the duration between visits was longer than those arbitrary and government-assigned weeks, time enough for the apartment to fall into such an advanced state of decay, maybe a collection of years, lost years, had passed, or epochs only measurable by fossilized bodies, bones, and teeth.

"What are you doing here?" Jody's voice is frayed, an exposed wire, quick with its electricity but weak enough that it'll break or flame out at any moment.

Joe steps over the rubble of her apartment. The place smells of sweat and burnt chemicals. Joe walks inside the study. Jody sits on the floor, cross-legged, huddled next to a small fire, a mini-pyre set up on the hardwood floor stained black. Mounds of papers, books, and photographs surround her and the fire. She wears a white bra and black underwear along with black marks that are either bruises or smudged ash. She's too thin. Her bones are a story written in Braille, but the story is too big and horrible to be contained by her skin. Joe puts a hand into his jeans pocket, touches the tinfoil, and he knows how she spent their time apart, and he knows this is all his fault.

Jody's eyes can't focus, and they roll around the room. Her breaths are fast and irregular, as are her twitchy movements. She says, "You still have it, don't you, Joe. You still have it. . . ." Her voice trails into whispers, and the words come too fast, fumbling over each other, letters placed inside of letters, making new sounds.

He says, "I do."

She says, "You didn't forget to give the tooth back, you kept it on purpose, you made it all up, that story you told me is bullshit, all bullshit, you kept it on purpose. You didn't forget, no way, no way you forgot."

"I did forget, Jody."

She laughs. Then says, "Look at this. Another note. *Misery is manifold*, Joe. It's true. Steve wrote that on this letter over here, and stuck it in my English Lit book. It's right over here. There. You wanna read it?" Jody picks up a slip of paper and drops it into the fire. Jody turns toward him, and her hair is frayed thread. She smiles, shows her meth mouth, her teeth, blackened and decayed, pieces missing, an incomplete jigsaw puzzle, jagged and eroded canyon boulders, each tooth or what was a tooth is a bombed and burnt-out building that cannot be repaired.

"You know what? A tooth fell out last night, Joe. It was cracked and loose, and I played with it, wiggled it around with my tongue and fingers, like we did when we were kids, I wiggled it, pulled on it, and it hurt a little but not much, nothing I couldn't take, nothing I couldn't deal with, and it just kinda popped out. Do you wanna see it, Joe? I saved it for you because you're collecting teeth now, right?"

Joe needs to do something, say something, anything that will close her terrible mouth. "I don't know why I kept the tooth. I don't know why I do what I do, anymore. Don't know if I ever did."

"You're a junky, just like me." She smiles again, flashes her intimate, private devastation. "Like me, Joe. See? Get that fuckin' tooth out of your pocket, you fucking junky. *Misery is manifold*, Joe, and you're a junky, the worst kind, the one who won't ever admit there's a problem even when the signs, the signs, the signs are there, big as fucking billboards, billboards in your pocket, not a billboard, a headstone, headstone in your pocket, Joe, you have a headstone in your pocket, Joe. Joe, fucking, Joe, take it out, tell me what is says, what does it say? I know what it says but I want you to tell me, Iwantyoutotellmetellmetellmetellme . . ."

Joe says, "I'm sorry, Jody. I didn't mean to do this to you, to us. I'd forgotten about him. Really, I did."

He isn't strong enough to tell her that he forgot on purpose and that he worked at it and that he was good at it, better than she was, and it's why she's like she is now and it's why he's like he is now. He wants to run out of her apartment, to run away, as he's always been running away even if he never left home, where there's still room enough to hide, there's an all-encompassing desert in which to hide.

At the southwest edge of Nogales, there was a stretch of desert near the border—and at the time, almost twenty years ago, a generally unsupervised border—where local teens would ride their dirt bikes and mountain bikes during the day and then later reconvene at night to light fires and bottle rockets and drink cheap six-packs. Joe and Jody were only eight and not allowed to go to there, but they went anyway. They told each set of parents they were riding to the playground for the afternoon and then would ride their bikes to the edge of the desert.

It was late afternoon, the sun low and lazy in the west, a half-shut eye, and they were knee deep in their summer routine; climbing on rocks, turning over smaller stones looking for scorpions and small lizards, filling small burrows with sand and dried grass. Two high-school-aged kids on dirt bikes showed up in their desert, kicking up dirt and filling the air with their engines' whine. Jody pulled Joe behind a rock, their roles shifting from desert explorers to spies, skulking around and hiding behind boulders and saguaro cactus.

The dirt bikes were chipped paint and dented metal. The riders didn't wear helmets. One kid was white, short and pudgy, wore a sleeveless black T-shirt with a bald eagle that was all talons and beak, and he had a mop of unkempt, dark hair, like a dead tarantula on his head. The other teen was a blond beanpole with a crewcut, wearing a baggy white T-shirt with large, slashing letters and baggier shorts that hung down to his shins when he stood up on his pegs. The teens rode up a ridge that was 100 yards or so away, a ridge that may or may not have been a part of Mexico, and then back down.

Joe and Jody didn't say anything or do anything, afraid of the teens, but both secretly wished for the thrill of being caught, of having to jump on their bikes, and then somehow outrunning the dirt bikes, cutting through yards and short cuts that only they knew. They moved carefully, exchanging cactus for boulder, and crept closer to the ridge.

While tearing through another run, the chubby kid grabbed his left shoulder like it'd been stung, then swerved, and jumped off his bike, which landed on its side and slid halfway down the ridge. Three Mexican boys popped up from behind a boulder at the ridge's crest; two kids threw rocks and a third pointed and shouted something, then they all took off running down the other side of the ridge. The blond sped over and helped get his friend's bike back on its wheels.

Their conversation was animated and brief. The high-pitched whine of engines was too loud for Jody and Joe to hear anything.

The teens went over the ridge. Jody pulled Joe from out of their hiding spot and said, "Come on!" She ran ahead, and he followed her up the ridge. They stopped at the top and could see everything below.

The three boys alternated fleeing with throwing their small stones at the circling dirt bikes. The teens swore and shouted epithets from the top of their mechanical steeds, and they both cradled a rock in the crook of one arm. The smallest and presumably the youngest trailed far behind the other two retreating boys. The teens focused on the straggler, tightening their circle, revving their engines and spraying dirt on the boy with their spinning, angry tires. The boy was trapped and crying, and scrambled onto a large, jagged boulder. He shouted to his friends, cupping his hands over his small mouth, but they hadn't stopped running, were too far ahead to hear his pleas. The chubby kid, the one with the eagle T-shirt, threw his rock and hit the boy in the back of his thigh. There wasn't much behind the throw, but the boy lost his balance, windmilled his arms, and fell off, behind the craggy rock, out of view of Jody and Joe.

The teens didn't stop to investigate. They tightened their formation, parallel to each other, shared an awkward high-five, and rode triumphantly back up the ridge. Joe and Jody crouched, praying they wouldn't be seen, or they'd be next, chased down the ridge, into Mexico, and then knocked off a boulder, but the teens didn't see them and didn't stop. They sped away, out of the sand, and onto the main drag and out of sight.

Silence, the voice of the desert, replaced the screaming boys and dirt bikes. Joe and Jody listened and watched for a sign from the boy who fell and there was none. They waited. The sun drooped lower in the west. The other two boys did not come back for their friend.

Wordlessly, Jody and Joe climbed down the ridge. They crept behind the jagged boulder and found his body, lying adjacent to the flat rock upon which he landed. The boy looked like Joe and the boy looked like Jody, but only smaller, younger. The left side of his head was dented, caved-in, and was missing a flap of scalp. His left arm was held out stiffly and twitched, beating like one wing of a broken hummingbird. The lower half of his face had crumbled, ice cream melting over a cone. He was breathing, but irregularly. They crouched, hands over their mouths, but not over their eyes. His chest inflated sharply, then deflated slowly, a sagging balloon. The right side of his face was perfect, asleep. His left eye was swollen shut, or missing. It was hard to know for sure with the orbital socket broken, pushed in, along with the area around his temple. Everything leaked slowly. There were too many colours on his face. And his teeth, his *teeth*, they were baby teeth, as small as seeds, and they peppered the sand and dirt around his head, those miniature headstones in the sand. Then there was one long sigh and the boy stopped breathing and his arm stopped moving.

His suspension is over but Joe does not report to the Tucson office in the morning. He manages to drive his Jeep into the Tohono O'odham Reservation and into its desert despite his near total exhaustion, his being purposefully drunk, and the pain that fills his head. He deposits a mix of aspirin, ibuprofen, and little blue pills he took from Jody's apartment into his dry, copper mouth, and grinds them up as best he can. It hurts to chew, but he won't use his water yet; he needs to conserve it.

He stops the Jeep in approximately the same area where he helped rescue the Nicaraguan woman, but he didn't save her. He knows he hasn't saved anyone and can't save anyone. This trip into the desert isn't about saving anyone. He's going to find Guillermo and give the man back his son's tooth. Joe crawls out of his Jeep and walks, slowly, due south, toward the border. He doesn't have a compass, but he thinks he knows where the border is.

Joe allows himself to remember that day in the desert. He remembers the slow walk back to their bikes, their pile of metal and chains, and the ride home. They didn't tell anyone about what had happened, didn't tell anyone about the boy. They were afraid of the teens, afraid people would think it was their fault, afraid because they were only eight and didn't know what to do. They didn't tell anyone about their desert silence.

The sun is only beginning its climb in the east, but it's midday hot. Joe's pulse throbs in his temples and inside his cheeks. His backpack of meagre supplies already feels too heavy.

There was never any word or news about the little boy. They did not go back over the ridge and to that boulder. They didn't talk about it, didn't make up stories about coyotes dragging the boy away, didn't fool themselves into believing he was alive, didn't discuss the possibilities or probabilities of the police finding him or the teens coming back for the body or the boy's friends and family laying belated claim and bringing him back to Mexico. They didn't turn the boy into a legend for the neighbourhood kids, didn't tell anyone that the boy might still be there. They agreed to forget, their secret, bury it inside themselves, beneath as much passed time as they could.

Despite the heat and his headache, which is a fire inside his brain, Joe walks for hours until the sun is directly above him and discerning direction becomes impossible. He finds a Desert Ironwood and sits under its thin canopy, desperate for shade. He has drunk half of his water supply already. Joe takes off his small backpack, drinks, and again goes back to that day all those years ago in another part of the same desert. Joe remembers the urge to pick up the boy's teeth, those headstones, and put them in his pocket, an urge as inexplicable now as it was then.

There are teeth in his pocket now: a small one lovingly wrapped in tinfoil, and another tooth, adult and big and ugly with roots like talons. That tooth is not wrapped in tinfoil or anything that would protect it. Neither tooth is his.

Joe fights waves of dizziness and nausea. His fistful of pills isn't helping. His gums are still bleeding and his right bicuspid is loose. If he pushes on the tooth with enough force there's a wet sucking sound inside his mouth. There are pliers in his backpack. Earlier this morning, the pain was too much, unlike Jody, he couldn't deal with it, and he stopped pulling on the tooth, but he'll try the pliers again later, maybe when the sun goes down and when the pills kick in.

Joe falls in and out of sleep throughout the afternoon and the temperature begins to drop. Maybe a quarter of a mile beyond his tree is a ridge, and just beyond that ridge is Mexico, he's sure of it, and despite everything, he's sure he can make it over that ridge. And maybe he'll be strong enough to make it through the desert, his desert, and give back the teeth.

IT'S AGAINST THE LAW TO FEED THE DUCKS

Saturday

Ninety-plus degrees, hours of relentless getaway traffic on the interstate, then the bumps and curves of Rural Route 25 as late afternoon melts into early evening, and it's the fourth time Danny asks the question.

"Daddy, are you lost again?"

Tom says, "I know where we're going, buddy. Trust me. We're almost there."

Dotted lines and bleached pavement give way to a dirt path that roughly invades the woods. Danny watches his infant sister Beth sleep, all tucked into herself and looking like a new punctuation mark. Danny strains against his twisted shoulder harness. He needs to go pee but he holds it, remembering how Daddy didn't say any mad words but sighed and breathed all heavy the last time he asked to stop for a pee break.

Danny says, "Mommy, pretend you didn't know I was going to be five in September."

Ellen holds a finger to her chin and looks at the car's ceiling for answers. "Are you going to be ten years old tomorrow?"

IN THE MEAN TIME

"No. I will be five in September."

"Oh, wow. I didn't know that, honey."

Tom and Ellen slip into a quick and just-the-facts discussion about what to do for dinner and whether or not they think Beth will sleep through the night. Danny learns more about his parents through these conversations, the ones they don't think he's listening to.

It's dark enough for headlights. Danny counts the blue bug-zappers as their car chugs along the dirt road. He gets to four.

"Daddy, what kinds of animals live in these woods?"

"The usual. Raccoons, squirrels, birds."

"No, tell me *dangerous* animals."

"Coyotes, maybe bears."

Their car somehow finds the rented cottage and its gravel driveway between two rows of giant trees. Beth wakes screaming. Danny stays in the car while his parents unpack. He's afraid of the bears. They don't celebrate getting to the cottage like they were supposed to.

Sunday

They need a piece of magic yellow paper to go to Lake Winnipesauke. Danny likes to say the name of the lake inside his head. The beach is only a mile from their cottage and when they get there Danny puts the magic paper on the dashboard. He hopes the sun doesn't melt it or turn it funny colours.

Danny runs ahead. He's all arms and legs, a marionette with tangled strings, just like Daddy. He claims a shady spot beneath a tree. He doesn't know what kind of tree. Ellen and Beth come next. Beth can only say "Daddy" and likes to give head butts. Tom is last, carrying the towels and shovels and pails and squirt guns and food. Danny watches his parents set everything up. They know how to unfold things and they know where everything goes without having to ask questions, without having to talk to each other.

Danny likes that his parents look younger than everybody else's parents, even if they are old. Danny is a round face and big rubber ball cheeks, just like Mommy. Ellen has a T-shirt and shorts pulled over her bathing suit. She won't take them off, even when she goes into the water. She says, "You need sunscreen before you go anywhere, little boy."

Danny closes his eyes as she rubs it all in and everywhere. He's had to wear it all summer long but he doesn't understand what *sunscreen* really means. *Sunscreen* sounds like something that should be built onto their little vacation cottage.

Danny is disappointed with the magic beach because there are too many other people using it. They all get in his way when he runs on the sand, pretending to be Speed Boy. And the older kids are scary in the water. They thrash around like sharks.

Lunch time. Danny sits at the picnic table next to their tree, eating and looking out over Winnipesauke. The White Mountains surround the bowl of the lake and in the lake there are swimmers, boats, buoys, and a raft. Danny wants to go with Daddy to the raft, but only when the scary older kids are gone. Danny says Winnipesauke, that magical word, into his peanut butter and jelly sandwich. It tastes good.

A family of ducks comes out of the water. They must be afraid of the older kids too. They walk underneath his picnic table.

Ellen says, "Ducks!" picks up Beth, and points her at the ducks. Beth's bucket hat is over her eyes.

Tom sits down next to Danny and throws a few scraps of bread on the sand. Danny does the same, taking pieces from his sandwich, mostly crust, but not chunks with a lot of peanut butter. He eats those. The ducks get mostly jelly chunks, and they swallow everything.

Tom stops throwing bread and says, "Whoops. Sorry, pal. It's against the law to feed the ducks."

He doesn't know if Daddy is joking. Danny likes to laugh at his jokes. Jokes are powerful magic words because they make you laugh. But when he's not sure if it's a joke or not, Danny thinks life is too full of magic words.

He laughs a little and says, "Good one, Daddy." Danny is pleased with his answer, even if it's wrong.

"No really, it says so on that sign." Tom points to a white sign with red letters nailed into their tree. Danny can't read yet. He knows his letters but not how they fit together.

Ellen says, "That's weird. A state law against feeding the ducks?"

Danny knows it's not a joke. It is a law. The word *law* is scary, like the older kids in the water.

Danny says, "Mommy, pretend you didn't know it was against the law to feed the ducks."

"Okay. So, I can just go order a pizza and some hotdogs for the ducks, right?"

"No. You can't feed the ducks. It's against the law."

Danny eats the rest of his sandwich, swinging his feet beneath the picnic table bench. The scary older kids come out of the water and chase the ducks, even the babies. Danny wants to know why it's not against the law to chase the ducks, but he doesn't ask.

Their cottage has two bedrooms, but they sleep in the same bedroom because of the bears. Danny sleeps in the tallest bed. There's a ceiling fan above him and after Daddy tells a story about Spider-Man and dinosaurs, he has to duck to keep from getting a haircut. That's Danny's joke.

Beth is asleep in her playpen. Everyone has to be quiet because of her.

Danny is tired after a full day at the beach. His favourite part was holding onto Daddy's neck while they swam out to the raft.

Danny wakes up when his parents creep into the bedroom. He is happy they are keeping their promise. He falls back to sleep listening to them fill up the small bed by the door. He knows his parents would rather sleep in the other bedroom by themselves, but he doesn't know why.

Danny wakes again. It's that middle-of-the-night time his parents always talk about. He hears noises, but gets the sense he's waking at the end of the noises. The noises are outside the cottage, echoing in the mountains. He hears thunder and lightning or a plane or a bunch of planes or a bunch of thunder and lightning and he is still convinced you can hear both thunder and lightning or he hears a bear's roar or a bunch of bears' roars or he hears the cottage's toilet, which has the world's loudest super-flush according to Daddy or he hears a bomb or a bunch of bombs. Bombs are something he has only seen and heard in Spider-Man cartoons. Whatever the noises are, they are very far away and he has no magic words that will send his ears out that far. Danny falls back to sleep even though he doesn't want to.

Monday

The beach lot is only half full. Ellen says, "Where is everybody?"

Tom says, "I don't know. Mondays are kind of funny days. Right, pal?"

Danny nods and clutches the magic yellow paper and doesn't care where everybody is because maybe this means Daddy and him can spend more time out on the raft.

They get the same spot they had yesterday, next to the tree with its against-the-law sign. They dump their stuff and boldly spread it out. Beth and Ellen sit at the shore. Beth tries to eat sand and knocks her head into Ellen's. Tom sits in the shade and reads a book. Danny takes advantage of the increased running room on the beach and turns into Speed Boy.

By lunch, the beach population thins. No more young families around. There are some really old people with tree-bark skin and a few older kids around, but they are less scary because they look like they don't know what to do. The lake is empty of boats and Jet Skis. The ducks are still there, swimming and safe from renegade feeders.

Tom swims to the raft with Danny's arms wrapped tight around his neck. Somewhere in the middle of the lake, Tom says, "Stop kicking me!" Danny knows not to say I was trying to help you swim. Danny climbs up the raft ladder first, runs to the middle then slips, feet shooting out from beneath him, and he falls on a mat that feels like moss. Tom yells. "Don't run, be careful, watch what you're doing." Danny doesn't hear the words, only what's in his voice. They sit on the raft's edge, dangling their legs and feet into the water. Daddy's long legs go deeper.

Tom takes a breath, the one that signals the end of something, and says, "It is kind of strange that hardly anybody is here." He pats Danny's head, so everything is okay.

Danny nods. Commiserating, supporting, happy, and grateful to be back in Daddy's good graces. He's also in his head, making up a face and body for a stranger named Hardly Anybody. He can't decide if he should make Hardly Anybody magical or not.

They wave at Mommy and Beth at the shore. Ellen's wave is tired, like a sleeping bird. Ellen wears the same shirt and shorts over her bathing suit. Danny wonders how long it takes for his wave to make it across the water.

They leave the beach early. On the short drive back, Tom makes up a silly song that rhymes mountain peaks with butt-cheeks and it's these Daddy-moments that make Danny love him so hard he's afraid he'll break something.

Back at the cottage. Beth is asleep and Ellen dumps her in the playpen. Danny sits at the kitchen table and eats grapes because he was told to. Tom goes into the living room and turns on the TV. Danny listens to the voices but doesn't hear what they say. But he hears Tom say a bad word, real quick, like he is surprised.

"Ellen?" Tom jogs into the kitchen. "Where's Mommy?" He doesn't wait for Danny's answer. Ellen comes out of the bathroom holding her mostly dry bathing suit and wearing a different set of T-shirt and shorts. Tom grabs her arm, whispers something, and then pulls her into the living room, to the TV.

"Hey, where did everybody go?" Danny says it like a joke, but there's no punch line coming. He leaves his grapes, which he didn't want to eat anyway, and tip-toes into the living room.

His parents are huddled close to the TV, too close. If Danny was ever that close they'd tell him to move back. They're both on their knees, Ellen with a hand over her mouth, holding something in, or maybe keeping something out. The TV volume is low and letters and words scroll by on the top and bottom of the screen and in the middle there's a man in a tie and he is talking. He looks serious. That's all Danny sees before Tom sees him.

"Come with me, bud."

Daddy picks him up and plops him down in a small sunroom at the front of the cottage.

Tom says, "Mommy and Daddy need to watch a grown-up show for a little while."

"So I can't see it?"

"Right."

"How come?"

Tom is crouched low, face to face with Danny. Danny stares at the scraggly hairs of his moustache and beard. "Because I said it's only for grown-ups."

"Is it about feeding the ducks? Is it scary?"

Daddy doesn't answer that. "We'll come get you in a few minutes. Okay, bud?" He stands, walks out, and starts to close sliding glass doors.

"Wait! Let me say something to Mommy first."

Tom gives that sigh of his, loud enough for Ellen to give him that look of hers. They always share like this. Danny stays in the sunroom, pokes his head between the glass doors. Ellen is to his left, sitting in front of the TV, same position, same hand over her mouth. "Mommy, pretend you didn't know that I could see through these doors."

Mommy works to put her eyes on her son. "So, you won't be able to see anything in here when we shut the doors?"

"No, I can see through them."

IN THE MEAN TIME

Tuesday

It's raining. They don't go to the beach. Danny is in the sunroom watching Beth. His parents are in the living room watching more grown-up TV. Beth pulls on Danny's shirt and tries to walk, but she falls next to the couch and cries. Ellen comes in, picks up Beth, and sits down next to Danny.

He says, "This is boring."

"I know, sweetie. Maybe we'll go out soon."

Danny looks out the front windows and watches the rain fall on the front lawn and the dirt road. Beth crawls away from Ellen and toward the glass doors. She bangs on the glass with meaty little hands.

Danny says, "Mommy, pretend you didn't know we were in a spaceship."

There's a pause. Beth bangs her head on the glass. Ellen says, "So, we're all just sitting here in a cottage room, right?"

"No. This is a spaceship with glass doors."

Beth bangs on the glass harder and yells in rhythm.

Ellen says, "If we're in a ship, what about Daddy?"

"We'll come back for him later."

"Good idea."

Ellen and Beth stay at the cottage. Tom and Danny are in the car but they don't listen to the radio and Daddy isn't singing silly songs. Danny holds the magic yellow paper even though he knows they're going to the supermarket, not the beach.

They have to travel to the center of Moultonborough. Another long and obviously magical word that he'll say inside his head. There isn't much traffic. The supermarket's super-lot has more carts than cars.

Inside, the music is boring and has no words. Danny hangs off the side of their cart like a fireman. He waves and salutes to other shoppers as they wind their way around the stacks, but nobody waves back. Nobody looks at each other over their overflowing carts.

The line isn't long, even though there are only three registers open. Tom tries to pay with a credit card. Danny is proud he knows what a credit card is.

"I'm sorry, sir, but the system is down. No credit cards. Cash or check." The girl working the register is young, but like the older kids. She has dark circles under her eyes.

Danny points and says, "Excuse me, you should go to bed early tonight."

Tom has a green piece of paper and is writing something down on it. He gives it to the register girl.

She says, "I'll try," and offers a smile. A smile that isn't happy.

In the parking lot, Danny says, "Go fast."

Tom says, "Hey, Danny."

Danny's whole body tenses up. He doesn't know what he did wrong. "What?"

"I love you. You know that, right?"

Danny swings on those marionette arms and looks everywhere at once. "Yeah."

Then Tom smiles and obeys and runs with the full cart. Danny melts and laughs, stretching out and throwing his head back, closing his eyes in the brightening haze. There are no other cars between the cart and their car.

Wednesday

They spend the day in the cottage. More sunroom. More grown-up TV. When Tom and Ellen finally shut off the TV they talk about going out just to go out somewhere anywhere but the TV room and sunroom and maybe find an early dinner. Danny says, "Moultonborough." They talk about how much gas is in the car. Danny says, "Winnipesauke." They try to use their cell phones but the little LCD screens say *no service*. Danny says, "Pretend you didn't know I say magic words." They talk about how much cash they have. Everybody in the car. Tom tells Danny it's his job to keep Beth awake. There are no other vehicles on the dirt road and more than half of the cottages they pass are dark. Beth is falling asleep so Danny sings loud silly songs and pokes her chin and cheeks. They pass empty gravel driveways and the blue bug-zappers aren't on. Beth cries. Danny is trying not to think about the bears in the woods. Ellen asks Danny to stop touching his sister's face and then says it's okay if Beth falls asleep. They don't have to look left or right when pulling out of the dirt road. Danny still works at the keep-Beth-awake job Daddy gave him and there's something inside him that wants to hear her cry and he touches her face again. They're into the center of Moultonborough and there's less traffic than there was yesterday. Beth cries and Ellen is stern but not yelling. She never yells telling Danny to stop touching Beth's face. Maybe the bears are why there aren't as many people around. Beth is asleep. There's a smattering of parked cars in the downtown area but they don't look parked; they look empty. Danny gently pats Beth's foot and sees Daddy watching him in the rear view mirror. The antique stores, gift shops, and hamburger huts are dark and have red signs on their doors and red always means either stopped or closed or something bad. Tom yells did you hear your mother keep your hands off your sister! They pass a row of empty family restaurants. Ellen says Tom like his name is sharp like it hurts and she says I only asked him to stop touching her face I don't want him to be freaked out by his sister he's being nice now why are you yelling when he was just doing what you asked him to do you have to be consistent with him and she is stern and she is not yelling. They pull into a lot that has one truck another empty restaurant this one with a moose on the roof and they stop. Then Tom is loud again this time with some hard all rights and then I hear you I get it okay I heard you the first time. Tom gets out of the car and slams the door and an older man with white hair that could mean he's magic and a white apron walks out the restaurant's front door. Danny waves. The older man waves them inside. Ellen gets out of the car and whispers but it's not a soft whisper not at all it's through teeth and it has teeth she says don't you dare yell at me in front of the kids. Beth wakes up and points and chews on her rabbit. They go inside. The older man says they are lucky he was just cooking up the last of his non-frozen food so it wouldn't go to waste and it was on the house. Danny thinks about the moose on the house. They walk by the bar and there's a woman sitting on a stool staring up at a big screen TV. Tom asks if they could shut that off because of the kids. The old man nods and uses a big remote control. Danny doesn't see anything again. The old man serves some BBQ chicken and ribs and fries and then leaves them alone. The lights are on and nobody says anything important in the empty restaurant.

On the way back to the cottage they see a lonely mansion built into the side of a mountain. Looking dollhouse-sized, its white walls and red roof surrounded by the green trees standout like a star even in the twilight.

Danny says, "What is that?"

Tom says, "That's called the Castle in the Clouds."

"Can we go see it?"

"Maybe. Maybe we'll even go and live there. Would you like that?"

Danny says, "Yes," but he then he thinks the Castle is too alone, cloaked in a mountain forest, but too open, anyone can see it from this road. He doesn't know what's worse, being alone alone or watched alone. Danny doesn't change his answer.

It's past Danny's bedtime but his parents aren't ready to put him to bed.

Ellen is on the couch reading a magazine that has a tall, blonde, skinny woman on the cover. Tom sits in front of the TV, flipping channels. There's nothing but static. The TV is like their cell phones now.

Tom says, "Well, at least they've stopped showing commercials for the *War of the Worlds* remake."

Danny wants to laugh because he knows it's what Daddy wants. But he doesn't because Mommy isn't. Danny has a good idea what *war* means even though no one has ever explained it to him. Tom shuts off the TV.

There are pictures of other people all over the cottage. Now that

IN THE MEAN TIME

Danny is allowed back in the TV room, he's looking at each one. Strangers with familiar smiles and beach poses. He looks at the frames too. They have designs and letters and words. Maybe magic words. Danny picks up one picture of a little girl and boy hugging and sitting on a big rock. He doesn't care about those kids. He wants to know what all the letters etched onto the wooden frame say. Those letters wrap all the way around the photo.

"Read this please, Daddy."

"Children are the magic dreamers that we all once were."

"Mommy, pretend you didn't know I was a magic dreamer."

"So, you dream about boring, non-magical stuff, right?"

"No. I'm a magic dreamer. Are you a magic dreamer?"

Ellen sleeps with Beth in the small bed next to the bedroom door, Danny sleeps in his Princess-and-the-Pea tall bed. Tom sleeps in the other bedroom. Alone alone.

Thursday

A perfect summer day. The corner Gas 'N Save is open. The pumps still work. Tom fills up the car's tank and five red two-gallon containers he took from inside the market. Danny is inside, running around the stacks. No one tells him to stop. He climbs onto an empty shelf next to some bread, though there isn't much bread left, and he lies down, breathing heavy from all the running.

Tom makes multiple trips from the market to the car. On the last trip, he plucks Danny off the shelf. He says, "Hmm, this melon doesn't look too ripe." Danny giggles and squirms in Daddy's arms. "But I'll take it anyway."

The older woman behind the counter is smoking a cigarette and has a face with extra skin. She looks like the girl from the supermarket but 1000 years older. Tom extends a fistful of money and asks, "Is this enough?"

She says, "Yes," without counting it. Danny thinks she is lying and that she just wants them gone like everyone else.

Tom buckles Danny into his seat. Danny says, "What would you do if you were a giant?"

"A giant? Well, I'd use a mountain as my pillow and the trees as a mattress."

Danny thinks about a Giant Daddy lying on a mountain, crushing all the trees and bears and other animals and the Castle in the Clouds with his back and arms, and his legs would be long enough to crush Moultonborough and the other towns too, maybe his feet would dangle into Winnipesauke and cause huge waves, drown the poor ducks, flood everything.

Danny says, "That would hurt."

At night the electricity goes out, but it's okay because they have two lanterns and lots of candles. They sit in the backyard around a football-shaped charcoal grill eating hotdogs and holding sticks with marshmallows skewered on the tips. The smoke keeps the bugs away. They sing loud to keep the bears away. Danny sits on Mommy's lap and tells stories about magic and the adventures of Speed Boy and Giant Daddy. Then Tom carries him to bed and Ellen carries a candle. They kiss him goodnight. Danny closes his eyes. He almost knows why they are still here when everyone else is disappearing, but he can't quite get there, can't reach it, like the night he tried to send his ears out to the noises.

Danny tries to send his ears out again and this time he hears his parents in the hallway. They speak with one voice. He hears words that he doesn't understand. They might be arguing and they might be laughing and they might be crying but it doesn't matter, because Danny knows tonight was the best night of their vacation.

Friday

Danny wakes up before anyone else and goes into the sunroom. There's morning mist and a bear on the front lawn. The bear is black and bigger than Danny's world, although that world seems to be shrinking. Danny thinks bears, even the dumb-looking teddy bears, always know more about what's going on than the other animals and it's part of what scares Danny. He's scared now but he wants a better view so he opens the front door and stands on the elevated stoop, his hand on the door, ready to dash back inside if necessary. The bear runs away at the sound of the door and it disappears. Danny hears it crashing through some brush but then everything goes quiet. Why would a bear be afraid of him?

Now that it's gone Danny steps outside, the wet grass soaking his feet. He says, "Hey, come back." He wants to ask the bear, where are all the people? The bear must know the answer.

Danny and Ellen sit out back, playing Go Fish at the picnic table. Tom went shopping for supplies, a phrase he used before leaving, by himself. He's been gone most of the morning.

Danny loses again but Ellen calls him the winner.

Danny says, "Mommy, pretend you didn't know it was a beautiful day."

Ellen shuffles the cards. "So it's really rainy and cold out, right?"

"No. There're no clouds. And the sun is out and super hot. It's a beautiful day."

They play more card games. They play with Beth. She's almost ready to walk by herself but she still falls, and after she falls, she rips out fistfuls of grass and stuffs it in her mouth. They eat lunch. They nap.

Tom comes home after the naps. Supplies fill the car, including a mini-trailer hitched to the back. Tom gets out of the car and gives everyone an enthusiastic kiss and puts Danny on his shoulders. Ellen shrinks as he goes up.

Ellen says, "Did you see anybody."

Tom whispers an answer that Danny can't hear because he's above Daddy's head.

Ellen says, "What you got there in the trailer?"

"A generator."

"Really? You know how to set one of those up?"

"Yup."

Danny comes back down.

"Where'd you learn how to do that?"

"I just know, okay?"

Ellen goes back to the picnic table with Beth, Tom to the trailer and the generator. There are no more enthusiastic kisses.

Danny watches Tom setting up the generator. He says, "Daddy, pretend you didn't know this was a beautiful day."

"It's not a beautiful day."

"No, it is! There're no clouds. And the sun is out and super hot. It's a beautiful day, Daddy. I just know, okay?"

Saturday

They leave the car at the cottage and walk the mile to the beach. They don't carry much beach stuff. Beth is asleep in the stroller. Danny has on his swimming trunks but his parents are wearing shorts and T-shirts. The trip to the beach is for him. His parents don't know it, but Danny has the yellow magic paper folded up in his pocket.

Danny asks, "Is today supposed to be the last day of vacation?"

Ellen says, "I think we're going to stay here a little while longer."

Tom says, "Maybe a long while longer."

Ellen says, "Is that okay?"

"Sure."

Tom says, "Maybe we'll go check out that Castle in the Clouds tomorrow."

Danny almost tells them about the bear. Instead he says, "Mommy, pretend you didn't know we were still on vacation."

They pass empty driveways of empty cottages. Danny, for the first time, is really starting to feel uneasy about the people being gone. It's like when he thinks about why and how he got here and how are his parents his parents and how is his sister his sister, because if he thinks too much about any of that he probably won't like the answers.

The beach lot is empty. They stake out their regular spot next to the tree and its duck sign. There are ducks on the shore scratching the sand and dipping their bills in the water. It's another beautiful day.

Tom says, "I don't get it. I thought this is where everyone would want to be."

Ellen finishes for him. "Especially now."

The ducks waddle over. They don't know the law. Tom pulls out a bag of Cheerios, Beth's snack, and tosses a few on the sand. The ducks converge and are greedy.

Ellen pushes the stroller deeper into the shade away from the ducks and says, "Are you sure we can spare those, Mr. Keeper-of-the-Supplies?" It walks like a joke and talks like a joke but it isn't a joke.

Danny says, "Daddy! Don't you remember the sign? It's against the law to feed the ducks." Danny looks around, making sure the people who aren't there still aren't there.

"It's okay now, buddy. I don't think anyone will care anymore. Here, kiddo."

He takes the Cheerio bag from Daddy. Daddy pats his head. Danny digs a hand deep into the bag, pulls it out, and throws Cheerios onto the sand. The ducks flinch and scatter toward the water, but they come back and feed.

WE WILL NEVER LIVE IN THE CASTLE

polar coaster

Mr. Matheson lives over in Heidi's Hill, we confab every three days in the old mist tent between the World Pavilion and my Slipshod Safari Tour, but today he's late for our date, he scurries and hurries into the tent, something's up.

Mr. Matheson says, She took over the Polar Coaster, he says, I don't know if Kurt just up and left or if she chased him off or killed him but he's gone and now she's there.

I thought we'd never be rid of that retarded kid, he used to eat grass and then puke it all up.

I say, Who is she, what's she look like, does she have a crossbow?

He says, She's your age of course, medium-size, bigger than my goat anyway, and quiet, I didn't get a great look at her, but I know she's there, she wears a black cap, she just won't talk to me.

Why would she say anything to him, I only talk to him out of necessity, necessity is what rules my life, necessity is one of the secrets to survival, I'll give other secrets later, maybe when we take the tour.

Mr. Matheson and me have a nice symbiosis thing going, he

gets to stay alive and enjoy a minimum base of human contact, he keeps an eye on my Slipshod Safari Tour's rear flank, last year he saw these two bikers trying to ambush me via Ye Olde Mist Tent, Mr. Matheson gave me that goat's call of his, he is convincing, I took care of the burly thunderdome bikers, they tried to sneak down the tracks and past the plastic giraffe, the one with a crick in its neck and the missing tail, typical stupid new hampshire rednecks, not that there's a new hampshire anymore, live free or die bitches, their muscles and tattoos didn't save them, little old me, all one 132 pounds of me, me and necessity.

Mr. Matheson is clearly disappointed she won't talk to him, whoever she is, he's probably taken stupid risks to his own skin, and by proxy mine, trying to get her attention, it's so lame and predictable, because of the fleeting sight of a mysterious girl the old man would jeopardize my entire operation here, Mr. Matheson is down to his last goat, the house on Heidi's Hill is a small one room dollhouse with a mini bed mini table mini chair, no future there, it's a good place for a geezer with a white beard going yellow, straw on his face, getting ready to die, no place for a girl, she needs space, the Polar Coaster is a decent spot, back when Fairy Tale Land was up and running the Polar Coaster was one of the most popular rides, I never got to work it, they kept me over on the Whirling Whales, a toddler ride.

At the Polar Coaster the fiberglass igloo and icebergs are holding up okay, they make good hidey holes, warmth and shelter in the winter, shade in the summer, some reliable food stores, wild blueberry bushes near the perimeter of its northern fence, birds nest in the tracks, free pickings of eggs and young, small duck pond in the middle of it all and with ample opportunity to trap smaller critters, the Polar Coaster might be the third best spot in the park behind my Slipshod Safari Tour and Cinderella's Castle, of course, third because it's a little too out in the open for my tastes, everyone who comes to Fairy Tale Land always goes to the Castle and then the Polar Coaster.

I ask, Do you know her name?

Mr. Matheson says, She won't talk to me, remember.

Yeah, I remember, but sometimes it's hard when every day is the same.

tour: north

I'm not using magnetic north, I know how to use it, gridlines and a map and a steady hand, I'm using the entrance as due south, so in the park's north you've got the Crazy Barn, Farm Follies Show, and Turtle Twirl, no one's lived in those areas since the big freeze last winter, too much damage from the initial lootings for there to be enough shelter, the Crazy Barn used to lift off the ground and spin real slow, too slow, like the rotation of the world slow before that changed, before it stopped.

There was the panic, the Crazy Barn was uprooted off the hydraulic and picked apart, lots of rides suffered similar fates even if they didn't deserve it.

Going in order walking back toward my Slipshod Safari Tour, the Whirling Whales, which I keep cleared out of any potential residents, purely an egomania kind of gesture on my part, everyone needs a hobby, the Oceans of Fun Sprayground with its submarine that was destroyed by three feuding squatters to be, then the Great Balloon Chase, which is a ferris wheel of hot air balloons, empty now, early on there was a guy named Mr. Philips living in one of the balloons, I called him Dick behind his back, it was late spring and I don't think he was planning on staying there because it would've been too cold in the winter, with the mountains shooting up directly behind the park we always remembered winter, Dick would tell me stuff about his life, not that I cared, he used to sell lawn mowers and motorcycles on the weekends and was twice divorced from the same woman, that's all I remember, that and he had big yellow horse teeth, he didn't breathe, he chewed on the air, I didn't trust him one bit with how he climbed up into the highest balloons to spy on me, there was how he talked too, he always had something to say about how short and skinny and pale I was, he bragged about being a fisherman and hunter and how he used to watch those survivalist shows and he could still do one-hundred push ups easy, even if he was on the sunny side down of forty, Dick was all talk and no chalk, he didn't know anything about his surroundings, he didn't know magnetic north, he didn't listen to what the park and the forest and the mountains had to say, you need to stop and listen, he was a total ass, he listened to me though, he asked how I knew about all the edible wild plants, I give him fiddleheads first, then he ate *amanita phalloides*, death cap mushrooms, next.

polar coaster

I belly crawl from the mist tent to what used to be the waiting area in front of the Polar Coaster, Mr. Matheson is probably taking a nap, the old fool always plans eight days in advance, not seven days, he doesn't do anything by the old ways which I do kind of admire, Mr. Matheson leaves me his plan inside one of the Dutch Shoes, a kiddie ride just north of the Polar Coaster and its pond, the plan is usually written in crayon, he wrote his latest plan in burnt sienna.

I don't care if he's taking a nap, I didn't make any sort of pact with him that I would keep away from the new girl, even if we did, I'd break it, I just want to make contact, see what her deal is, see if she presents a danger to my Slipshod Safari Tour.

I say, Hello? Is there anybody out there in the Polar Coaster? Or is it just some funny walking penguins?

I should've probably worn my best threads for the introduction, underneath my jacket is a vest of bamboo that I clipped and ripped from The Bamboo Chute, a water flume ride that took a picture of you before you plummeted down, would never want to work that ride, the line moved too fast, but I liked that the ride exposed a truth, in those pictures where everyone was screaming at the big drop, everyone looked so happy when they were scared, the bamboo vest should stop any arrows or other projectiles that might be flung at me.

I say, Just want to say hi, and that me and Mr. Matheson over there in the Heidi House are friendly, we're not like those monkeys in the south of the park, by the castle, those frauds aren't in it for the long haul, like us, they'll all be gone in a week and then be replaced by other marauders and barbarians, a never-ending cycle, and for what? stupid Cinderella's Castle, it's nothing but a status symbol, no practical reason for surviving there, you'd think we'd be beyond that now, right? will people never learn!

I stop, drop, and listen, she doesn't say anything, yells and screams and other battle noises float up from the park's south, it's like a low cloud that's drawn in, tucked away in Mr. Matheson's crayon-blue sky.

I cup my hands as if that ever makes them stronger, and say, We're living fine in these parts, we help each other out up here, I say, I've killed three bad guys over at The Bamboo Chute with my bamboo spring traps, they shoot bamboo spears out of a panda bear's eyes and clean through the victim's chest, I mean, I've never seen it triggered live, but I've heard it go off, and there were these sick blood trails going away from the chute after, so cool.

A small rectangular chunk of the igloo pops out, so does the tip of an arrow, or a spear, then her voice, the sound of it makes me want to put the old act back on, makes me remember the kid I used to be at the Whirling Whales.

She says, What do you want?

That's a good question, didn't think I'd get this far, really, or, I just haven't admitted to myself what it is I do want.

I say, Just want to make friends, be neighborly, borrow a cup of sugar or something every once in a while, right? I can help, give you information, a tour of the park, what to know what to avoid what to eat where to sleep, you can probably help me too, I live there, Slipshod Safari Tour, we can watch each other's backs.

She says, I don't need help.

I say, Fair enough, how about I give you the Slipshod Tour, the works, haven't done it in a while, we can fix it up for tomorrow, still got some gasoline for the tractor, it'll be fun, Mr. Matheson can drive us around, be our chaperone.

IN THE MEAN TIME

I'm done talking and my hands don't know what to do, they snap and slap into each other like triggered snares.

tour: boulder

There's this one-ton sphere made of granite right outside my mist tent and the World Pavilion next door, the World Pavilion is where everyone got their overpriced burgers, fries, and sodas, there's no food left there, the boulder sits on a thick, square base a few feet off the ground, when Fairy Tale Land was up and running the base filled with water and a kindergartner could spin the boulder with his kinder-hands in the thin layer of *agua*, all that weight supported by a puddle less than a quarter-inch thick, I used to visit the boulder on my breaks, nudged kids out of the way so I could put my hands on the wet rock and spin it in any direction I wanted, I'd get all wet, there was nowhere else to get that sensation, the power of moving all that impossible weight with my pencil fingers, I liked to stop that rock from turning too, pushing against all those other little hands until it was still, that was more exciting, daring, felt like I was doing something spectacularly deliciously wrong.

Of course, that big old rock doesn't move now, but you knew that.

whirling whales

Truth is, before everything happened, I wouldn't have wanted to work the Polar Coaster, the gig was boring, people on and off too fast, no time to talk to anyone, not like the Whirling Whales where I took my time checking the kiddies' seat belts, making jokes about how whales weren't supposed to fly, no one laughed, the other joke I used all the time was something I'd say to whoever was supposed to sit in whale number nine, you see, there was no whale number nine, only eight whales, get it? when kids and parents filled the eight whales I had to shut off the waiting line with a thin white chain that only came up to a toddler's chin or just above a parent's kneecap, it was small but no one dared to cross.

Whoever missed out on whale nine and had to watch the whales fly from right behind that chain I'd say to them, It's not your lucky day, is it? I knew by looking at you, you weren't lucky.

It wasn't much of a joke, I thought it was back then, funny I realize how awkward I used to be when there were all these people around but now that almost everyone's gone I know better, okay it's not funny, it's odd, they all thought I was odd Todd, they were right, I was, I didn't have much back then to hold onto so I made the Whirling Whales my domain, I was the star, I strutted around that ride when I checked the seat belts, sometimes I'd push a whale up and down pretending that I was performing some structural integrity test, I always pushed the fly button with flair, then I'd pretend to not watch the ride and chat up the parents in line, talk tough with the dads, flirt up the moms using my odd looks and leers, arching my barely-there eyebrows into the craziest spots on my forehead, with the kids I tried be the cool teenager, the one they looked up to, wanted to be even if they were too young to know what cool was, but that isn't right, they knew what cool was, just wouldn't be able to articulate it, right? none of them ever took me seriously, and why should they have? I was a short skinny bleached white kid with curly orangey-yellow hair and probably the physically weakest and geekiest teenager in the state, I didn't play football or go hunting or fishing, I got harassed all the time, I was the runt of the state's litter, my Fairy Tale Land shirt never did fit right, always so baggy, made me look thinner than I was, couldn't wear a wristwatch because it'd slide off my wrist, I wore Dickies that were too tight and too small for me because Mom wouldn't buy me new ones, some of the older kids at the park used to ask where the flood was, they don't ask that anymore, do they?

I knew, even then, my act wasn't working, but I committed to it, you have to commit, always, it's how I survived then and how I survive now, you see, I've come a long way since then and really, it didn't matter if no one bought my act back then because it only mattered that I believed in it myself.

IN THE MEAN TIME

slipshod safari

She creeps under the entrance canopy that I've worked hard to maintain, I had to replace some of the plastic palm leaves with fir and maple branches, the effect is almost the same, it stays dark in here.

I say, Hi, Joyce, welcome to the Slipshod Safari Tour! go bananas on your trek through the jungles of africa! please do not feed or pet the animals, same goes for the tour leader.

I bow, take off my safari hat, my blond curls bounce and rebound, Slinkys on escalators, my hair isn't all that blond anymore, more like the colour of the diluted Tang Mr. Matheson is always trying to get me to drink, no thanks, she stares at my hair, my Tang, so I put my hat back on, I look ridiculous either way, but in this new world, the one that doesn't turn or spin, what I look like is irrelevant.

She says, I'm supposed to sit in there? with you, in there? with you?

The tractor coughs out turds of black smoke, Mr. Matheson is at the wheel of the open air rig, wearing a white T-shirt with yellow pit stains and overalls that are three sizes too big for him, I know what I said already about looks being irrelevant but I can't help but be embarrassed for him, the tractor pulls a cage on wheels with damp hay bales as seats, the cage is the punch line, it was supposed to protect everyone in the park from the safari animals.

I say, I know it's a lot, it'll be fun, an escape from the daily survival grind.

Joyce takes it all in and says, Do we really need to waste the gasoline on this?

Not sure what she means by **we** but I like it and don't like it at the same time, my palms are sweating like they did when I saw a girl anywhere near my age in line at the Whirling Whales, then it got that much harder to press the fly button with my practiced and patented button flair, hiding those old feelings is impossible sometimes, even as useless as they are to me now.

I assure Joyce that we, **we**, we can spare a gallon, and I make a joke about my unlimited supply.

Mr. Matheson was right for a change, she is my age, give or take a grade, she wears an olive-green shirt and jeans, she's lost somewhere inside of both, black wool cap mushrooms her head, I don't know where hat ends and black hair begins, her crossbow is slung across the back of her shoulders, she talks real fast about this being dumb and it'll attract attention from all the assholes in the south end of the park, and she's right, it's true, the sound of the tractor might raise some curiosity in our little neighborhood, but we're in my area, I've made sure we're safe here.

She says, I'm korean.

I say, What?

Her confession is abrupt and I'm caught, guardless, I don't know if she's making fun of me, or not, I used to be used to that feeling.

She says, I'm korean, just wanted to get that out of the way, this morning our chaperone asked if my parents were chinese or japanese, or from vietnam or something, to quote him directly, I figured you and he might share the same brain.

I say, We don't share that lame brain or anything like that, and besides, it doesn't matter to me what you are, or were, I just see a person like me.

She says, Glad that you're able to dismiss my personal identity and thousands of years of cultural experience so easily, how big of you.

Hey, sorry, I didn't mean it like that, really.

How did you mean it?

I shrug and say, You're right, I'm sorry and should've been more sensitive, I've been spending too much time around Mr. Matheson, my discourse skills are rusty not trusty, my tongue is all feet, left feet, club-footed left feet, with painful corns and bunions.

I turn away, not sure if she'll follow me, I duck inside the cage and sit, the hay bale is a bit damp and tied too loosely together, falling apart, it'll do for now, there's a machete and a field knife underneath mine in case I need them, the hunting blade is almost as long as my forearm, serrated, lots of nasty little teeth, across from me on the most level bale is an old red tray that I scrounged from the wreckage of the World Pavilion, two plates of wild greens, apples, and charred goose meat covered in some of the shake-n-a-bag spice I rationed, only three bags left now, two canteens with sugarless lemonade mix, some good and bad mushrooms in my pocket if I need them.

I say, Are you coming? the tour leaves with or without, and soon.

the great balloon chase

Mr. Matheson thought Mr. Philips died of a heart attack despite the clear physical evidence to the contrary, he only sees what he wants to see, that's true of almost everyone, you too.

Oh, I found Mr. Philips, I found Dick leaning up against one of his grounded balloons, it was red and he was dying, drool spilled out between those horse teeth of his, it was gross and he was gross, there was no one else around, I was going to cut off his feet with my machete and use them as bait in a bear trap, but I wouldn't know what to do with a bear if I caught one.

Dick saw me and said some gibberish then he closed his eyes, his puffy eyes, then gathered himself for a clear moment, he said, you and me are a lot different.

He was right but I think he meant it as some sort of insult, implicating my moral character or lack thereof, whatever, fuckface, he was wrong and I told him so, I told him we are different, I told him about a road deemed worthy of the label **scenic route**, it was near my house, near where I grew up, that scenic route had a chunk of it washed out into a sink hole during a rainstorm, they closed a half-mile section of route to all through-traffic in both directions, confusing detours branched out for miles, that simple patch of washed-out blacktop was like an octopus, it had a reach in every direction, my mother swore about it all the time, how it would never be fixed, how they might need to have an emergency town vote on a budget override but not everyone would vote for it, how inconvenient getting around town was, she never got how cool it was, and you would never have got how cool it was either, that's part of the difference, our difference, listen, whenever I could, usually during the day, during working hours, I rode my bike to the route and past the **road is closed** signs and barriers, breaking the law, right? there were homes on the road but the driveways were usually empty, if they weren't empty no one seemed to be out, I rode my bike up and down the closed stretch until my legs shook, riding in the middle of the busy thirty-five mph route, that stretch had no more rules, I traced the yellow lines with my tires, it was so quiet and empty, I listened to the birds, that's all I would hear, I used to pretend the world had ended and that I was the only one who survived, that's not why we're different though, I know your secret, you've fantasized about that too, everyone fantasizes that they're important enough to survive, more than survive, to be the last one left, right? it's why you read those books or watched those Will Smith movies, you imagined how important the last one left would feel, but here's how we're different, I actually wished and wanted that fantasy to come true, and you, you only indulged in the fantasy because it was safely impossible in your mind, sort of like daydream sex with somebody you're not supposed to be daydreaming about, you indulge in the danger until you start thinking about the consequences, until you start really thinking about the big what if, what if it **really** happened? the difference between me and you, you and me, the only one that matters now, is that I wanted it, I wasn't as strong as you were, I wasn't stronger than anyone, I was a frail little ridiculous-looking boy riding a bike, all elbows and knees and nose and bad skin and stupid curly hair but I wanted it, I knew it would happen too, I'm not lying, not a revisionary Larry, that stuff is for you, I figured that if a little rain washing out a small square of road could mess up the everyday lives of the town and commerce routes and anyone else who needed to use that road, well then, it really would take a whole lot less than most people thought to trip up everything, put an end to it all, I knew it was just a matter of time before everything stopped turning.

I was right, I wanted it, I was ready for it, you weren't.

IN THE MEAN TIME

tour: slipshod safari

She's very distrustful of me, but we eat, the goose is as good as goose gets, I don't think I'll need the mushrooms, things are going well, she's cooperating, tolerating, the tractor struggles and muggles through the overgrown tour path, the tall grass whispers on the bottom of our cage, sometimes I dream about being on a small wooden boat, a life raft, a dinghy, I'm by myself, everyone in the world is below the water, all those fingernails tapping and scratching on my hull, the grass sounds like a ghost version of that, it's creepy, it's perfect.

I eat fast, finish before her, then give the tour, talking into the dead handheld microphone receiver, props are important for a successful tour, I tell her, Over there, in the creek bed, that alligator with the shit-eating smile had big pink sunglasses, a beach hat, and an umbrella drink in his claw, tore that stuff out when I moved in, found uses for them, you know, that giraffe who's supposed to be singing in the shower over there, his neck got bent in an attack I fended off a few years ago, now don't tell anyone but that giant fiberglass elephant is my winter bedroom, it's very well insulated, very well supplied, I sleep in its belly and made lookouts and breathe holes through its trunk and asshole, yin and yang, baby, the elephant entrance is hidden, just below its pink skirt, warmer months I sleep in the cage or inside the baseball playing bear, more breezy in there, I can show you the elephant if you'd like? moving too soon, too much too fast? I know, ha ha! okay, I let this next area grow over a bit, the ol' fishin' hole (with the **f** backwards and in kid-script), nothing but a few frogs and crawdaddies in there, and the kiddie statues are kind of creepy looking, and annoying, Huck Finn kind of caricatures in unbuttoned overalls, straw hats, and big smiles, so I just let it grow over.

She says, Why didn't you take them down?

Tour interrupted! She keeps on about if it bothered me so much, why didn't I take the statues down, take them apart and reuse them like I did with the alligator parts.

There's a string tucked behind my hay bale, I reach back, pull on it twice, the other end is tied around Mr. Matheson's ankle, he stops the tractor like he's supposed to, I say, That's a good idea, come on, let's go, you can help me knock them over and perform a field autopsy, not that I mean to make that sound so grim, think of them as piñatas instead, who knows what we'll find inside when we crack them open, I'll let you take their fishing poles, I don't need them, they're made out of bamboo, bamboo is real strong stuff, very useful.

Joyce puts down the charred flank from a goose that never laid any golden eggs, that attraction is in the south of the park, she says, You want me to go into that thick brush with you? why would I go in there with you? I'd probably get ticks too.

Come on, it'll be fun.

I don't find wanton destruction fun.

No, not wanton, we're destroying to create, that's the big idea, like you suggested, we're harvesting parts to help us survive, we will survive! we'll be Gloria Gaynor! as long as we know how to love we'll always be alive! I sing/say to her, which was likely a too bold too goofy too weird thing to say, but I'm feeling good.

She says, Oh, gross.

Come on, I'm just kidding, pulling your leg, pull pull pull.

Stay away from my leg!

Let's go, let's chop 'em down and chop 'em up.

No.

Okay, all right, I drop my chummy tone, there's too much of my charisma and charm to handle, so I get formal, soothing, I say, Tell me, Joyce, from whence did you come? how'd you get to the yonder Polar Coaster?

She rolls her eyes at me, and that's all good, of course, she says, Does it matter? I'm new, that's it, I'm new here.

Completely new to the park, are you? I say, and then I cross my legs proper.

She says, No, I tried a couple nights in the south end of the park, in Miss Muffet's Market, but I was displaced.

She's answering my questions, finally, she's digging my

formalized speak, I say, Displaced? how fascinating, do continue.

She says, Thrown out, a mob of jerks wearing football pads and helmets chased me out, broke up and stole what little stuff I'd collected.

Mr. Matheson shuts off the tractor engine, sighs loudly, I flash mad, feel hot blood pooling in my cheeks, red, ruddy, we might not get that tractor started again, composure, though, must com-pose, I say, That's what those football guys do, they try to clear out and claim that area, they're a joke, an annoying one for sure, they never come up here, though, never.

She says, I know that now, but it doesn't make sense, Muffet's Market is at the very southwestern tip of the park, still a good distance away from the Castle, probably as far away from the Castle as this place is, whatever, the south end was too crowded, too loud, and not good enough for me anyway, I could've fought off those assholes if I really wanted to.

I say, I know you could've, you're a bad mo fo, whoops! shut my mouth.

Joyce eyes me up and down and sideways, she's not sure whether to laugh or stab my thigh, whether she needs to take me seriously or not, she says, I left the market of my own free will but I'm heading back to that area soon, I deserve the Castle, I want the Castle.

I'm disappointed, it's always about the Castle, always, about, the, Castle, I don't know why, everyone goes there, they sleep and fuck and fight on the front lawn if they can't get in and if they do get in the stay is never long, I haven't had word trickle up here of a permanent resident, the Castle is always under siege, stuck in a permanent coup loop.

I say, I thought you were better than the Castle, you wanting to live there, I have to say, is so cliché, thought there was more to you than that, Joyce, really.

She says, Fuck you, don't even pretend to know me, so typical, I want what I want and I have my own reasons for what I want.

Okay, I'm sorry, I take it back, I say and pretend to catch the words out from the air and stuff them in my mouth, I say, Mmm, tastes like goose, let's talk later about the Castle, maybe we can work something out, now, don't be freaked out but I have a machete on board with us, we can use it to clear us a little path to the fishing hole, right there, I only keep machete here because I'm always prepared, prepared always.

Joyce stands and doesn't have to crouch in the cage, pulls her hat down tighter, unsheathes her own machete hidden inside her pant leg, strapped around her calf, she says, Fine, we'll do this, but after you and me are going to talk about the Castle, seriously talk.

We jump out of the cage and hack two separate paths in the brush, Mr. Matheson pretends not to watch us like a good chaperone, maybe I'll forgive his shutting off the tractor, I swing the machete wildly, freely, and all the other ly-ies, I'm losing control, it's a good feeling, I catch the back of my knuckle on the recoil and open up a bright cut, skin opens as easily as the brush, the shrubbery, the lean green, I'm at the fishin' hole's edge, so is Joyce, she pushes her sleeves up, smiles at me, she says, We could do this over near the Castle, make a path, sneak in the back, it would work.

She takes a mighty hack at the freckle-faced all a-okay usa fisherboy, loosening the right arm at the shoulder, I know she's pretending the kid is one of those footballers who chased her off, I hack away at his buddy, punch through the plaster chest, cave in his always happy face, Joyce and I are daydreaming about what we can do, together, it feels good, it feels more like practice than daydreaming.

IN THE MEAN TIME

professor wigglesteps's loopy lab

Mr. Matheson couldn't start the tractor again, we ditched him there, his head inside the engine trying to figure out why everything falls apart, breaks down, good luck with that, I invited her back to my elephant, show her my supplies, I think Joyce sensed how nervous I was, I am, that neither of us were ready for that, she declined, I was relieved, instead we jogged out of the Slipshod Safari, past the Great Balloon Chase.

Joyce was a self-described average student but very intelligent, there's a difference of course, she was quiet, no friends, accepted school as her great trial, a personal gulag she said, then when it all ended she lost her parents during the great panic, all of the state became a refugee camp pressing up against the canadian border, it was epic and sad, maybe her parents were trampled during a border rush, Joyce remembers being squeezed so tight, face pressed into someone's sweaty back, her feet didn't touch the ground, her movements determined by the tide of humanity coming in from every direction, it was no way to die, it was no way to live, she swam out, kicked punched clawed out, climbed on top, walked on heads and scalps, away from the border, she hiked back down through the state to Fairy Tale Land, she doesn't really know for sure if her parents died under a million desperate heels, it feels true, it's what she fears but at the same time it makes living here by herself easier, wondering if they were alive or if they missed her would be too difficult to bear, care bear, or maybe the truth is that Joyce's parents were overbearing snot-jobs she couldn't kick to the curb fast enough, for her the great panic was the day she was born, the great panic was an opportunity, like it was and is for me.

I'm not sure, I don't really know anything, Joyce doesn't tell me any of this, but the border-scenario is what I imagine for her as we walk to Professor Wigglestep's Lab.

The lab is an empty but cavernous building that has been stripped, just a few hunks of two-by fours lying around, and stray red-blue-green-yellow plastic balls from the ball pit, we rustle up the

stray balls, corral them into the pit, less a pit than a depression in
the floor, the balls are hard and brittle, and deflate easily into hard
shapes with uncomfortable nubs and corners but we sit on them
anyway, Joyce puts her hands behind her head and closes her eyes, I
just start talking, tell her everything I know about the park, give her
an oral tour of the north section, tell her about the stilled boulder
at the World Pavilion near the Polar Coaster, she's seen it but hasn't
tried to spin it, I tell her about me and my mom, about the Whirling
Whales, about the washed out road, about how I took care of Dick.

She says, Stop it, the kids down near Muffet's Market told me
about Mr. Philips, how he died of a heart attack.

That's the story Mr. Matheson told them, I'm giving you the real
deal, I say, and I pout, blood filling my cheeks again, blood always
wants to break out from beneath the surface, that's what I think
about while picking at the splintered edge of the ball depression
with my pocket knife.

Joyce must feel bad for calling me out like that and finally starts
telling me stuff, she talks about some books and blogs she used to
read, Jungian treatises on the nature of reality, stuff on cultural
appropriation and radical politics, she tells me her utopian visions
for the park, she makes it all sound so cool, I'm mostly listening and
she uses the word **opportunity**, I do envy her big social ideas, her
ability to include everyone who deserves to be included, but I can't
go fooling myself or anyone else, not anymore, I'm in this for me and
no one else, then I think about Mr. Matheson and wonder if he's still
working on the tractor, working on it by himself.

I'm still picking at the frame, twisting the knife, turning the wood
dust, still more than a little sore that she'd dismiss my dispatching
of Dick story so quickly, and just when I'm thinking that maybe she
doesn't understand me at all, we're somehow back on the subject of
Cinderella's Castle, she has a plan on how the two of us could take
it over, not for personal glory, no never, we claim it so we could lead
the park, instill some order, the right kind of order, a new golden age
of civilization, a pax Fairy Tail Land-a, Joyce doesn't use those exact
words but it's what she means.

IN THE MEAN TIME

I say, Okay, what's the plan, Stan? I'll be your Achilles to your Helen of Troy, I'll be your Rasputin to your Anastasia, she doesn't laugh until I say, I never was any good at history, we should just re-write it all now anyway, no one cares.

Joyce digs underneath her legs and pulls out a red pit-ball, it's not in ball shape anymore, caved in, a half-moon, a half-eaten rotted poisoned fruit, she says, Okay, this is the Castle.

tour: south

It's early dark, the dark before, everything covered in dew, I walk by Muffet's Market, there are two dudes in football or lacrosse gear, asleep, maybe drunk or stoned, toad or leaf lickers, snores echo in their helmets, cleated feet stick out the market front door, too bad it wasn't that someone dropped a house on them, wish I was that strong, my machete is out, I think about having some pre-Castle-coup fun, a little hacky hacky, but I'm not working alone today, stick to the plan, a two-pronged attack, with me walking to the Castle's front door and Joyce sneaking in through the back, it'll never work.

Down by the south end of the park, by the old entrance, I hate it down here, it's easy to get sick, it's commoner than the cold, thick in the air here, like pollen, common, the want the need, to be seen with everyone else, to be park popular, park important, to live in the Castle, or settle near it, to be in its shadow, as if that's enough, I mouse it past the Old Woman in the Shoe, Humpty Dumpty, Three Bear's House, and Granny's Cottage and weak, curled-up thoughts of relocation fill my head, oh my poor little head, no, I'm staying where I am, we will never live in the Castle, I'm only helping Joyce get to where she wants to go and then I'm going back, recede into the background, a man behind the curtain is something to be.

Past the Cuckoo Glockenspiel, the empty Storybook Animals pen, the petting zoo, to the Swan Boats, and there, across the bridge and up the hill is the Castle, I sit at the foot of the bridge, I could be the grumpy old troll who lives under the bridge, I really don't care about other people answering my questions three, it's hours past midnight, waiting for the sun to rise from the east, waiting for the sign.

cinderella's castle

Something went wrong, Joyce must've got caught, failed, bailed, I don't see her anywhere, everyone on the grass hill is awake, this was a mistake, what was our plan exactly, anyway? a mistake I'm going to make worse, I run across the footbridge, the hero who knows he's going to die, a Grimm or Aesop hero, not fucking fraud Disney, I run in slow motion, show my import, the weight of the hero's every step, machete raised and sharpened, hungry, greedy, the tip cuts off chunks of sunlight that fall to the ground, everything dies, the green hill ahead of me is a hive, crawls with people, everyone fights each other, every person for himself, they'll be ready for my army of one.

At the other end of the bridge, my first combatants, a tall girl wearing a plastic but reinforced viking helmet and brandishing a wooden chair leg versus a short hamburger of a dude in a suit of armor made of duct tape, he swings a metal fence post, I yell and offer some manic machete swings that connect with no one, nothing, the two combatants join forces to face and fend my attack, she whacks my arm with the chair leg, fucking ow! I drop the machete, it clangs like a gong, get the hook, the hamburger dude is slow with his bulky fence post, he doesn't swing so much as he pushes, he nudges, nudges me aside so they can finish the serious fighting, I've been dismissed as a threat so easily, it's because I'm out of my element, out of my elephant? why am I here?

I'll have to do this without my weapon, the machete gone, someone swooped in and took it already, damn, a costly casualty I wasn't expecting, I run up the hill and don't stop for the plethora of battle engagement invites thrown my way like casual insults, I run past warriors sporting the everyday household items as shields, as weapons, blunt instruments most of them, but there's one person waving around a whisk-spatula combo that looks sharp enough to pierce through pseudo duct tape armor.

Word of my gauntlet-run passes through the epic unending battle scene, the word is a virus, a worm, I sense it more than hear it, everyone here is here every day, fighting the same person or the same people, they're a group, a whole, an entity, they know when there's an intruder, interloper, outsider, a me making a go at them.

Near the top of the hill, almost off the grass, just ahead is the rotunda where Cinderella's pumpkin cart pulled a u-ey, turned around and went back down the hill, I'm close, the front door isn't far, the Castle is a cartoon capping on a hill, gleaming white with purple and teal spires and turrets, it's shaped like a crown with a swirl of marble staircase leading to its great wooden doors, the doors are closed, I'll open them, I will.

I'm still on the grass, haven't made the swirl, the front stairs where the fighting is the most intense, a blur of the thwarted and the thwartees, a cluster of jousters and their tree-branch or golf-club lances demand that I halt who goes there, these masked riders riding piggy-back on their masked rides block my path, circle me, shepherd me backwards, lost sheep, I'm blinded by someone's pocket laser pointer, I stumble and bumble, then broadsided by two park-issued baby carriages, the trundling plastic wheels take my legs out at the knees, I'm down, I lose my breath, I'm effectless useless and all the other-lesses, this might be it, everyone moves in, picks me up, swallows me whole, spits me out, rejected, I roll down the hill, I roll down forever and into the pond, I can't swim, it's only knee-deep.

I limp home, the battle renews behind me.

heidi's hill

He let me in but this place isn't big enough for the two of us, he let me in but he isn't talking to me, he pretends to be busy whittling something, a goat maybe, what is it with fucking goats?

I sit at the mini table, my chin plays the bongos on my knees, I say, She never showed, she's not at the Polar Coaster either, she must've made it without me.

Mr. Matheson sits on his bed, it's small enough to be a couch cushion, he shrugs and almost hits his head on the ceiling, he says, I'm sure she's fine, you should probably just leave her alone, you're going to have to leave, I'm sorry, but I'm busy.

I'm a cast of a thousand questions, I say, Maybe I was enough of a distraction out there on the hill for her to get into the Castle, I mean, don't get me wrong, I don't really care about the Castle, the Castle can suck it, those damn dirty apes can have it, but I hope she made it, maybe she's still waiting for me to show up, should I try coming in from behind like she did?

Mr. Matheson is wearing his park-issued Heidi's grandfather outfit, his brown hat is too small, his legs too white and veiny, he says, Visiting hours are over, kid, scram.

Mr. Matheson gets in moods, funky funks, he probably has his lederhosen in a bunch because I left him with the broken-down tractor in the middle of the Slipshod Safari, I say, You blew it by shutting the tractor off, don't even remind me.

I stand up, tall as Paul Bunyan, and lurch around the place, I say, What if Joyce ditched me, used me? if I let that happen, if I allowed that happen to me, it's so stock, cliché, right out of a middle-schooler's YA novel of the week, it's like Jill pushing Jack down the hill, or something.

He says, Just go.

I'm still soaking wet from the dunk in the pond, I lost my machete, he has one tacked onto the wall, a real big knife sitting there on the replicated and miniaturized wall, Heidi's wall, Heidi was a story about an orphaned girl being taken care of by her grandfather, a grandfather who lives like a recluse in the swiss alps, Mr. Matheson isn't the grandfather, he just plays one in the park, he told me the story once about Heidi's grandfather learning to love her and there's other crap about Heidi helping some girl in a wheelchair walk because of goat milk and the mountain air, but I stopped listening, stopped caring about Heidi, the story was as stupid and small as the Heidi House, everything is so stupid and so small.

I say, All right, Mr. Happy Pappy, I'll go, I know what to do now anyway.

It's true, I do, I know what to do, I say, Thanks for helping with the tour earlier, really, I appreciate it, I brought you a bounty, more a snack than a bounty to be honestly honest, your favorite kind of snack, picked just for you.

I empty my pockets onto the mini-table, my pockets were full of mushrooms, a mix with a fix, a medley of mushrooms, it takes all kinds, a bit soggy and loggy but he'll eat them, even the ones he shouldn't eat, the ones with the great green caps, big as garbage can covers.

end of the tour: boulder safari castle boulder

I'm back here, outside my mist tent and the World Pavilion, opposite the Polar Coaster, I'm back here, at the center of the park, its core, the heart, the one-ton heart, this here granite boulder is my crystal ball, in it I see my past, the past is passed.

The past, I left Heidi's Hill and went back to my the Slipshod Safari, avoided the booby traps and snares and crawled inside my elephant, it's the elephant in the park, inside the elephant was my room, darker than any closet, inside were the supplies, and the surprise, inspired by Mr. Matheson I put on my old Fairy Tale Land uniform, the one I had worn when I was that little shit working the Whirling Whales, it all still fit, the baggy blue shirt was still baggy, the tight pants were still tight, I walked to the Castle, my arms loaded with barrels and bullets, fingers itching triggers, I walked to the Castle as determined as an earthquake.

Even through the lens of my handy-dandy boulder crystal ball, my assault on the hill and the Castle is fuzzy, it was like that scene in the cartoon movie about a secret society of rabbits, cartoon movie but not a kid's movie, not some anaesthetized fairy tale that you'd find here or in other parks, this movie was real, there was this scene near the beginning of the movie, the end of it all came at the beginning, the farmers ploughed the rabbits and their warren all under, there was rabbit screaming, wide bulging rabbit eyes, rabbit terror, frozen rabbit expressions gone all swirly in a flood of torn throats and blood and dirt and bodies, my ears ringing afterward, just like after my run up the Castle hill, and after, it was all quiet, the park cleared, I was alone, I was alone, dripping the rabbit blood, standing outside the great wooden doors, at the top of the swirled marble staircase, I was alone, dripping the movie blood, knocking on the great wooden doors, no one answered my knocks or my calls, Cinderella wasn't home, she didn't live there, I knew this, standing there alone and outside the great doors yelling **let me in** felt like the end to a different story, a different fairy tale, the wrong one, so I opened the doors even if I wasn't supposed to, inside the castle everything was small, it made me angry to think that this is what everyone was fighting over, it was only one room with mirrored walls, some fake suits of armor, a dingy red carpet, a shoddy throne, Joyce was there, huddled and hiding behind the throne along with the pumpkin driver dressed in service orange and a phony Cinderella with painted-on apple cheeks and a few other kids that used to work the park, Joyce was wearing her old Polar Coaster outfit, the one with the penguins, she wouldn't look at me, but tried to talk me out of whatever it was I was trying to do, she tried to tell me it was okay that we could still live in the castle like she promised, I knew better, and I made like that movie again, I ploughed her and the rest of them rabbits under, the end came so quickly, and then I just left, I've learned it works that way sometimes, I came back here and covered the boulder with the blood from my hands and my clothes and my hair, there was enough blood so that I could turn and spin the boulder again, it's a wheel and has always been greased with blood.

The boulder, the one-ton boulder is my mirror mirror on the wall, it's showing me the future now, I will survive, no one will care or come after me for what I did because there's no one left, I told you that already, there's no one left, I'm the last one, it has to be that way, what I'll do is this, I'll dig out my bike from out behind the employees shack out behind the World Pavilion, the bike is beat up, a little small for me, the spokes and chain will have some rust but the gears will still work, still turn, it'll be the only thing that still turns, I'll get my bike out from behind the shed and ride it around Fairy Tale Land, ride it around the park for a lark, to wherever I want, and it'll be just like when I was riding my bike up and down that closed road, you and no one else will be there.

ACKNOWLEDGEMENTS

Thank you first and foremost to my family, most of whom make it into these stories whether they want to or not.

Thank you to Erik, Helen, Sandra, and everyone at ChiZine Publications. Extra-hot-sauce thanks go to el presidente Brett Savory, who is shorter than I am. Brett has always believed in me, even when I was talking ridiculous trash about winning contests and the like. Brett is one of the good people.

Thank you in particularly alphabetical order to friends, editors, and co-conspirators who have all helped me and these stories in some large way: Jessica Anthony, Stephen Barbara, Laird Barron, Kevin Brockmeier, Mort Castle, Michael Cisco, Neil Clarke, F. Brett Cox, JoAnn Cox, Dave Daley, Don D'Ammassa, Ellen Datlow, Kurt Dinan, the Elitist Horror Cabal, Steve Eller, Brian Evenson, Neil Fallon, David John Gutowski, Jack Haringa, John Harvey, Stephen Graham Jones, Nick Kaufmann, Brian Keene, Mike Kelley, Matt Kressel, Carrie Laben, John Langan, Sarah Langan, Jennifer Levesque, Seth Lindberg, Nick Mamatas, Paul McMahon, Stewart O'Nan, Helen Oyeyemi, Kathy Sedia, Charles Tan, Lee Thomas, Jeffrey Thomas, M Thomas, Ann Vandermeer, Sean Wallace, Kevin Wilson, Dave Zeltserman, and Your Pretty Name.

COPYRIGHTS

ABOUT THE AUTHOR

Paul Tremblay is also the author of the novels *The Little Sleep* and *No Sleep Till Wonderland*. He is the author of the short speculative fiction collection *Compositions for the Young and Old*, and the novellas *City Pier: Above and Below* and *The Harlequin and the Train*. His short fiction has been nominated twice for the Bram Stoker award and won the Black Quill editor's choice award. Stories have appeared at *Weird Tales*, *Last Pentacle of the Sun: Writings in Support of the West Memphis Three*, and *Best American Fantasy 3*. He served as fiction editor of *ChiZine* and as co-editor of *Fantasy Magazine*, and is also the co-editor (with Sean Wallace) of the *Fantasy*, *Bandersnatch*, and *Phantom* anthologies. Paul is currently an advisor for the Shirley Jackson Awards. He still has no uvula, but plugs along, somehow.

www.paultremblay.net, www.thelittlesleep.com